The Intoxicating Mr Lavelle

Neil Blackmore never had any intention of becoming a writer. He wrote his first novel at work to fill time at a boring job. He published his first novel in his twenties but then spent most of his thirties travelling the world. *The Intoxicating Mr Lavelle* is his third novel. He lives in London.

The Intoxicating
Mr Lavelle

Neil Blackmore

WINDMILL

1 3 5 7 9 10 8 6 4 2

Windmill Books
20 Vauxhall Bridge Road
London SW1V 2SA

Windmill Books is part of the Penguin Random House group of companies
whose addresses can be found at global.penguinrandomhouse.com.

First published by Hutchinson in 2020
First published in paperback by Windmill Books in 2021

www.penguin.co.uk

A CIP catalogue record for this book is available from the British Library.

ISBN 9781786090997

Typeset in 10.73/14.60 pt Sabon LT Std by
Integra Software Services Pvt. Ltd, Pondicherry
Printed and bound in Great Britain by Clays Ltd, Elcograf S.p.A.

The authorised representative in the EEA is Penguin Random House Ireland,
Morrison Chambers, 32 Nassau Street, Dublin D02 YH68

To Zahid Mukhtar
with my endless, endless thanks

If all good, respectable people had one face,
I'd spit in it.

Jean Rhys

AUTHOR'S NOTE

When writing this novel, I wanted it to be authentic to the period – as any historical novel should be – but for it also to speak to modern readers. My characters reference the terms the 'Enlightenment' and the 'Renaissance', which did not come into common usage until the nineteenth century, but have since become a shorthand for us to understand entire cultural movements. Please forgive these occasional anachronisms ('medieval' wouldn't have been in use then, but we've been referring to 'the Middle Ages' since the 1610s) and enjoy Benjamin's travels and travails. Benjamin and Lavelle aren't based on real people, but a love story like theirs wouldn't have been allowed to be told at the time.

PART ONE

Dearest Mother —

A short note with an engraving showing how one traverses the Alps. In truth, it was not nearly so bucolic and charming. The passes to Italy are treacherous, and everywhere are English people hollering from their coaches, first about the cold and then the lack of wine! Benjamin says this is very funny. I am not sure why. But you know Benjamin – he sees the world differently to us!

Your loving son,

Edgar

LONDON, 1763

*M*y mother was sure that in the future, I would be a good person. Or she was sure that I – or rather my brother, Edgar, and I – might *meet* good people, and become their friends.

My mother had a plan for our social advancement that was based on culture and erudition. All she had to do, she was sure – and my mother was *always* sure – was train us well in her twin holy tenets: Englishness and the Enlightenment. If we followed her plan, we could not fail.

We were not sent to school but educated at home by tutors my mother found in periodicals. She recruited an émigré German named Herr Hof to teach us Latin grammar and Greek philosophy, Descartes and Diderot, conversation and *contredanses*. We were not allowed to acquaint ourselves with any other boys, and their mothers did not come and sit with ours to take tea. We were isolated, but we were content within the world that my mother created. It never occurred to us that to live so secluded an existence could be dangerous.

My mother was convinced that by nurturing our minds and perfecting our social poses, we would be accepted into English society. She planned for Edgar and me a glorious future as perfect Englishmen. But now, half a lifetime later, I see the paradox of her ambition. She was preparing us to be great successes in the world – but her every effort had been expended on keeping us cloistered away from it. She believed that if we just followed her plan, Edgar and I would be accepted by the firmament of fashion and influence that London adores: dukes and duchesses, earls and princesses. Unfortunately, my mother was wrong. Even more unfortunately, being wrong never stopped my mother.

The source of my mother's ambition – or rather my parents' ambition, for we very much had two parents – was the fact that neither she nor my father was English. They both wanted us to belong in England in a way they never could. My father, William, was to English eyes almost the lowest type of person: a Welshman. He was also the founder of the Bowen Maritime Company, the first passenger-liner firm to ship fashionable Londoners direct to New York. My mother, Rachel, was a Dutchwoman. We knew she had been born in Amsterdam, yet she said Spanish was her first language. She was intelligent, highly educated, could quote philosophers and recite Latin poetry from memory with ease. Our parents had met while my father worked for her first husband's shipping house. Then the first husband died and my father married my mother and established his own passenger business, the Bowen Maritime. She was ten years older than my father, though as children we didn't recognise this as unusual. This was *almost* all we knew of her.

My mother had a great admiration for the English – she thought them paragons of fairness. But, despite this, she did not understand her adopted nation one bit. English people, no matter what they pretend, hate knowledge and hate education. They hate books. They hate people who learn, and who speak with curiosity and openness about what they have learned. And they especially hate anyone who asks for acceptance among their number but who has no right to ask for it. No, my mother understood none of this. And that was why, among the English, I was never going to be a good person.

The night our future arrived, my brother, Edgar, was twenty-two and I was twenty-one. We loved each other dearly and were physically very similar: both tall, thin, with dark hair and dark eyes. My mother called us her 'two halves' and we did not yet question that. She also called us her 'boys' and she was right to do so. For although we were past twenty, Edgar and I had learned nothing – no experience, no responsibility – that could be conceived as adult.

On the evening that would set the rest of our lives in motion, my parents, my brother and I ate together in the long, light drawing room that looked out over Red Lion Square. My mother was seated near the leaded bay window which faced the square's leafy trees and bushes. It was summertime; we had a few more hours of light still. As usual, my father was seated next to my mother. He loved her absolutely. If the Company was the great love of his life, then our mother was the greatest. After a long day of work, all he had to do was come home – at six o'clock, every day without fail, and he never went back out again – and spend the evening gazing at her. She made him happy – completely happy.

Supper that evening was served with wine, brandy and coffee, in what my mother called the English style. Most nights, nearly full glasses of wine would be cleared away. Now and then, I caught the servants glancing at each other, but I did not yet know that there was nothing English in leaving wine undrunk. My mother talked of the book she was reading: *The Social Contract*, by Rousseau.

'He says that kings are not divine!' Edgar declared, making my mother nod. She liked us to be correct – but not to correct her.

'More than that,' my mother added, 'he says that men are collectively responsible for their society. All men are equally free. They must agree laws by consensus, not have them imposed on them.' I wondered if this was true. Are all men equally free – an emperor and a slave, a man and a woman, a mistress and her servants? I watched my mother as she spoke, watched her confidence, her certainty. Would I dare question her? Of course not. To question her aloud was unthinkable – but perhaps not internally.

My father smiled, eyes shining. 'I should not like that when I am running the Company,' he said, as cheerfully as he could manage. My mother looked at him sharply. I was glad he had been the one to speak, rather than me. He always let her speak; our mother's voice reigned in that house. Edgar asked her sculpted questions about the book, and said that he thought whatever she had said was very good. He was not being obsequious; he genuinely worshipped our mother. 'I should like to read it, too, Mother,' he continued and my mother seemed pleased. She liked us to agree with her. But her delight was short-lived. After a moment her jaw clenched and she looked at me directly. 'What about you, Benjamin?' she asked, her voice instantly cold. 'Do you have no thoughts?' When exercised, my mother's foreignness always came out.

I had to think. Did I mean to annoy her? 'I think such words are probably the future, Mother. I think that it is a very intelligent, perceptive set of thoughts about men's freedoms. And responsibilities.' I said nothing about emperors and slaves, men and women. My mother smiled. My words had satisfied her, and I was happy about that.

'Do you wish to read the book too, Benjamin?' she asked.

I smiled and nodded. 'Of course, Mother.'

When the conversation came to a natural end, my mother took what seemed to be a very significant pause, one which drew attention to what she was about to say. In response, the three of us fell into a respectful hush.

'Boys, your father and I have come to a decision. It is time for you to go on the Grand Tour.'

When Edgar spoke, his excitement was clear. 'What, Mother, it's time?'

She gave him a slow, regal nod. 'Yes, my two halves. It is time.' My mother had often spoken of her dream that we should, once we'd come to the end of our education, go off on Tour. She had rhapsodised of how we would see Paris, Germany, the Italian cities, go as far as Rome and Naples. She had eulogised how the Tour was the culmination of a refined and erudite education. It would signal the end of the first phase of life, and mark the start of the second, for which the first had prepared us. In the second, we would be true successes.

We had always understood that the purpose of our going on Tour was twofold: social and educational, yes, but also strategic, commercial. One day, Edgar and I would inherit the Bowen Maritime Company. The Tour would be our chance to develop the social network our parents did not possess. We would go and meet English people, the 'good' kind of people, and they would become not just our friends, but also our future customers. This was clearer to my father than my mother perhaps: while he was pragmatic, she had more romantic notions of the project. Our mother continued: 'It will be so beneficial for your refinement and connections.'

My brother, like my father, was a devotee of the world my mother had created. He knew what she had planned for us, and he wanted what she wanted. 'Oh, Mother,' he gushed. 'Oh, how exciting. Benjamin and I have longed for this day. How many years we have been waiting, and now it is here.'

My brother spoke for both of us but I had not said anything myself, and my mother knew that. She heard every statement – and every silence too. 'And what about you, Benjamin?' she asked then. 'You don't seem much excited!'

I paused a second or two. I let the moment hang, the possibility of dissent. Edgar's eyes were on me, hesitant. I knew I could make him feel anxious near my mother.

8

Rebellions in that house were barely comprehensible. He only ever wanted to please her, just as my father did. My father coughed and pulled forward in his seat. 'Why don't you speak up, Benjamin?' I heard his soft, rolling Welsh syllables. 'Why don't you tell your mother what a good idea you think this is?'

My father's voice made me jump. His was a different presence in the house to my mother's: quieter yet darker. 'Oh, yes, Mother, I am really very excited,' I said.

My mother was gazing at Edgar and me, a smile hovering on her lips. 'All this knowledge –' she raised her hand towards the bookcases lining this and every other room in the house '– has led to this moment.' She sighed and added, 'You will be great successes,' and nodded to herself in agreement with what she had just said. 'You will see all the vestiges of the classical world, and the triumphs of the Renaissance. You will experience first-hand the foundations of our enlightenment.' Then she clapped her hands together: 'Now, my sons, we will play the Minute Game.'

'Oh, yes,' said Edgar. 'Let's! But on which subject?'

The Minute Game was my mother's invention, devised long ago – no one remembered when – to test the fruits of our intense study. Suetonius or Spinoza! Pliny or Petrarch! In sixty seconds, we were to demonstrate what we had learned on a historical, literary or philosophical subject of Mother's choosing. She believed nothing was more crucial than the ability to demonstrate one's knowledge.

'Why, on the two most important subjects for each of you in the coming year,' Mother said. 'For you, Edgar, the Renaissance.'

Edgar was immediately on his feet, clearing his throat. When playing the Minute Game, he adopted a pose like an actor on a stage, declaiming to a great audience that was only ever we four. 'The Renaissance,' he began, 'is from the French for rebirth, and in turn from *Rinascimento*, the Italian, the land of its origin. It is the great rebirth of classical study after the long barren interlude of the Dark Ages, and the elevation of refinement, learning and achievement in the European mind and culture. It begins our own current apotheosis as the finest moment of humanity, and for this, we often call the intellectual currents of the Renaissance "humanism". The Renaissance began in the fourteenth century in northern Italy. Then, the country was fragmented into a number of small city states, whose rulers had become rich with trade and who, in a desire to show their elevation and authority, began to encourage scholars and artists to make new strides, and to re-engage with the lost knowledge, writings and technical expertise of the Romans and the Greeks. Technological advances such as the invention of the printing press rapidly increased the transference of knowledge among peoples and centres of study and art. For whom shall we give credit to the Renaissance, not just these forward-looking merchants –' I looked at my father, who nodded supremely '– but also to the great fathers of the new learning, such as Dante and Petrarch; and the innovators of new painting, from early masters through to the likes of Botticelli, who were interested in capturing the real and the physical, the dimensional, and stories that were not strictly religious, but philosophical, dramatic or sensual—'

Whilst my parents were watching him, my brother glanced at me momentarily. As he did, I closed my mouth and filled my cheeks until they popped out round, flicking my eyes left and right, left and right. Edgar let out a short, sharp laugh. I saw my mother turn to look at me, but I was quick enough to return my expression to one of a bland composure, and smile and nod to her.

'Are you two boys playing at goats?' she asked.

'No, Mother,' I said, 'I am not a goat. I am not sure about Edgar.'

My brother started to laugh, pointing at me: 'He put me off! It's not fair, he put me off!'

When we were young, Edgar liked to remind everyone that he was a year my senior, but now it was he who sometimes acted – was even seen to be, perhaps – as a child. My mother giggled a little at his protest. She was not a martinet. She liked fun and she liked to laugh. We all did. This was her world, however, and we all had to understand that. 'Now you, Benjamin,' she said, 'you shall speak on our own dear Enlightenment ...'

My mother was the greatest devotee of our Enlightenment and clung hard to its beliefs. She held its values – of reason and reform, of fairness and progress – in the highest regard. She expected Edgar and me to do so, too. I will say this, quite openly. There was much to respect in my mother's modernity. She disapproved of absolute monarchs and of the slave trade. She wanted people to be free across Europe – and she was a great admirer of the freedoms of her adopted country.

I began to speak: 'Our era of Enlightenment is the manifestation of the advances of the Renaissance. In bringing European civilisation to its apex, it has produced the greatest flowering of human understanding and knowledge yet. Descartes laid the foundation for our

Enlightenment ideals with the development of his rational way of thinking, breaking decisively with the dominance of the Church.' My mother tilted her head to one side and nodded, now and then briefly closing her eyes. 'This was the end of a long period of religious war in Europe in which conflicting churches had used their power to slaughter millions of Europeans. People no longer tolerated church dominance. Locke's *Essay Concerning Human Understanding* was an important milestone.'

Mentioning my mother's favourite writers was always an easy win, and she loved John Locke very much. I could just about see Edgar arching an eyebrow, but I kept a straight face. 'In it, he stated that newborn humans were *tabula rasa,* blank slates, and could develop their senses through education. Locke has been much challenged, for instance by Leibniz, who argued for the innateness of idea in an innate soul. And Spinoza disputed Descartes over matters such as the separation of the mind and the body in the conception of a soul, and the nature of God. But these challenges formed a new language of debate and enquiry into the nature of existence that over time led to a different way of thinking, in which the human mind, and not the existence of God, was of paramount importance for civilisation. These advances led to the development of ideas of individual liberty, freedom of expression, and saw the end of theology as a basis for morality. People have freed themselves from the Church.'

My mother opened her eyes. I smiled at her, and she at me, happily. Then I looked at Edgar; I would never have dared wink, but let my eyes linger on his as if to say, 'Oh, you think *you* can slather it on? Watch this.' I inhaled dramatically. 'It was our own dear Voltaire who first argued that society must be based upon reason and not faith; that natural law must inform civil law, not religion; that society must be democratic and must protect the vulnerable, and that science be based on experiments and observation. Voltaire uses both philosophy and fiction to explore his ideas and transmit them to a wider audience. In our age, we may look to Diderot and others, of course, but always we must return to Voltaire.'

My mother loved Voltaire above all others. She did not wait for his works to appear in English but ordered them, by letter, from Paris as soon as they were published. Her favourite line of his was 'We are all of us fallible. So let's forgive each other's follies.' She held this to be true, held it very close.

To show I was finished, I took a bow. I looked first at Edgar, who now had his eyes wide, and then at my mother, who had hers closed once more. She was nodding calmly with her left hand laid flat on the table. My father placed his hand over my mother's, gently rubbing her skin with his thumb. She opened her eyes and smiled at him.

Later, in our shared bedroom, after our parents had said we may retire – two men in their twenties being told to go to bed – Edgar talked extensively about what the Tour would be. He spoke breathlessly about all the good people we would meet, and the good experiences we would have. Now that our mother was nowhere near, he hardly mentioned the Enlightenment. He was fantasising about parties and balls, fashionable society, excellent chaps and pretty girls.

Lying on my bed, as I let Edgar chatter around me, I stared up at the ceiling. A long crack ran through it, created by the settling of the house over many years. As Edgar was gushing about our futures with an enthusiasm at once beguiling and a little silly, I traced the line's shape with my eyes and imagined it as a route that the two of us would follow. At points, it shifted direction slightly – south to Paris, then east towards Lorraine – or ran into a squiggling fissure – the journey through the Alps' narrow valleys – and then arched out perfectly, as if drawn by a draughtsman's hand – in the direction of the Italian cities.

'Do you think there will be lots of pretty girls?' Edgar asked, his question urgent and heady with possibility. Now and then my brother talked of girls, but I did not join in with him, and I did not do so now. I am not interested in girls.

As a boy, I would occasionally borrow a book of etchings from my mother's library and, in the middle of the day, take it up to our bedroom, softly turning the key in the lock. Staring at the rippling muscles and taut bellies rendered so beautifully by the hands of the Old Masters, my cock would grow hard and I would feel ashamed.

Edgar and I knew nothing of girls. But there were things I knew about myself, in all my lonely innocence. Once, I overheard one of the kitchen maids saying that Edgar and I were 'probably both sodomites'. I asked Herr Hof what the word meant. He refused to tell me then, but the next day a street pamphlet was left, upside-down and unacknowledged, on my bedside table. It reported how two boys, aged seventeen and fifteen, had been found in the Park. They claimed they had been there only to rob, but they were found guilty of importuning men for sodomy. They were to be hanged. The story reported how the court gallery cheered when the boys were sentenced to die for their sin – a sin that was also a capital crime. I read the pamphlet in horror, knowing I had those same impulses. I felt that horror pulse through me: was this the fate awaiting someone like me? The next day, Herr Hof asked me to tell him which maid had said 'that thing'. He would get her dismissed. I said I did not know which. He insisted, but I maintained I did not know, although in fact I did.

'Benjamin! Benjamin!'

'What?' I groaned, turning on my bed to look at my brother.

Edgar's eyes were as bright as torches. '*Do you* think there will be lots of pretty girls on the Tour?'

I laughed. 'Yes, I expect so.'

'Yes,' Edgar sighed. 'English girls are the prettiest in the world.'

'Are they?' I asked, laughing. 'How would we know?'

Edgar faced me, then, his brow furrowed, a curious look in his eye. He did not see things as I did, perhaps.

A footman came and knocked on the door, saying that our father had sent him to check that we were undressed for bed. So we changed into our night things and slipped under the covers. Edgar and I had always shared a room; even though there were sufficient rooms in our house for us each to have our own, it did not occur to us that we might not. I lay in the darkness for a long time. Eventually, I realised that the rustling sound I could hear was not the mice who came through our floorboards at night: it was Edgar, masturbating. I turned on my side, pushing my ear deep into my pillow. Two minutes passed, I heard a sharp little breath, then nothing, until finally the sounds of Edgar's shallow sleep-breathing.

I opened my eyes and, as I got used to the darkness, stared back up at the ceiling until I could again see the crack. I was thinking of the world that was out there, beyond Red Lion Square, beyond London, and I was both excited and afraid.

Perhaps parents always choose to deceive their children. Perhaps the lies a mother tells her sons, or a father tells his daughters, are as natural as air. Sometimes deceptions are direct, harshly known. Only when we went on Tour did I come to understand that in that house, Edgar and I were not raised in the spirit of the truth.

The first deceit might have been my father's violence. He was violent in his mind, in his utter belief that the Company, and our role in its future (more than it in ours), was all that mattered. How he used to rage at us during our visits to the Company offices on Moorgate, when we did not understand, or did not care enough! 'Do you have any questions, Benjamin?' 'Nothing about the implications of depreciation on the older ships?' 'You have to take this seriously, Benjamin! This is going to be the rest of your life, and the Company has to be the most important thing in your life! It is going to be every day for the rest of *your* days, and your brother's!'

As I have said, my father's presence was both quieter and darker than my mother's. But the truth was I was afraid of my father – physically afraid. When we were children, even for minor infractions he would whip us with his belt, or hold us down on a bed and knock our skulls together until we were dazed. 'Don't tell your mother!' he would warn us, whenever he went too far.

As we grew older, he ceased beating us in that way. I do not know why he stopped. He could not possibly have been afraid of us. Once, when I was about thirteen, I saw my father beat a debtor to the Company half to death in front of his staff. He punched the man repeatedly until his face was covered in blood: my father wild with fury, out of control, unable to restrain himself, like a dog with bared teeth; the debtor, in seconds, a bloodied ragdoll hanging from my father's raw-knuckled fists. It was the most frightening thing I had seen in my life. What I re-member most harrowingly were my father's eyes connecting with mine as his rage wore down and he let the debtor go, the man crashing to his knees. I will never forget the look in his eyes then: that mix of fury and shame, anger and regret. He made me swear not to tell Mother or Edgar, and I kept his secret, and in doing so I became his con-spirator, his accomplice. I hated him for asking me to do so, but I obeyed.

My mother's untruths were wholly different, for they were not coercing me into lies but rather omitting the truth. In fact, perhaps it was my mother's mystery that affected me more. For years, right up until I went on Tour, I used to keep a locked box under my bed, hidden amongst other boxes. I kept the key to it under a floor-board. My mother, even if she had found the box, would never have been able to find the key. But I was sure that she might become angry enough to force the lock open with a knife, and sometimes I worried she might. What would she say, finding what was inside?

I collected secrets – mine and hers. Inside the box were two pages torn from my mother's book of etchings, the ones of Apollo and Mars. (I burned the rest of the book on a bonfire the servants had built in the back garden.) The newspaper article I found about the two boys hanged for sodomy, I kept that too.

And what of my mother's past? There was so little evidence, and what I possessed, I had accrued slowly over years and kept like relics. There was a book on my mother's shelves on the history of England, in Spanish, in which the words LA PROPRIEDAD DE SOLOMON FON-SECA were written. A letter from 1742, which I found one day in the records room of the Company offices, which confirmed the transfer of ownership of the Fonseca Shipping Company from 'the late Solomon Fonseca' to the newly incorporated Bowen Maritime. The new owner was listed as William Bowen, and the letter mentioned the inheritance of the first company by 'Mister Fonseca's widow, Rachel'.

I stole the letter from the records room and hid it away. I waited for my father to complain bitterly about its loss, but he never did.

Another time visiting the Company, I found in the archives, written again and again, a name and an address in Paris: CARDOSO, RUE DES ROSIERS. I knew that 'Cardoso' was my mother's maiden name. That, together with the existence of the first husband and the fact that she grew up in Amsterdam, was literally all we knew of her. Of parents, or sisters, brothers or cousins, we knew nothing. It was the weight of her mystery, its totality, that made me write down the name and address on a separate piece of paper, and hide that in the box under my bed too.

I think of the boy who did these things. In part, I see a boy with desires, unaware of anyone else in the world who shared them. I also see a boy who spent his life concealing things: his own secrets, and those of others. How should he make sense of them? By keeping them in a safe place, where he could retrieve them, and study them for himself. Or *maybe* it was just a small act of rebellion in a house that allowed none.

Seven months separated the night of that supper on Red Lion Square and the date of our departure. At first, it seemed impossibly far away, but the day soon neared – and our sense of urgency increased. In the final few months, we had a wave of shopping of the sort that only London truly provides. Wigs – white and black and grey – and men's face powder suitable for French society, bought in a shop in St James's. On the cheek, the proprietor said, it was like a deadening snow. Tailors came and pinned us up for fitting; coats, waistcoats and breeches were cut and cut again. My mother would say that one styling was too manly, too short, or too tight, too revealing, 'inappropriate for boys' – but we were not boys, of course. She would ask which silk we liked; sometimes she would agree with our choice, and sometimes she would sniff and hold another: 'No, this one is better.' And that would be the end of that. We had always dressed in the fashion of twins – the possibility that we might not had never even occurred to us – so everything was ordered in sets of two. Trunks were bought, two large, for jackets and shoes; two small, for shirts, breeches, stockings and cravats; wig and hat boxes in good number; bags to hold boxes of powder and scents. We were not taking our own servants – we were not that level of society – but would hire porters and carriers as we needed en route. Mother believed we would make the greatest impression as a pair.

For the most part, the preparations were fun – every bit for our mother as much as for us, perhaps even more so. Based on her own knowledge of the Continent and with the help of our tutor Herr Hof, she had already prepared our itinerary. She excitedly guided us through the concertinaed map our father gave us. 'The western half looks much like England: France, Spain and Portugal, these are big countries like England itself,' she said, showing borders relatively unchanged for many years. 'But go east, go south, and Europe – literally – shatters,' she explained. 'Italy is just a cluster of tiny states: Florence, Modena, Genoa, Padua, Parma, Rome and Venice.' She showed us the Empire and we saw how Germany was even more atomised, a pulverised rubble of territorial shards, Holsteins Gottorp and Gluckstein, Brunswicks Celle or Wolfenbüttel, very many Saxonies, a Bavaria and a Bayreuth.

I have never loved maps. But for our mother, to gaze at the map of Europe was to read a scripture. It was to see all of the Continent's history and thought in a single glance. We were channelling not just the names of countries and capital cities but also of our Enlightenment saints:

Cicero and Tacitus, Dante and Erasmus, Descartes and Voltaire. My mother adored all of it, and sincerely and openly and lovingly wanted us to do the same. Her joy in knowledge was her truest quality; I admit that, even now, all these years later.

We were to leave in March, the very start of spring in London. On the eve of our departure, I remembered the box under my bed. I did not want my mother to find it while I was away, in asking the maids to give our room a good clean. I did not want her to get that knife and force it open, to find inside stories of young men hanged for sodomy, pictures of rippling male bodies torn from a book only then would she realise she had lost; her first husband's name, Solomon Fonseca, inscribed on its endpapers. I decided that I would finally have to dispose of the contents of this box. My childhood was ended, and those small, unknown acts of rebellion must be too. I took the key from under the floorboard and went back to my bed, knelt down and retrieved the box. There was a fire lit in the bedroom – it was still cold this time of year – and one by one I burned my secret artefacts on the flickering coals. The last thing I came to was a name and address in Paris, written by me on a slip of paper, another clue about my mother's past.

CARDOSO
RUE DES ROSIERS

I stared at it. Were we not about to go to Paris? Were we not about to be in the vicinity of some truth about our mother? I slipped the paper into the pocket of my coat. Then I closed the now-empty box and put it on a high shelf, where no one would even notice it.

That evening, we ate supper in a strange, uncertain mood that would not shift no matter how much we proclaimed excitement at what lay ahead. We had always been together, the four of us, and soon we would not be. That frightened us. To avoid the truth of our agitation, my mother fussed about whether we had enough clothes. We each had three large oak chests, two of which were filled solely with clothes, wigs, kerchiefs and fans, and the third half filled with ten pairs of shoes apiece. My father told her not to worry. He said, 'You've done everything, *cariad*,' the Welsh word for one whom you love absolutely, 'everything.' Towards the end of supper, my mother rose from the table and went to a sideboard. On top was a large leather-bound book, which she handed to Edgar. 'Open it, please.'

Edgar glanced up at me. His brow twitched a little, a hint of a smile on his lips. 'What is it, Mother?' I asked. I moved some plates to one side so Edgar could lay the book on the table without fear of it being dirtied. He opened it, and inside on the first page was written in upper cases, in our mother's neat hand:

A LIST OF INSTRUCTIONS, IN OTHER WORDS,
A GUIDE TO OUR GRAND TOUR

PART ONE: FRANCE (PARIS)

'"Our" grand tour?' Edgar asked, with much amusement. 'Mother, you are not coming with us.'

He laughed giddily, scandalised that he might play with her so.

'Oh, I am,' Mother said, very seriously. She touched the centre of her chest. 'In my heart, I am with you every step of the way.'

Edgar began leafing through the book. I moved closer to his side so that we might look at it together. On each page was written out, with a location at the top, the entire itinerary our mother and Herr Hof had devised for us: Paris, Germany, the Italian cities – Venice, Florence, Siena, Rome, all the way to Naples. From Naples, Edgar and I would sail home. We would be away not quite a year.

We continued leafing through the pages. Here and there, our mother had glued something she had cut from a published guidebook: a map, a diagram, an etching of some work of sculpture or architecture. Of course, she could have just given us the original guidebook herself (she did give us plentiful maps), but then she would not have been able to shape the experience exactly as she saw fit. I see it now that she wanted to mould the trip precisely, to leave nothing to any error that we two boys might allow, if we had any say of our own. My poor mother did not understand that it is possible to guide a hand too much.

'I want you boys to make me a promise,' she said, her eyes iridescent with tears. 'You must make an oath to protect each other and love each other and never to let the other come to harm, to never let the other out of your sight – not for a day, not even for an hour – so that you will come home to me. Together you will seek out good people, and make them your friends, and then you will return home, safe, to me.'

Edgar and I said yes in turn, and so we all laughed – happily, nervously – hardly noticing that an oath had been made. And the whole time, a magnificent, beautiful, heartless cuckoo was out there, waiting in the nest of that perfectly-planned future my mother had devised: *Lavelle*.

Darling Mother —

Please find enclosed a drawing of the monuments of Paris. Paris is not actually like this but quite another sort of place, yet wonderful nonetheless! I asked Benjamin if you had been to this city, but neither of us could remember. Did you ever tell us if you had? We have your precious guidebook and it 'guides' us everywhere. We have met some marvellous people – absolute Quality – and I shall write you a longer letter to reveal all!

Benjamin and I both in tremendously good spirits, Mother!

All my love, your son,

Edgar

PARIS

At first, Paris seemed a marvellous thing. The city was so beautiful in spring; everywhere birds were chirruping and blossoms opening. If Paris was elegant – the neat garden squares and pretty royal parks, the famous palaces of the French royal family, the spectacular domes – its people were even more so. We quickly understood that you could not be a galumphing, hollering Londoner in Paris. Mother's book had informed us that Parisians whispered politely and discussed poetry, soberly. We should avoid too much laughter or smiling, which the French abhor. It was imperative (and this was underlined) that one should be seen as a 'paragon of elegance'. When promenading, one should nod, nothing more, to other people of Quality. And the Quality of the city were always immaculately turned out, never seen without *maquillage*, their wigs higher than any hat, beauty spots and fans adorning the cheek of every woman and man. It was intimidating, I admit, and there were many, many rules.

Days appeared to be strictly prescribed, filled with endless diversions and pleasures: opera or dances early evenings, gambling and drinking late into the night, indulged hangovers in the morning. The afternoons were designated the 'strolling time'. On our third day in the city, Edgar and I went to the Tuileries Garden, near the river, to take part in *la promenade*. In the royal garden, the Quality moved slowly, crunching the pale gravel walkways that divided the rectangular palace grounds into squares. Each section was decorated with pretty spring flowers in ornate pots, tiny trees or topiary bushes. To stroll from one end of the garden near the Tuileries Palace to the other took just fifteen minutes, but the task was to walk around and around, over and again, until several hours had passed. In this time, one would encounter new people, then see them again, and maybe again, until one might feel compelled to nod or even wish them a good day. But herein was the trick.

This was a world of instant judgements: on dress, on wigs, on gait, on countenance, on sincerity of smile. All around was light conversation, punctuated by sharp little hoots of recognition or derision. *Oof! Ha! Oof!* People held fans to their faces to hide their mouths, but above the fans, eyes flirted or remonstrated. Everyone watched everyone else for the first signs of a nod. Breaking first could be interpreted in many different ways: sometimes, those who nodded first were the social victor, sometimes the humiliated.

Edgar and I watched, fascinated, observing the occasional word that accompanied a smile one would struggle to recognise as sincere. And then there might be a moment of hesitation around a pair of eyes, flashing towards a nearby friend, as absolute as it was unspoken: an emphatic, utterly silent, *no*. We had grown up in a world without society; suddenly, we were thrust into it. I felt so unprepared for this world. These people, I reflected, knew things I did not understand, things that were not revealed in guidebooks. Lost in my thoughts, I was shaken from them only when Edgar nudged me in the arm. 'Benjamin, *look*!'

A strikingly beautiful lady and two gentlemen appeared to be walking towards us. That they had no doubt at all they were the finest of specimens, one could see from how they moved, talked and delicately smiled. As they neared, my brother touched my arm:

'They are speaking English.'

'So?' I asked. 'They will never want to speak to us.'

'I think we should nod to them,' Edgar said, his voice full of confidence – a confidence I did not share. 'I think we have to be brave.' He shot ahead of me and a second later, they were only a few feet from each other. The man at the front – exquisitely turned out in a powder-blue suit with a high, curled off-white wig – smiled cautiously at Edgar, awaiting the nod. But my brother did not nod. He bowed, so deeply that the group appeared a little shocked – or as shocked as people this perfect ever dared look.

The young woman was dressed exclusively in the softest yellow, almost entirely without any depth of colour; colourlessness being a very smart thing. She held a folded fan to her lips, the height of refinement. In her stillness, I could see quite how beautiful she was. Her eyes were a deep, English blue – so unlike our dark little things – which lingered on Edgar as she studied him.

'What jolly fellows do we have here?' asked the man.

'We are the Messieurs Bowen, from London,' Edgar said. *Messieurs?* I thought, but Edgar kept glowing with the same confidence. 'I could not help but hear that you are English, sirs. And I thought that I should make my introduction ... I mean, our introduction.'

The man had an air of amusement. 'Why, we were terrified that *you* were going to cut *us*.' A little hum fizzed out of his chest. Was he being sarcastic? 'But now I see you are bowing good and deep.' The woman's eyes were as attentive as a bird's. The man continued: 'These rules of introductions are awful hard. In London, it is much simpler, for everyone just ignores one another and barges right past until they point out that you met them once at Blenheim Palace!'

Everyone laughed. 'Blenheim Palace!' Edgar repeated, awed, like a child before adults.

'I am Sir Gideon Hervey,' the man introduced himself.

'*Sir* Gideon,' Edgar said, adding his own emphasis. The man then turned to indicate his friends.

'This is Miss Augusta Anson. And this is Mister Frederick Anson, her cousin and companion.'

'Are you brothers?' the woman asked, her mouth pursed in the same expression of amusement as Sir Gideon's.

'We are,' Edgar said. He was blushing ever so slightly. 'This is my brother, Benjamin. I am Edgar.'

I stepped forward. Miss Anson took a long breath. 'I was wondering when you might introduce us.' She flicked a finger in my direction. 'He was hiding, hoping we might go away.'

I shook my head. 'Not at all, miss.'

She held my eyes for a moment and in her gaze was something so unremittingly knowing, I had to drop my gaze to the ground, and as I did so, I heard it: her chuckle, softly pretty, yet deeply cold. 'I am teasing you, Mister Bowen. You mustn't take me seriously.'

Now I was blushing, too. 'Would you care to walk with us a while?' Sir Gideon asked and Edgar agreed so readily that it could have knocked us all flat. I don't know why, but I felt a reluctance.

We strolled, all of us together, around and around the geometric patterns of the gardens for perhaps half an hour. Edgar chattered brightly and enthusiastically about any and every subject. Sir Gideon laughed and laughed as he did so, and appeared genuinely to find my brother amusing. Now and then, stylish French people walked airily past us, their faces frozen in a permanent, ironic misery. Each time one of these gloomy, fashionable people passed, Sir Gideon pulled a mocking grimace to show his amusement. Edgar laughed loudly, enthusiastically, a perfect mimesis of Sir Gideon. With the tip of her fan pressed into the flesh of her lips, Augusta Anson leaned towards my brother. Her lips were painted a glossy, pert pink. Edgar's eyes focused on them as they drew near his face. She whispered into his ear, loud enough for all to hear:

'The French do not expect to be mocked. That's what makes it so delicious to poke fun at them.' The fan pushed harder against her mouth, and her upper lip plumped sensually around it. How quickly Edgar and I forgot that we had, only moments before, cared deeply how the French behaved. There was nothing wrong with that, perhaps: after all, we were here to meet English people. In terms of our parents' plan, the French were quite irrelevant. It was the likes of Sir Gideon and Augusta Anson whom we were here to impress. Miss Anson pulled back and let the fan fall to her side: 'But, of course, none of them speak English.'

'I hear that is changing now,' I said, because I thought I should say *something*. 'I hear that the Dauphin himself is learning our language.'

Her eyes flickered to mine. I felt that flicker in my chest. 'How extraordinary!' she cried. I was not clear if it was extraordinary that the Dauphin was learning English, or that one might think it something worth reporting. I coughed a little, embarrassed, and she smiled the smallest possible smile.

Our little group continued its promenade. Edgar almost immediately seemed so effortlessly a part of it. Did I feel jealous as he chattered on, unencumbered by doubts, telling some story about something we had seen, some person who had made us laugh? Now and then, in my silence, I felt Augusta Anson watching me, which only served to silence me more. I kept expecting her to say, 'Do you have nothing to add, Mister Bowen?' but she did not. Whatever her thoughts of me, for the moment she kept them to herself.

Sir Gideon was saying how 'darling' it was that we were all such friends now. My brother's eyes beamed with happiness. Yes, he said, yes, it was 'darling'. 'There shall be all sorts of invitations,' Sir Gideon declared. 'You shall come with us and be our friends. It will be a kind of dream.' A dream for whom, he did not say.

We said goodbye near the Pont Royal, as our new friends were due to attend a viewing of portraits by Boucher of various ladies of the Court. 'All of them King Louis' whores,' Sir Gideon joked, causing Augusta Anson to give a throaty, worldly purr. Edgar was laughing too, more innocently, of course, nodding eagerly. Cards were exchanged so that notes could be sent later. There was talk of a party and then of another stroll. You *will* come. You *will* come, Sir Gideon kept saying. My brother's eyes shone with unconcealed joy.

Sir Gideon proved to be an alchemist of social opportunity. Every day, folded notes with our names written in his rolling cursive hand arrived at our lodgings, numerously, note after note, saying we should go here or we should go there. As we became known in society, printed cards of invitation, edged in gold or purple, started appearing. *Les messieurs Bowen ... Nous demandons votre présence ...* It was beyond anything we could have imagined, and it was all Sir Gideon's doing. There were invitations to go and see this painting by Leonardo da Vinci and that sculpture by Bernini at the house of this fine prince or that notorious marquis. There were balls and parties and receptions and card games *très intime*. And there was a stroll most days, usually in loud, good humour at the Tuileries Garden.

Knowing Sir Gideon and Augusta Anson meant there were more introductions: to a Lady Montagu or an earl from somewhere. Most days, Edgar wrote to our mother with long lists of names of the people we had met and the outfits we had worn to do so. He did not tell her how much wine we'd drunk, or how few of her prescribed cultural sights we'd seen. 'Isn't it wonderful?' Edgar wrote. 'This new life of ours. How I wish you were here to see for yourself. I dare believe that even you could not have imagined we'd be such an instant success!'

Sir Gideon said that we simply had to go to a salon, that it was the Parisian experience *par excellence*. Edgar agreed this would be wonderful. Heavily made up and dressed in brocade, I was sweating underneath my powdered wig as we stood in a sudden burst of springtime heat outside La Comédie-Française. Sir Gideon strolled up to us, a quarter of an hour late. On his cheek, over layers and layers of white chalk, was stuck a huge black, silk beauty spot, so that it looked like a great bug had alighted on his face.

'Oh, such a treat today, my good fellows!' he cried.

'Where is Miss Anson?' I asked.

'Oh, poor Gussy! She drank too much champagne last night after the opera. She insists that she ate bad shrimps, but that doesn't explain why she reeks of wine!' He laughed, and Edgar laughed too. I marvelled at Sir Gideon's privilege in being able to say such things about the lady. I am sure we were not. 'Today, we are going to the salon of la Duchesse du Maine.' This sounded very important, but Sir Gideon could see that we did not know who she was. 'She is the bastard daughter of old King Louis. The fourteenth. She is as old as Methuselah now, but at one time was a great beauty. Well, that's what they say. I'm sure she looks like a side of beef these days. She keeps a salon at the Palais-Royal.' He pointed up the street. 'Up there.'

'Who goes to her salon?' I asked.

Sir Gideon glanced at me and took a moment to look at what I was wearing. 'Oh, I don't know. Writers. Philosophers. Nobody interesting. But it is your chance to go and stare at the progeny of the Sun King himself. Don't you want to do that?'

'Oh, my goodness, yes!' Edgar cried. 'A princess.'

'A *bastard*!' Sir Gideon corrected, but then grinned. 'Albeit a royal one.' Then he clapped his hands. 'Excellent. Then *on y va*!'

The palace was all Palladian symmetries in glowing golden stone. Sir Gideon waved a note of introduction to the royal guard. We were ushered into the wide, beautiful garden, which was said to have been planted by a sister of Charles II of England, who had married Louis XIV's brother. I did not know it then, but her husband was interested in men, not women.

From the garden, we walked up flights of marble stairs until we were shown into a large, light-filled room. Elegant people – they were always elegant, I began to realise – stood around, in periwigs and gleaming silks. Their eyes fell on us judgementally as we entered, then flitted off, ostentatiously bored already. At the end of the room, on not-quite-a-throne, sat Madame la Duchesse herself, eighty years old, regal, exhausted-looking. She wore a bright pink wig with long ringlets that tumbled suggestively over her low décolletage and nestled into the finely creased crêpe of her powdered bosom. 'A vision!' Sir Gideon declared, and I found it oddly cruel, though Edgar laughed. Then my brother turned to me, whispering:

'Can you believe it? We are here to meet a *princess*! Who can imagine such a thing?'

'A *bastard*,' I observed ironically, arching my eyebrows, 'albeit a royal one.' Edgar did not laugh.

A line assembled before the Duchess, who nodded in precisely the same way at anything said to her by those who queued: 'I am here from Alsace.' 'My father is dead.' 'I am your long-lost cousin.' 'I am visiting from the moon.' Each time, no matter what was said, the same stately nod. I realised she was not even listening; she had, quite literally, heard it all before. As each person bowed and departed, the line shuffled along, until we were next. An usher whose wig was crisp like spun sugar asked our names so we could be presented. '*Les messieurs Bowen,*' I murmured. '*D'Angleterre.*' The usher, puzzled by the pronunciation, practised it back to himself: 'BOW-WANG. BOW-*WANNN.*'

'*Les messieurs Bow-wang,*' he declaimed. '*D'Angleterre!*' He then added, softly in French: 'These young men have come all the way from England.'

Madame la Duchesse did not seem impressed by this at all. 'Ugh, I see.'

The usher then turned to us and asked, still in French: 'Her Highness would like to know how you find Paris.'

Madame la Duchesse had asked no such thing. 'Oh, marvellous!' Sir Gideon replied. Edgar and I stood mute at his side. 'It is quite marvellous! All the parties. All the cake.'

The usher turned back: 'They said that it is an incomparable vision, quite unlike their home city. They add that the highlight of their visit is coming to meet you.'

'I see,' said Madame la Duchesse, nodding. 'Yes, I hear London is nothing but shops. All trade. How vulgar. How can London compare to Paris? *Of course* it cannot.' She sounded rather animated. I wondered if all those who had preceded us resented this. She had not been nearly so rude when discussing Alsace or the moon. 'Do *they* think London is vulgar?'

She looked at us through narrowed eyes, her ancient cheeks caked in powder, sticky with rouge. Edgar grinned and bowed. Did he not hear what she had said about trade? Were we not trade? The usher bowed again to his mistress and then turned back to us: 'Her Highness wishes you a prosperous visit.' We all of us spoke French, but were pretending that the usher had indeed translated what the Duchess had said. Then he extended his hand to one side in dismissal. I stared at the princess, the dust-thick powders of her wig, a *maquillage* one could have cut with a butter knife. Then Madame moved forward in her seat and cried: 'Wait!' The usher froze. 'Ask them if they have philosophers in England.'

'Yes,' I said, causing Sir Gideon to flash me a look, as if, in implying I knew anything about philosophy, I had said the wrong thing. Some irritation sparked up in me, so I could not stop myself. 'Has Her Highness heard of Sir Francis Bacon? He had many of Descartes' most famous ideas first.'

The usher looked bilious and asked me, in English: 'Can you mean to suggest to the great-aunt of the King of France that Descartes was not the most original thinker of the seventeenth century?' Pah! went the usher, before adding sharply, still in English: 'All Englishmen are liars. That much is plain!'

The Duchess, who adamantly spoke only French, was confused by the sound of odd English words over which she had only a slim grasp.

'Bacon?' she cried. '*Comme lardon?* I don't understand what these fools are going on about. It is all quite confounding!' The princess now turned her gaze on me, and I saw in her eyes not recognition, not connection, but a

37

cold, contemptuous anger. 'And do you know *Rousseau* in England?'

'Yes,' I said, my rebellious spirit unbowed, 'Your Highness, of course.'

The Duchess's anger seemed only to swell at the idea that people might have heard of Rousseau in England.

'And what about *Piron*?'

'No!' Edgar interjected before I could say any more. 'We have never heard of Piron in England!'

At this, Madame la Duchesse seemed satisfied.

'*Pfft*, these English,' she spat, 'they have never even *heard* of Piron! What barbarians!'

The three of us glanced at each other, stifled our giggles, bowed and shuffled off. Behind us, the usher was introducing the next visitors.

*T*hree weeks after we made the acquaintance of Sir Gideon and his circle, Edgar and I were invited to a party in the city palace of an elderly cardinal to celebrate the recent death of the King's all-powerful mistress, Madame de Pompadour. We had made no other real connections, so this invitation was purely thanks to Sir Gideon, of course: indeed, I could not help but feel that we belonged to him. Sir Gideon informed us that the Pompadour's enemies were having a wonderful time now she was dead. 'Can you imagine?' he cried. 'Can you imagine how amusing it is?' It did not seem so to me.

The party was held in a large salon hung lavishly in cream and pink drapes, its ceiling decorated with rows of silver birdcages suspended above the partygoers' heads. Inside each cage was a different songbird; forty-three in total, one for each year that the Pompadour had lived, and each was singing a different song, the individual calls uniting in a screeching cacophony. French doors from the salon led to a quiet courtyard, lined with potted orange trees in bloom. Someone said that at the end of the night, the birds would be released in the courtyard and shot by a master marksman brought in from Rambouillet especially for the occasion. And so the joke about Madame de Pompadour was revealed: eventually, every songbird has to die.

Everyone was in splendid dress. No one danced but rather whirled about in an endless exchange of pleasantries, ceaselessly turning from person to person. Edgar launched himself in headlong, talking on in his buoyant, fluent but accented French. Watching him, I felt a great affection for his optimism and lack of guile. I wanted Edgar to succeed and be happy, and so I decided to make good efforts to be social as well. I strode up to strangers and attempted conversations in good faith. But how I hated it, how unnatural and forced it felt. It is all very well to know how one should stand, or how to talk about Petrarch, but nothing had prepared me for the bell-chime of horror I felt as I looked at one person after another and wondered: would they speak to me?

And what was worse was that people *didn't* want to speak to me. Each time, hearing my French, they asked: 'Are you English? Yes, of course one can tell. What is your title? You have no title? Is your father in the army, a general? My goodness, what is he, a lawyer?' When foolishly I explained that he was in shipping, they would instantly turn away to another companion. 'As I was saying, Monsieur le Duc de Rochefoucauld was truly very *elegant* in his response ...' pretending I was not there. Yet whenever I turned to look at Edgar, his brio remained undimmed. He did not seem afraid. He was sure that people would talk to him, and so they did. Did he not tell them that our father was in shipping? Did he tell them,

I wondered, that he was a baron with a family pile on a wet Welsh hillside?

I wanted to escape for a moment, away from the silken crush of fine bodies. I stepped out into the quiet courtyard, and sat down on a low stone bench. I closed my eyes, resting my back against the cool wall, breathing in the heady scent of the orange blossom. Soon, the party would be over and the birds inside would be released from their cages and blasted to their deaths. Then we would return to our palaces and boarding-houses, and wait until we all had to meet again. All of us were tied up in our endless social exchange: another party, another conversation, another invitation, and for what? I knew what, of course: for the realisation of my parents' plan.

'I say, Mister Bowen, what are you doing out here?'

I opened my eyes: the magnificent Augusta Anson stood above me. Her dress was a shade of lilac so pale it was almost silver, her hair powdered in that same lilac-silver, with strands of ivy, also painted silver, woven through it. Her lips and cheeks were coloured a soft pink. She looked like a theatre-stage ghost: exquisite, ethereal: a beautiful harbinger of some unknown doom. She moved towards me, turning the width of her dress to navigate the orange trees. I stood up.

'I am taking a break from the conversations, Miss Anson.'

'Do you find the French to be a strain all day long?'

'Not the French. I find the conversation a little ... repetitive.'

She looked at me with hazy unease, a studied express-ion that I had previously noticed her assume in a moment of not understanding. She smiled confidently. 'When do you leave Paris, Benjamin?' she asked, changing the subject. She used my first name with feline authority.

'Soon, Miss Anson. Next week, perhaps.'

When she was near, she touched the back of my hand with her folded fan. She then moved the fan to her mouth as if my skin had just touched hers. Its end pressed against her lip, sank deeply into the pink-painted flesh – just as it had that first day at the Tuileries.

'I shall miss you, Benjamin, when you have left us.'

Her words surprised me. I always expected that she thought of me very little, if anything at all. I wanted to grasp at something one should say in situations like these. 'Have you enjoyed the party … *Augusta*?' I gulped as I said her name. She did not correct me.

'I think I am growing bored of Paris. Paris is like a big, beautiful wedding cake, whereas London is the kitchen that made it, teeming with those who supply it, I mean the *tradesmen*' – she emphasised the word – 'and the people greedily clamouring to eat it. After all this polite chatter, one rather longs for a riot, don't you think, Benjamin?'

'How strange,' I said. 'I was just thinking something rather similar.'

She let out a long, humming breath. 'Is it so surprising, Benjamin, that intelligent people share a view?'

Her blue eyes sparkled as they ran over my face. She opened her fan with a sharp shake and fanned herself a little, though there was no need; the air out in the courtyard was cool enough. 'Your brother thinks *you* might be bored in Paris.'

The moment popped around me. 'Does he?' I asked. Did I believe Edgar had said that, or did I think she might want me to believe that? She gave a little shrug and sighed as prettily as she could – so very prettily indeed.

'I am teasing you, Benjamin.' I waited for her to say that Edgar had not said these things about me, but she did not. 'I am teasing you, because I know that you could never regret *our* acquaintance.'

Those blue, bird eyes were watching me. Then she turned and moved off, doing a strange little dance through the pots of orange trees. They were covered in small white flowers, heavy with sweet-sharp pollen, and as she moved, like a huge lilac-silver bee, the pollen collected on the fabric of her dress. Pollen on silk: a catastrophe. But Augusta did not seem to care. The moment was what mattered: there are always more dresses to be bought. Eventually she circled back towards me until she stood only inches away. She looked first into my eyes. Then at my lips. Her eyes focused on my mouth and I could not breathe at all.

'Should you like to kiss me, Benjamin?' she asked, still staring at my lips. I felt my chest contract. 'Should you?' she asked again. Then, brightly, she looked up at me. She let out a breath, softly, sensually slow. I felt the blood move at once to my cock. Then she snorted cruelly, derisively. 'Do you presume to *even* think of it, *Mister* Bowen? Ha!' she snapped. 'Your nasty little father ships his own vulgar type to New York in a rowing boat and yet you imagine that you could kiss *me*. My father is a hereditary baronet, sir, and you and your brother are vulgar little innocents to think I would deign to do so! Why people like you are even *on* Tour, truly, I do not understand it! You wonder why those people inside ignore you and cut you? Why, sir, it is because you are most *obviously* a merchant! Why would those who have been in the presence of the French king speak to *you*, except perhaps to borrow money at a good rate?'

She stood above me then, a glorious, evil warrior-queen. I was struck mute with terror, with her superiority. 'Do you know where Gideon and I were before we came here? We went to a luncheon with the Earls of Lincoln and Cardigan. Do you truly think we would have taken you with us? Earls don't eat with trinket-sellers and boat-rowers – do you and your *silly* brother not understand that?' She tossed back her head and started laughing. I glanced sideways, for fear Edgar might have wandered near. It would have crushed him to hear her call him that. Then suddenly we heard shouting from inside. We each looked around, as though we were secret lovers intruded upon unexpectedly. People began to pour out through the French windows into the courtyard. Augusta moved away from my bench, vanishing into the mass of bodies. Footmen mingled among the Quality, holding aloft the cages of songbirds for everyone to see. One cage swung close to my face. Inside, a nightingale had been painted gold. The paint was stuck to its feathers and had got into its eyes. The bird wheezed on its perch; its feathers tarred with poisonous gold. It struck me that in that moment, the bird and I were in some awful community, both of us contaminated and condemned.

Another shout went up. *Hoop-la!* The marksman from Rambouillet was brought in to begin the shooting. He was enormous, broad-shouldered and tall, dressed in

44

expensive leather boots, linen shirt and an antique hunter's hat with a long pheasant-tail feather, an aristocrat's fantasy of the peasants' garb. A wide grin was spread across his face as he nodded to the silked-and-wigged spectators, who parted before him. As one they began to applaud lightly, while the birds, wheezing and golden, were tipped out of their cages and attempted to fly.

I had already lost all sight of Augusta among the cheering partygoers. There in the middle of a cardinal's festivities, to celebrate the death of a woman I had never met, I only wanted to see my brother, my other half. I began to push through the crowd back into the salon, trying to find Edgar, and when I finally did, he looked at me angrily:

'What did Augusta say to you? What did you say to her?' My brother's eyes were red-raw, round with unexpected rage. 'Have you spoiled things? Good grief, Benjamin, why must you always spoil things?'

Always? I thought. The room suddenly shook with a loud bang. The glass in the French windows rattled. The marksman's gun fired out, birds and wings and guts were blasted and scorched, falling among the applauding guests and the orange blossom. I looked out across the courtyard. I could see Augusta Anson, standing with Sir Gideon Hervey, staring at us, a look of amusement on her pretty face. There was an air about them of gossip just revealed. Both of them pursing their lips like it was all such fun. I turned back to Edgar, who was furiously looking away. He had not seen his friends – or their cruelty.

Edgar and I returned to our room in grim silence. I slept poorly, turning and sweating. I did not understand why he was so angry with me. I had no intimation of the resentments he might feel. He was awake too, but neither of us spoke. In the morning, when I opened my eyes, Edgar was already dressed before I had a chance to get up. He said he was going out to get breakfast. I called his name, but he did not turn back. 'Edgar, please wait.' He left, not quite slamming the door, but an echo reverberated in the room. Throughout our childhood, the two of us squabbled as brothers do, but very rarely had we had serious fallouts.

At ten o'clock, I sat alone in our room. My brother still had not returned. We were due to take a tour of Paris by coach that day. Over a silvered pot of coffee gone cold and half a stick of bread untouched, I wondered what I should do. I picked up our mother's guidebook, but I did not want to read what she had ruled we should visit. I put on my coat: the same one I had worn the night before we left London. Only then did I remember what I had kept inside its pocket: the scrap of paper I had rescued from the box under my bed. Now I pulled it out and read the words I had long before copied onto it. 'Cardoso': my mother's maiden name. The address: 'Rue des Rosiers'. I had quite forgotten about it. I returned the paper to my pocket.

At ten-thirty, I went out to the street to meet the carriage, and there was Edgar, sitting on some stone steps opposite, and the driver waiting for us. The man nodded and my brother saw me, got to his feet, sauntered across the street and got into the carriage, not saying a word.

We went first into the heart of the city, near the Tuileries again, and then beyond the Louvre down the busy Rue de Rivoli. The carriage circled over the bridges and the islands, where the traffic was moving in a slow file. From the window, I looked up and down the Seine, choked with boats. Boys on the right bank sat with fishing poles but did not seem very interested in catching fish. They called to each other and ran barefoot along the stone ledge of the river wall. The whole time, neither Edgar nor I spoke. I wanted to, but I did not know what I felt afraid of. Perhaps it was that I had nothing good to say of Sir Gideon, or particularly of Augusta Anson.

We passed the Hôtel de Ville. The carriage came to a momentary stop. My brother, alerted by our stillness, shifted in his seat. 'Are you all right?' I asked. 'Hmm,' he replied, non-committally. But then his air changed again.

'I am sorry that I was vile yesterday, Benjamin,' he said. It surprised – and pleased – me that he should say it. Our eyes connected. 'I don't know why I did it.' He sighed. 'I know I am too excited by everything that's happening here but I shouldn't be vile to you. It's just …'

He stopped, and for a moment, I thought he might be on the verge of tears.

'What is it, Edgar?' I asked.

'It's just that you are so clever, Benjamin. You have always looked at Mother with your ironic eye. And I know that none of this matters to you, really.'

'I don't think that's true.'

'*Pfft!* Of course it's true,' he replied. 'I don't think you care anything about the future, about the Company, about any of that. You don't care about meeting good people, about *being* good people. You simply *don't*.'

Up until that moment, I would never have thought that of myself. But sometimes, another person will utter something about you, and you realise that it is probably true. 'I know you look at it all, Benjamin, and tut and think it's just Mother telling us how to live our lives. But it matters *to me*. I want to be a success. I want to have friends. I want to go back to London with an address book full of invitations. I want Gideon and Augusta to ...' He sighed. 'Well, just to like me.'

I was tremendously moved by his words. Maybe I could have disabused him of this idea – *maybe* I should have told him about Gideon and Augusta enjoying watching us argue, but that would have hurt him, and I had no wish to do that. 'I think they do like you, Edgar.' Oh, I know it was a lie. 'I wouldn't worry on that score.'

He sighed again and I felt so sorry, and wished things had been different. Above us, I heard the driver call to the horses, and then his whip crack in the air. The carriage began to pull away. I put my hand inside my coat, into the pocket, and felt the folded paper between my fingertips.

'I have something to show you,' I said.

'What is it?'

I took out the paper and handed it to him. He examined it for a moment, then unfolded it. 'It's an address.'

'Yes,' I said. 'Not far from here. Do you see the surname?'

'Cardoso.' He thought for a second. 'What kind of strange name is that?'

'Spanish, I suppose.' I took a breath and felt my nerves. 'It is Mother's maiden name.'

'What?' he whispered. 'How do you have this?'

'I have had it for some time. I don't know why I brought it but …'

Edgar's eyebrows lifted. 'Mother's maiden name?' he said, with some wonder.

'Yes, like I say, I don't really know why I brought it.'

He chuckled to himself. 'Oh, I know why.'

'Why?' I asked.

'Because, for you, Mother is a mystery.' He paused and gazed at the paper in his hand. 'How do you have this?'

'I found it,' I said, 'a long time ago. I copied it down. I always knew about it.'

Edgar laughed. 'You are such a frightful sneak, Benjamin!' He looked down at the paper again. 'Cardoso,' he sighed. He stared at the name for a while. 'Do you think that's a *grand* sort of name?'

'I don't know,' I said. 'Mother is a very educated person. Refined, I suppose.'

'Perhaps,' he began, in his hopeful little way, 'Mother is quite grand. If she was grand and had married down –' he looked up, both apologetic and conspiratorial '– to Father, I mean, that would explain a lot, wouldn't it?'

I felt my brow knit. 'I have often wondered who she really is,' I said.

'Maybe Mother is very grand. She is secretive like you.' I found it strange that he should compare us, let alone call me secretive. I always compared *them*. A light danced in his eyes. 'Maybe Mother comes from a noble family in Spain.' He mouthed the name to himself: 'Cardoso … Cardoso …'

'You are fantasising,' I said, happily, teasing, the light still dancing in his eyes.

'Do you want to go there, Benjamin?' my brother asked. He was looking at me. 'Maybe she is really a *marquesa*,' he continued, his eyes expectant. 'Wouldn't that be a thing to tell Augusta!' Edgar sprang up in his seat and tapped the carriage roof.

'Edgar!' I cried.

'Rue des Rosiers!' he called up to the driver.

Minutes later, the carriage pulled into a narrow throng of dark streets. We turned a corner onto another street and from above us the driver huffed down: '*Ici.*'

My brother and I got out of the carriage and stood in the gloom of the long, narrow street. We walked along a little. 'Look!' Edgar cried, pointing up. Above a door, a few houses ahead, hung a wooden sign with the words carved into it:

CARDOSO
NÉGOCIANT

Négociant: a merchant. 'This is it,' I said. Before I could say anything more, Edgar ran forward and loudly knocked on the door. 'Edgar!' I cried and he just grinned and shrugged at his own *fait accompli*. I rushed up behind him just as the door opened, only slightly, and an elderly man appeared behind it.

'Yes, what do you want?' He spoke in heavily accented French, but I could not recognise from where. He glared at me with undisguised suspicion. I leaned forwards and he pushed the door even closer to its frame. 'What's your business, hmm?' he cried.

'We are Cardosos,' Edgar said, brightly in French.

The old man frowned, looking up and down our bodies: 'Who, *you?*'

'Yes,' Edgar answered as I looked past the man and into the darkness of the interior.

'Is there anyone to whom we can speak?' I asked. 'One of our relations? Are you a Cardoso?'

'Me?' the old man groaned. 'Pah, I should be so lucky.' Edgar glanced at me. Maybe our mother was going to be grand after all. Reluctantly, the man ushered us inside. 'Me,' he muttered to himself, 'a Cardoso. Ha!'

The house was much like any other. In the fashion of business, the ground floor was an office. Dusty scrolls and wooden folders were arranged in teetering towers on top of mazes of desks and drawers, labyrinths of disorder. The old man scuttled forward, clinging to desks and shelves to stop himself from falling. We were led up the stairs and into a small, elegant sitting room on the first floor. 'Do you want coffee?' he barked. I did not know what the right answer was: yes or no? When we did not reply immediately, the old man croaked: 'Or is *our* coffee not good enough for you?'

'Coffee would be very nice,' I said.

'Nice?' the old man groaned. 'Nice? Pah!'

He went back out into the hallway he had led us through, mumbling complaints to himself. Edgar and I sat in silence. Then the door to the sitting room opened again. In walked a tall, elegant man, rather handsome, dressed in a good though subtle dark blue suit, his hair not wigged but in a turban. He bowed as he entered and spoke in French, also accented:

'I am sorry, *messieurs,* but I am not sure if I know ...'

We both got to our feet and bowed. I began to explain that we were on the first stage of the Tour, having sailed from London. I listed the cities to which we hoped to go, and he told us which of those he knew, mainly because of commercial connections. As we exchanged pleasantries, my brother began to look around the room at the little oriental oddities. The old man bustled in again, and behind him a boy of about thirteen, carrying a tray of coffee. 'They said they wanted coffee,' he complained to the turbaned gentleman. 'I told them, I don't have time to make coffee, but they insisted.'

I looked to our host who smiled at me as though resigned, a request for patience towards the old man, I supposed. We sat back down and received our coffee cups. 'Forgive me, *messieurs*,' the Cardoso fellow tried again, 'but I am not sure I understand why you are here.'

'*Monsieur*,' I began, 'our mother's maiden name was Cardoso. And I have never met or even heard of another Cardoso. I know nothing of the surname's provenance.'

The man bowed his head forward a little, with the air of one confused.

'And I thought I knew every Cardoso in the world,' he said, clearly a joke. 'But we are a disparate group, it's true. Amsterdam, Berlin, here, Riga, North Africa, Constantinople.' North Africa and Constantinople? I thought, amazed. What kinds of contact did this man have, and more to the point, what kinds of cousin? 'I did not know there were any Cardosos in London just now, at least not any connected to me.' His eyes were searching ours as if we were supposed to give some secret signal to show we shared some knowledge. 'Forgive me, gentlemen, but may I enquire your mother's name?'

'Rachel,' I said. Immediately Cardoso's face fell. He hesitated. I thought perhaps he might make to leave. '*Monsieur?*'

'Say your surname again, please?'

'Bowen,' Edgar said.

Cardoso got to his feet. 'I am sorry, gentlemen, but, uh, I have another matter to which to attend.' He bowed quickly. 'Good day.'

Edgar and I looked at one another before I turned back to Cardoso. 'Will you explain yourself, sir?' I asked. 'You do know our mother?'

It was then that Edgar said, 'Benjamin, perhaps we should leave.' I glanced between the two of them as if they understood some secret I did not. Edgar's face was instantly all agitation, horror even.

'*Monsieur,*' I said, not grasping whatever the two of them seemed to understand, 'can you explain ...?'

'Gentlemen –' he now spoke in crisp, clear English '– I would prefer that I did not speak any more on the subject of my cousin.'

'Your *cousin?*' Edgar spat. His fists formed tight balls as if ready to strike out. I had never seen him like this before. 'Benjamin, I want to leave.'

Cardoso flashed his eyes at me. 'You should listen to your brother. There is nothing I want to say about *Rahel.*' The name he used – *Rahel, Rahel* – seemed to blare mysteriously through the silence, as loud as a trumpet.

Edgar leapt up and swung at Cardoso. 'Scoundrel! Liar!' he yelled in English. Cardoso flew sideways out of his seat. I screamed Edgar's name. Our cups of coffee shattered into smithereens across the floor. I tore at my brother.

'Edgar! What are you doing?' I shouted.

My brother swung around as if ready to strike me too.

'Don't you see? Can't you tell?'

'What?' I cried. '*What?*'

'This man is a Jew, Benjamin! Are you so stupid you do not know? He is a Jew. That means he is saying that our mother is a Jew too, that *we* are—' The word died on his lips. It was choking Edgar to death.

Wiping his mouth with the back of his sleeve, our cousin got to his feet. I was restraining my brother, but my brain was reeling. Cardoso was holding the side of his face, perhaps where Edgar had struck him. 'Your mother has not earned the title of Jew, any more than you two ruffians do.' Edgar reared up upon hearing this, but I managed to contain him. 'Your mother was thrown out by her family, by her community.' The word lingered in the air.

'I don't understand,' I said, confused.

'Understand?' Edgar groaned, as our cousin began to spit the truth:

'Your mother was born into the poorest part of our family, clever but feckless, lost in books and not business. Her father found her a husband, a kind man with a good business in London, many years older than she, and what did she do? She seduced a Christian man – one of their employees – and when her husband *conveniently* died, she married this other man!'

Edgar had gone very still. Suddenly, the door to the room burst open and the old man and the young lad started tearing at us, yelling furiously in Spanish and French. I pulled my brother away with one hand whilst pushing back our assailants with the other. Seconds later, in a blur of fists and curses, Edgar and I fell blinking into the Paris sunshine. The door to the house – to our past – slammed shut and we stood in the street, the two of us, alone.

'We shall have to leave Paris,' Edgar cried, staring at the ground. He did not lift his face to mine. 'Tomorrow. We cannot risk encountering … *that person* again. I shall write to Sir Gideon and say that we have to leave and ask that we remain friends and meet up again, further along the route.'

'What are you talking about, Edgar?' I asked. 'Why does it matter?'

'*Why does it matter?*' he shrieked at the top of his lungs. People passing in the street stopped to stare at the two young Englishmen making fools of themselves in public. 'No one will befriend a Jew in London!' he said. 'Do you know nothing? Englishmen can have nothing to do with Jews! Every person knows it! If anyone finds out the truth about our mother, we will be destroyed! I cannot be destroyed!' He paused, and looked up at me. His eyes were red and misted. 'And you must never tell anyone, Benjamin. Not even in jest.'

'In jest?' I cried.

He shook his head, in anger and frustration. 'You must never tell *anyone*!'

I stood in that street and thought, but at least we have taken a step closer to the truth.

'Give me your word!' he thundered. '*Anyone!*'

'All right,' I said, not yet knowing that this was a promise I would not be able to keep.

THE ITALIAN ALPS

*A*osta was our first stop on Italian soil. It is beautiful there, in the high green pastures that fall away from white Alpine peaks. The sun sparkles on the snow; the air is pure. But Aosta is only the cusp of Italy. From there, Florence and Bologna and Venice and Siena and Rome – all the masterpieces of European civilisation – beckon. Visitors do not linger in Aosta. The young people who come on Tour, the English Quality, stand outside log-lined chalets above vast flower meadows, in high wigs, holding pet dogs, counting luggage and huffing loudly. 'How far is it from here to Milan? *Two days?* How can it be two days?'

On the day we arrived, our bodies sore from the coach rattling down the stony slopes from Zermatt and the Valais, Edgar hungrily eyed these splendid youths. 'We will soon make new friends. Don't worry,' he said urgently. 'Benjamin, don't worry.' But I hadn't been worried about that. What did worry me was the truth that we had come so close to in Paris, before Edgar had hastened us away. Whilst travelling through the endless, dull cities of

Germany, he had begun to imagine that we might see our friends from Paris again. But I knew one thing: I did not want to see Sir Gideon and Augusta. I hoped *never* to see them again.

On our second day in Aosta, Edgar was struck down with a sickness. He was one of several guests in our chalet poisoned by some spoiled yoghurt. The owner was mortified and called for a physician, insisting that he would pay the bill, although, in fact, he never did. I sat at the edge of Edgar's bed in our shared room, and asked him if there was anything I could do.

'You should go out,' he said.

'Go out?' I replied. My brother's skin was as green as mint jelly, and his eyes as white as lard. But now he told me to go out by myself, when I had never been outside on my own in my life.

'You can't stay here.'

'But don't you want to meet people with me? I am nervous to go on my own, Edgar.'

He let out a heaving, puking sort of groan. 'You can speak to people, Benjamin,' he said. 'Don't be such a child.' I had forgotten how, as children, he'd liked to advertise his year's seniority over me. I heard it again then. His annoyance was down to his sickness, but still, it worked. I agreed, and took my leave for the day.

That day and the next, I drifted around Aosta, whilst Edgar remained, liverish and sweating, in his sickbed. Even at that high altitude, the Italian summer sun was hard on an English wool coat. I ate alone in a tavern, a luncheon of air-dried meats and oily salad, and watched French diners twirling their hands and making appalled pronouncements on the quality of the cuisine. This seemed to somewhat bolster their mood. I shrank into the corner, hiding behind my table, and uttering no word except the occasional *grazie* to the serving girls. A group of English Tourists stood near me once. One raised a hand, recognising that I was one of their nation. I looked away, afraid that they might initiate any conversation. What little black thing inside me made me turn my face away? A voice in my head, saying, *they* won't want you. The voice, I imagined initially, belonged to Augusta Anson.

Keeping myself to myself, I decided to see what remained of the ancient Roman city. I stared up at old arches, remnants of a long-dead empire. I visited the amphitheatre. Inspecting it, I thought only: so much grey brick. The Porta Pretoria: more grey brick. The Arch of Augustus: yet more grey brick. Somewhere, in my mother's guidebook, were the instructions of what we should see, and implicitly, what we should think. Admire the Doric entablature! The symmetry of the triglyphs! I stared at grey brick, and thought, I hate Aosta. I hate this. I hate all of it. This voice surprised me too. It certainly was *not* the voice of Augusta Anson.

I dragged myself out to see the church of Sant'Orso. I had never even visited the churches of London. My parents were not churchgoers and certainly had not encouraged us to go rolling around the city *looking at things*. I therefore had no idea whether Sant'Orso was in any way noteworthy. I walked around its shadowed and candlelit spaces at a funereal pace, *looking at things*, but I hadn't a clue if they were significant or not. On painted panels, sad-eyed Marys gazed up at accusatory Jesuses. My mother, when talking about the history of art, would often speak of the 'mysteries' of religious artworks, yet we were never educated to experience that mystery. We merely observed it, repeating what renowned art historians had written.

Upon reaching the dull Gothic nave, I stared up into its featureless ceiling. Various gaunt and exhausted Christs in multiple states of dishevelment hung from crosses. Somewhere nearby, a group of despairing nuns stood gazing up. One of them whispered in Latin, 'He died for our sins.' What a bloody stupid thing to do, I suddenly thought. No one had asked him to.

I heard a voice at my shoulder: 'I say, are you English?' The voice was clear, bell-like. I turned. An unwigged, golden-haired young man was peering at me. His skin had the gilded pinkness of an Englishman in the South. I felt myself wince; my eyes flickered, even in the gloom of the church. He was a few years older than me, a man rather than a boy. He wore a royal-blue coat, so deep in hue it seemed to jump off his body. His cravat was badly tied. No one in Paris would wear their cravat other than tightly wrapped like a tourniquet around their Adam's apple. And he was handsome, very handsome; as handsome a man as I had ever seen. 'I am Mister Horace Lavelle,' he said, a marvellous half-smile on his lips. He was gazing at me, with amused intensity. 'You are English, aren't you? I can tell.'

'I am Mister Benjamin Bowen,' I said, my eyes glancing nervously across the floor of the church.

'Where are you looking?' His voice was all lightness. I looked up at him and now he was observing the ground, too. Then he lifted his eyes – they were like sapphires, very bright, very alert – and grinned at me. 'Were you admiring my shoes? They are rather lovely, aren't they?'

About what were we talking? I did not understand. 'Excuse me?' I murmured.

'My shoes. Do you know where I got them?' he said.

I simply stared at him, not sure how I should answer.

'I stole them. From the Elector of Bavaria,' he stated. I saw him watch my eyes widen.

'Truly?'

'No,' he said, 'of course not!' He must have seen my relief. He leaned forwards to whisper: 'It was the Queen of Poland.'

He rocked backwards and roared, a loud, glorious, shameless laugh. It rang up into the eaves of the church, echoing, and then fell back down – onto me. The Latin-speaking nuns watched us, their faces mean with a suspicion of … *something*. 'You are just arrived?' he asked. I said yes. 'I thought so. I have not seen you in this hellhole the last two weeks.'

Two weeks? No person of Quality stopped in Aosta for two whole weeks. Why had he lingered here so long? 'We have just been to Paris,' I said.

His brow twitched briefly. '*We?*'

'I am here with my brother. My brother, Edgar.'

With big, playful movements, Lavelle pretended to look around the nave, up and around, as if searching for something. Then he looked back at me, arching an eyebrow: 'I have noticed you these twenty minutes. I see no brother.' Twenty minutes? Had he been watching me, truly, for twenty minutes, and I had not noticed him all that while? 'You are quite alone. Do you have a brother *at all*?'

I knew that he was teasing me. He *was* amusing. But still, what was it about him that felt so ... perilous? 'My brother is ill,' I said. 'He has eaten some spoiled yoghurt.'

'Puking himself all the way to Rome, is he?'

He burst into loud laughter again, every bit as riotously as before. Now the nuns were wearing their annoyance like armour.

'You are making enemies,' I said.

He blew through his lips, to show his disdain. 'I don't care. Oh, how the Italians like to show their ill humour. It makes up for their lack of personality.'

'How can a whole nation lack personality?' I asked.

'Ha!' he responded. 'Haven't you just been to Switzerland?' The whole time he gazed at me, I felt his blue eyes burning.

'You must like Aosta if you have been here two weeks,' I said. I was becoming nervous under the intensity of his stare. 'Have you been to see the Arch of the Emperor Augustus?' I tried to be clever. 'It's all grey bricks.'

'Oh, sir, are you truly asking me about the Emperor Augustus? Truly, are you asking me about *some bricks* you saw once?' His face loomed towards mine. 'Boring grey bricks,' he said. And I began to grin, and he grinned again – again and again. 'Who cares?' he continued. 'I couldn't give a fuck. Next you will be quoting Montesquieu at me.' His grin turned devilish. 'If we are going to be friends,' he said, 'learn this: I do not give a *fuck*!'

He said the word so loudly, I was struck mute. And then I realised *what* he had just said as much as how he had said it. Did he truly mean that we were friends? How were we friends? He kept on talking, filling my brain with words. 'Would you not prefer to ask me about what the women are like in Aosta? Would you not prefer to know what they will do if you get them drunk?' He laughed in that same shameless way, in the way one might to show one was speaking in jest. 'Was it Augustus or Tiberius who kept a harem of young boys and girls that he fucked when he was an old man? And is it Suetonius or Tacitus who chastised him for being a sodomite?'

Part of me wanted him to shut his mouth. And the other part? 'Why are you in Italy?' he asked, when I had still said nothing.

'We are on Tour.' I hesitated. My mouth was dry. 'My brother and I.'

'Oh, this mythical brother of yours?'

'I do have a brother.'

He smiled mockingly. 'And a bevy of sisters too, no doubt.'

'No,' I said, stumbling over my thoughts. 'Just a brother. We came to Italy for the culture.'

'You are in Italy … for the culture? Oh, you fibber!' he cried merrily. 'Really, Italians? What culture do these sweaty morons have to speak of?'

I could hear my mother's voice in my head: Petrarch, Boccaccio, Dante, Leonardo, rhapsodising, hymning the names. Now he called them sweaty morons! 'The whole point of the Tour is to see the culture. At least, that's what most people think.'

He fixed me with his eye then shrugged nonchalantly. 'Mister Bowen, as I say, I do not give a *fuck*. Did you not hear me? And I particularly don't give one *solitary* fuck to what people think.' And then he smiled, and walked away, out of the nave. He did not look back. He did not need to. He knew I would follow him. Part of me thought, *turn and walk away.* But every other part of me yelled, *go after him.* So I ran to his side.

'Then why are you here?' I asked urgently. With perfect timing, Lavelle stopped so that I almost ran into him. He looked up at the ceiling. The muscles in his thick, hairless neck tensed. His face tilted back; the suffused light from the church windows fell on his face. Then slowly he breathed in, and licked his lips absent-mindedly. How beautiful he was. I thought of the two sinners captured in the Park. I was jealous of them then – no, not of their deaths, of course, but of their knowledge of men. The mysteries of sex to the virgin. Lavelle came nearer to me and I felt his magnetic glow. His skin was luminous, and his lips glistened. His breath touched my face. His eyes were alight with intention. It was like I was being drawn upwards, towards him, into him, my feet leaving the ground.

'You haven't answered my question,' I said, hearing the hesitation in my voice.

'No,' he replied. 'I haven't. I wonder what it means if I don't answer your question. What do you think?' To show that I was not to be played with – and I now have no idea how I had conceived that to be the case – I went to turn away, but he grabbed my arm. 'I am not letting you go,' he said, and started yanking me along the aisle. 'Where are we going?' I cried.

'I have had enough of this –' we were passing the out-raged nuns; he leered at them and the poor virgins all shrieked as one '– *shithole*!' he yelled in Italian. One of the sisters crossed herself, and all the others looked like they were going to wet themselves.

We tumbled outside into the brightly lit square. 'You must tell me,' he said as he frogmarched me away from the church, out into iniquity, 'everywhere you have been.'

And so, squinting in the sudden brightness, my mind racing, I listed the cities of Germany which Edgar and I had visited. 'Hole,' he cried at each I mentioned. Cologne. *Hole.* Aachen. *Hole.* Kassel. *Hole, hole, hole.* Karlsruhe. *Oh, for goodness sake, hooole!* I told him that I spoke German, as if that might impress him. 'Good grief, German? What for? What next, Norwegian?'

'Why not Norwegian?' I asked. 'Why not?'

He sniffed. 'Indeed, I suppose, why not? Why English? Why Latin? Why any tongue?'

Across the square, shaded by pungent fig trees, stood two young Italian women. Each was raven-haired, full-lipped, dark-eyed. They were rapt with the knowledge of their own beauty. 'Do you think those two lovelies care that you learned German?' Lavelle asked me. 'Do you think they care about fucking *Diderot*?' I looked at the young women. They briefly looked at us and then turned away. 'They couldn't give a fuck about the Enlightenment,' he whispered. 'Why, Voltaire himself would burn every book in his library to have the chance to put his thin, jabby little cock inside those beauties.' He made his first two fingers into a sharp little point, and jabbed it in the air three times, before loudly squelching with his lips. Voltaire had ejaculated disappointingly all over the main square of Aosta. I gasped, and then I laughed, and I saw that it pleased him that he had made me laugh.

We peeled away, deeper into the town. 'So, why are you here, in Italy, if not for culture?'

Lavelle raised an eyebrow as we walked.

'Firstly, my parents forced me to come. They thought it would do me good, stop me inseminating their maids.'

'Really?' I said, and he squawked.

'Of course not!' he laughed. 'I don't have a quiverful of country bastards.'

'Then why did you say so?' I asked.

He glanced at me as though I were a particularly slow child. 'For. Ironic. Effect.' The slowness of his words drew me in. For. Ironic. Effect. 'I have come to Italy for Beauty,' Lavelle continued. 'The pursuit of Beauty.' He looked back at me. 'But I have decided to find Beauty where I choose. I do not need a guidebook written by John Locke to tell me what to think.'

'My mother is a great admirer of Mister Locke.'

Lavelle gazed at me, quite openly, as if this was quite the most stupid thing he had ever heard. 'Of course she is.' Then with his finger and thumb, he caught my cheek, not tenderly but with a flick. 'It is adorable that you do not understand the rules of English cruelty.'

'What do you mean?' I asked.

He sighed mock-unhappily, mock-sympathetically.

'What do you mean what do I mean? Do you think the Duke of Fitzroy or the Marchioness of Shuttlecock give a damn about John Locke? They don't have a clue who John Locke was. They barely know who Sir Isaac Newton was. They don't even know how to wipe their own arses let alone the first bloody thing about Pico della Mirandola.'

He stopped, and smiled beautifully, and then began to recite from what I recognised as the *Oration on the Dignity of Man*: 'Let some holy ambition invade our souls, so that, dissatisfied with mediocrity, we shall eagerly desire the highest things and shall toil with all our strength to obtain them, since we may if we wish.' He spoke graciously and elegantly, and it surprised me, how cultivated and perfect his recitation was. He grinned and slapped my arm: 'What a load of bollocks!' He laughed and strode off into the sunlight. He stopped and turned back to me: 'Well, are you coming, or not?'

Turning to me as we walked, he asked: 'Did you make good society in Paris?'

'Yes, we were known.'

It was a very elegant thing to say that one was 'known'. Yet upon hearing the word, Lavelle almost clucked with derision: 'Oh, my God, and by whom were you *knoooown* in *Paaaaris*?' I spouted surnames – Ansons, Russells, Herveys – and Lavelle sniffed: 'My God, the whole thing sounds truly horrible.'

'Sir Gideon Hervey …'

Lavelle groaned. 'Appalling!'

'Do you know him?' I asked, realising that there was a game afoot but not yet understanding its rules. Lavelle came to a sudden dead stop. I almost banged into him again.

'I do not need to, Benjamin. May I call you Benjamin?' He did not give me a chance to say yes or no. 'Just putting together those three words – Sir, Gideon and Hervey – tells me everything I need to know about him. He sounds *awful*.' He paused spectacularly well. '*Was* he awful?'

'Well—'

'Come on, you can tell me.'

His eyes were alive, swimming with mischief. 'Yes,' I confessed. 'He was absolutely awful.'

Lavelle grinned. He began to address an audience of no one but me, declaiming as an actor, outwards, into the mid distance:

'Hear me, hear me, ladies and gentlemen! Sir Gideon Hervey, the cousin of His Grace the Earl of Arsehole, pronounced *Uzzell*, is absolutely awful. He is bloody appalling. He is a piece of filth that any truly clever man –' did he mean me? '– would wipe from his heel as though he had stepped into a fresh cow pat.' Then Lavelle smacked his lips as if blowing me a kiss, though he was not. 'Do you like to drink beer?'

That night, I drank it until my blood was the colour of amber. I drank until I was drunk, in a way I had not done before. He told me how he had been brought up in Ireland and how his family were ashamed of his pleasure-seeking. 'I think with my member, and not my head,' he joked, but everything he said was so hard-tuned, clearly designed to provoke, that I did not know what to believe. I told him about my upbringing, about my mother's devotion to learning, her faith in advancement, our seclusion from the world. 'You were locked in a room full of books when you should have been out running in the open air, when you should have been with your friends, when you should have been feeling alive. Did you feel alive, growing up?' he asked. His question was very serious.

'I didn't think about it at the time.' I was surprised that I felt emotional. 'But I didn't.' Maybe it was the beer talking.

Afterwards, the two of us walked back in the direction of my lodgings. As we walked, I watched the moon, yellow against the dark blue Alpine night. Snow-caps were tinged a luminous violet, Aosta's empty streets were given a thin wash of silver-white. 'And what does your family *do*?' he asked, that most English of questions. I told him about the shipping company. When I was done, he rolled his eyes and cried: 'But you are *trade*, so you must see that all those lords and ladies in Paris would have regarded you with the *utmost* contempt?' He said the terrible word 'utmost' as if it were a joke.

I took a breath. 'But now you know I am trade, will you still be my friend?' I went for arch amusement, but hearing my own voice slurring against the cooling night air, I knew that for the first time in my life – the first time – I wanted a person, an actual person outside my family, to be my friend.

'Indubitably!' he cried, and then he sniffed and pulled his coat straight. A smile cracked across his face. The moonlight shone all across his beauty, like it was honoured to cover him, and both he and the moonlight knew it. Abruptly he turned and began to walk, hard to the right, away from where I was going. I took two steps after him and called:

'Will I see you again?'

He swung around, without stopping, and was wearing the most glorious, the happiest, grin.

'You shall see me every day from now, Tradesman Bowen.' He winked at me. 'I have come to save you!'

'From what?' I cried, as he moved further and further away, walking backwards.

'Oh,' he sighed. 'From your fate, from your upbringing, from the world, I should think.'

And then he winked, and laughed, and turned forwards, running off into the night. He started jumping into the air, flapping his arms, like he was some huge, magnificent, vampirical bat.

For two more days, Edgar lay sick in bed. Left alone to enjoy each other's company, two new friends drifted around Aosta. One was a starlit performer, the other his amazed audience. What ran from the former was a torrent of witty observations, funny asides and, yes, cruel jokes. But it was the cruelty of honesty. Quickly, we fell into a tight two-step, into a rhythm of conversing familiar among those who know each other well. I would set up jokes and he would deliver the punchline. We developed a private language, a mosaic of codes designed to amuse only the other. By the end of the second day, I was deep under Lavelle's spell.

His lack of convention and his rejection of manners were apparent in his appearance. His cravat was always half undone so that the muscles of his throat would be revealed. He wore no make-up, no foppish beauty spot on his cheek. Without powder, you could see how his skin had become golden in the sun – an indecent thing, but it was so clear that he did not care. I found myself staring at him and he would catch me looking and grin. Without a wig, his fair hair had grown more fair in the southern sun. I asked him if he ever wore wigs.

'Would you prefer me to wear one?' I shrugged to show that I had no preference. But I realised that I did. Everyone wore wigs. It had not occurred to me that that had constituted my preference. 'I will wear one soon and that will show you just how *re-fined* I am.'

That word, in his mouth, had new, luxurious readings, so different from the sober clamour of Red Lion Square: *sophisticated*. The way he said the word literally tore it apart. When Lavelle used it, he offered only misinterpretations, deliberate and knowing. 'Of course,' he continued, 'the question is not, why do I *not* wear wigs? It is, why do other men insist on wearing them?' He nodded at the one I had right then on my head. 'The question is, why do *you* wear one?'

'Everyone wears wigs,' I said.

He looked at me, mock-appalled. 'Well, if everyone does it!' He chuckled knowingly to himself. 'I thought you were clever. Obviously not!'

I searched through all those pages my mother had made us read, year after sequestered year. 'We wear them because Louis XIV went bald.' This was meant to be a joke, but as soon as I said it, I realised quite how ridiculous it sounded.

I knew at once the kind of response that must follow. 'I couldn't give a shit,' he said, 'about what Louis XIV did, or Louis XIV said, nor about the colour of his piss. I. Could. Not. Give. A. Purple. Shit.' He laughed. 'Write that in a letter and send it to your parents.'

I had never encountered ideas like his before. 'The world is rotten,' he said to me one day, as we picked apart a stick of olive bread we had bought from a street-hawker. 'Do not pretend it is not. Lovers of books, do you think they do not rape their maids? And philosophers, do they not whip their slaves? They are every bit as ugly and nasty as me, but they laurel themselves with illuminated crowns and pronounce: "Oh, high-minded acolytes, do you not admire me?" And don't people rush forwards, bowing and scraping, and muttering, "Oh, yes, great poet, yes!" They claim to deliver freedom, but freedom strictly of their own design. Freedom conditional to rules – especially rules like politeness and fairness and being equal, all those horrors – is no kind of freedom at all. I will take my own freedom, thank you, where I please, and what philosophers offer me in consolation of my sorrows, they can …' He paused, sighed, smiled. ' … they can stick it up their puckered arses.'

He laughed and so did I, but in truth, I was overwhelmed. I was laughing not because what he said was funny, even if it was. I simply did not know what else to do, or to think, about him – about his presence in my life.

Edgar was very keen to meet Lavelle, although it took him a day or two more to fully recover. I felt two things simultaneously: firstly, pride, that I could show him my magnificent new friend; and secondly, fear. I knew who Edgar was and I knew enough of Lavelle to know that this might not be the best of matches. But there was no way I could avoid their meeting.

'Does he have a title?' Edgar asked and this made me laugh.

'Is that what we require now, Edgar?' I asked mischievously. 'Titles? Will we no longer countenance misters and misses?'

My brother laughed. 'I was only asking. I am looking forward to meeting him now.'

He did seem very excited. I should have been glad that he was, but instead I felt trepidation.

On our last night in Aosta, Edgar and Lavelle finally met for the first time at supper. That evening, I stood in front of the mirror in our shared bedroom. Edgar was getting dressed with great care behind me. He had hung up the red coat he was going to wear so that there would be no creases. He had sent for his cravat and shirt to be washed and pressed. He had polished his own shoes. In the mirror, I gazed at my naked head. It was more than a week since I had last shorn it. Now my hair stood in black bristles half an inch long so that you could no longer see my scalp. In the mirror I saw myself unmade-up, unwigged, skin touched by the sun; a young man in his prime. Could I be beautiful, like Lavelle? I wanted that so much. 'Have you patted down any loose hairs on your wig?' Edgar asked.

I hardly heard him; I was so distracted. 'What?'

'Have you done your wig?' he said again, with a fond impatience.

'I am not going to wear one,' I said.

As soon as I said it, he turned. I saw his reflection in the mirror, his open mouth, his amazed eyes. 'What do you mean?'

I shrugged, trying to seem nonchalant. 'I am not going to wear a wig. I don't see the point any more,' I said, in an attempt to sound light and serious at the same time. Edgar kept staring as if I were mad.

'What if we meet good people?' he asked. I could hear the edge of alarm in his voice.

I laughed. 'In Aosta?'

'Yes,' he said with some conviction. 'Even in Aosta.'

'I am not going to wear a wig,' I said.

'Wear it, Benjamin!' I said I would not. '*Wear it!*'

But again I said no, I would not, and my brother descended into an irritable silence that lasted almost until we went out.

When we got to the tavern I had chosen for us to meet Lavelle, I thought it was empty. Its large, low room was hung with huge sausages and legs of ham, and was hot with a great, crackling fire. The owner came towards us, bowing, jabbering in a mixture of French, Italian and Franco-Provençal, the language of the Savoyards. I replied that we were three diners. The man pointed to the far corner of the room, where in a dusky shadow sat Lavelle.

As my eyes found him, he nodded, already watching me as he had the first day we met. He was dressed spectacularly in purple and gold, the imperial colours. On his head – unbelievably – he wore a golden wig. It was all neat, perfect curls, absolutely the finest quality, tied with a deep purple bow. As I saw him, he was looking back at me. I knew at once that he had tricked me. He did not try to convince me otherwise. His gaze was on me, pressing and smart and full of humour: did you think I couldn't wear wigs? Did you really think I didn't know how to create … an effect?

Lavelle rose to his feet and elegantly bowed. Edgar and I approached the table, moving through the empty tavern. Then at the last moment, Lavelle gave a great flourish of the hand outwards as he rose from the bow, catching my hand and pretending to kiss it. Edgar startled, to see the scene.

'Excuse my levity, Mister Bowen,' he said. 'Your brother and I have a very *particular* sense of humour.'

Lavelle stared at me with such intensity that I had to look away, towards Edgar, so that I could introduce them.

'I have heard much of you, Mister Lavelle,' my brother was saying. 'Benjamin has had the fortune of making a great new friend.'

'Not at all,' Lavelle replied, his eyes passing over mine. 'The fortune is mine. I heard that you made many friends in Paris,' he said. Although I had recounted appalling stories of Sir Gideon and Augusta Anson, and – more treacherously – of my brother's toadying, I had not told Lavelle much of the circumstances of our leaving Paris.

'Oh, yes indeed,' Edgar said.

Lavelle pulled a mock-sad face. 'But you've lost them all now?'

Edgar's face changed, into uncertainty. 'I beg pardon, Mister Lavelle.'

'I mean to say, they did not come south with you.'

'Oh! No, they remained in Paris. No doubt we shall bump into them along the way.'

'No doubt,' Lavelle replied, his eyes liquid with a trickiness only I could see.

'Shall we sit down?' I said. 'I have never seen you so well dressed, Horace.'

Lavelle smiled at my brother. 'Your brother takes me for a barbarian, Mr Bowen. But I assure you, I am quite well trained.'

'I can see that you are no barbarian, Mr Lavelle,' Edgar replied. 'Your suit is exquisite. Where was it made?'

'Paris.'

Lavelle gave a regal, gracious nod, the sort that Augusta Anson would have given. But I knew him well enough now to understand that when he said 'Paris', or 'Sir Gideon' or whatever else, he was being sarcastic. Paris sounded so sweet in his mouth, but I knew it was not. Maybe I should have better heeded his satirical mood.

'Benjamin said you are from Ireland, Mister Lavelle.'

'Well, I do not dig peat if that's what you mean, Mister Bowen.' Edgar smiled, aware of the joke, but a little unsure of such immediate flippancy. 'My family is in the Irish peerage,' he said.

Edgar raised his eyebrows appreciatively. 'What is their title?'

Lavelle did not answer questions he did not wish to answer. 'As poor and lowly as you can get,' he said, not quite replying.

Edgar's smile grew tighter. 'And their title?' Again, Lavelle did not reply. Instead he looked up at the tavern-keeper, who was arriving at our table to suggest a particular wine. Being English, none of us knew a thing on the subject. So we said, oh, yes, very good. He named things that we should eat using their Italian names and we agreed, so that he would go away. I do not remember now if Edgar asked a third time what Lavelle's title was.

Plates of cut vegetables arrived with a simmering soup of garlic and anchovies kept warm in a pot over a flame.

The owner said its name, *bagna cauda*, 'a hot bath'. This seemed to amuse all of us. Local salamis were brought out, and blood sausages sliced very thin. A clay pot of pigs' feet stew, the meat falling off the bone. A whole jointed hare arrived, cooked in a sauce of wine and, Lavelle guessed, chicken livers. As the pretty tavern boy laid out the plates, leaning slightly over the table, Lavelle stared openly at his pert behind, two eggs in tight breeches. Then he glanced back at me, waggling his eyebrows.

He wanted me to laugh but I felt a curious kind of panic. I was with Lavelle, not on my own but out in the world, and more precisely, *with my brother*. Before, I had been alone with Lavelle, and I had laughed and laughed at whatever ridiculous thing he had said. But now I felt only peril. What if he said something embarrassing, scurrilous? What would I do with him, or with Edgar, when his irreverence was exposed before our reverent world?

We began to eat. I drank with haste, not so much that I was inebriated but quickly enough so that my head was swimming. I was still not yet quite used to drinking wine, although that would change soon enough. At first, the conversation remained polite, yet was run through Lavelle, of what I understood he could do with any idea, any received truth. When Edgar spoke of our connections in Paris, Lavelle asked me directly if we were not having more fun in Italy. 'Horace,' I said, 'stop it,' causing him to laugh and Edgar to ask, 'Stop what?' Lavelle only smiled. 'Stop what?' Edgar asked again, but neither of us answered.

Edgar started to speak about Sir Gideon and Augusta Anson, and Lavelle said that they sounded *divine*. He made the word sound like an insult. Edgar had no irony – he himself knew it – so he could not hear Lavelle's intent. But I did, and so my sense of the jeopardy he personified only sharpened. Still, my brother tried to impress. He did not yet understand that Lavelle was not like the other people we had encountered. He was, in fact, their antithesis. That was precisely why I liked him. 'So, please, Mister Lavelle, tell me what you are hoping to visit here in Italy. In Rome, or Siena, or Bologna, or Florence, what do you wish to see?'

Lavelle did not reply at once. He appeared to be thinking terribly hard about his answer. Then he sniffed sharply and breathed out. 'Nothing much,' he said.

My brother blinked, surprised. 'Nothing much?'

'Um,' Lavelle continued, as if thinking of a better answer. 'No, not really. I think it's probably all the same old rubbish.'

Edgar laughed nervously. Perhaps he was hoping it was a jest. Lavelle was a waggish sort of fellow, clearly. But Lavelle kept his face perfectly still, to show that he was utterly serious. Even I could not tell if he was or not.

'Oh,' Edgar said eventually, 'you are being serious.'

Lavelle bowed his head serenely. An extraordinary moment of silence descended upon us: Lavelle smiling supremely, all sweet faux-innocence; Edgar, in mute, genuine incomprehension at the nonsense tumbling out of this mouth I had praised so lavishly; and me, staring from one to the other, a foot in each world.

Lavelle laughed brightly then, and reached for the jug of wine, topping up all three glasses. 'Yes, I am just joking, Mr Bowen! I just want to have a bit of –' he waggled his eyebrows salaciously '– a bit of *fun*. But isn't that what everyone comes on Tour for? A. Bit. Of. Fun. It's not like anyone *really* comes for the culture.'

'What?' Edgar cried, finally beginning to crack under the assault.

'Oh,' Lavelle went. 'Come on, let's be honest. Who gives a damn about Boccaccio and Petrarch and all that shit?'

'Shit'? In polite conversation among strangers? Edgar's face soured. 'Well, *I* came here for the culture,' he said sharply. 'And I care about those things.'

At this, I thought, *enough*. 'Horace, stop being...' I struggled for the word but I knew what it was '... satirical. We all come on Tour for the same reasons, you know very well.' I looked at my brother. 'Pay him no heed, Edgar.'

Edgar was staring at me. I could see his growing distress. To what place had I brought him? I was not even sure myself. Lavelle sniffed: 'Where did Dante put the blasphemers in Hell?'

'What?' I asked, confused.

'Where did Dante put the blasphemers in Hell?' He was looking straight at me, as if he were actually asking me a question, and it wrongfooted me, to realise that I was supposed to be offering an answer.

'The Seventh Circle,' I guessed.

'Oh, indeed,' he went. 'Between the suicides and the sodomites.' He smiled at Edgar, widening his eyes in sedition. 'So, mixed company, then.'

Edgar was starting to look nauseated. '*Mixed* company, sir?'

'Well, yes,' Lavelle said. 'I mean, I'm sure the sodomites are a lot of fun – and *mostly* very accommodating – but certainly the suicides would bring things down.' He picked up his knife and stabbed at a pig's foot. 'Wouldn't you say?' He put a slice of meat in his mouth and I sniggered. I could not help it. Edgar turned to me, as if detecting treachery, and perhaps he had. I put my hand to the tip of my nose, hoping to disguise my laughter. 'But you were saying you came for culture,' Lavelle continued. 'May I ask you a question?'

Edgar bristled. It was the nearness of humiliation, the cat that stalks the bird of men's pride. 'Ask away,' Edgar said, with the brittleness of one who really means, please don't.

'You speak of coming to Italy for culture, and your brother said the same thing to me. But pray tell me, what do you think culture is?'

Edgar's face changed, into one of surprise. 'I beg pardon, sir?'

Lavelle repeated his question: 'What do you think culture is?'

The question seemed simultaneously foolish and profound. Even I did not understand at what he was driving. We had grown up under the ministrations of our mother, reading Voltaire, John Locke and all the rest as interpreted by her and Herr Hof. We were very clear what culture was.

'Well …' Edgar began. 'Books, the love of literature. The classics. Philology, of course.' The very word 'philology' paired with 'of course' seemed to make Lavelle's eyes shine with derision. 'Art,' Edgar said recovering himself. 'The truly great art, then, is painting, I suppose – what we have been given in these last few centuries.'

'But those,' Lavelle said, 'are the objects of art, the pretty things. If we set a standard and say, your poetry must be like this, or this good, or your paintings must observe these rules and achieve these layers of reference and reality, then that's fine. But it does not tell us what culture is *for*.'

'To refine the mind. To make a person reflect.'

'You mean the observer, or the reader, but they are not the person who created the art. Perhaps we could agree that the writer and the painter, and the reader and the observer – the one side of creation, the other of consumption – have together created culture. But that again, only tells us what purpose culture serves ...' he laughed to himself, deliberately speaking inelegantly ' ... culturally.'

My brother's eyes were fixed, his jaw set; he glared at Lavelle. 'Please, Mister Lavelle, tell me: what precisely are you insinuating?'

Edgar's irascibility only served to gratify Lavelle. 'By asking the question, what is culture?'

'Yes,' Edgar said.

Lavelle paused and closed his eyes. He seemed very serious for the moment, which surprised me, and when he spoke, it was with a long sigh. 'Culture is unhappiness,' he said.

It was me who reacted. 'Unhappiness?' I cried. Lavelle nodded without doubt.

'Culture is the product of unhappiness. Authors and artists, they are ambitious. They seek eternity. They seek acclaim. Poets and painters, they might as well be dancing on a stage, like the cheapest sort of singer in a burletta, screaming at the audience to love them.' He burst out laughing, in love with his own joke as he began to screech. 'Here's my poem! *Love* me! Here's my novel. *Love* me! It's in iambic pentameter! *Admire* me!' He sighed, allowing his eyes to pause on mine. 'What?' he cried. 'Too much?'

I felt the need to protest. It was me, not Edgar, who was becoming distressed. 'I think great artists have beauty in them, and they share that with the world.'

'Oh,' he groaned caustically. 'And whores have wonderful fundaments but nobody gives them a laurel wreath and a cup for first prize.'

Of course this made me want to laugh, but I resisted. Making me laugh was a device, of course I knew that. 'Even if we were to agree that these great men of beauty are not actually whores grubbing for money, for acclaim, for the pitter-patter of fools' applause, then consider this. Have you seen the prints of Caravaggio? Or Ribera or Rembrandt?' Of course we had. Either Edgar or I could have spoken eloquently of the violent physicality of Caravaggio's work, the burnished spiritual devastation of Ribera, the shaded mystery and out-of-the-ether innovation of Rembrandt. 'Do you think those look like the works of happy people?' he asked. I knew that they did not. 'You see, Benjamin? Culture is unhappiness end to end.'

Edgar leapt to his feet so fast, his chair smacked back against the floor, causing everyone in the room – the waiter, the innkeeper, us – all to jump as one. 'I have been poorly,' he snapped. 'I think perhaps it will not serve me well to continue eating and drinking. I must retire.'

'Oh, *dommage*!' Lavelle sighed.

Edgar looked back at me. 'Benjamin, are you coming?'

'What?' I said limply. 'The evening has hardly begun.'

Edgar gave this short shrift. 'I am not well!'

Lavelle leaned forwards and touched the back of my hand, his fingertips electric on my skin.

'Then, overtaking his cohorts at the River Rubicon, which was the boundary of his province, he paused for a while, and realising what a step he was taking, he turned to those about him and said: "Even yet we may draw back; but once cross yon little bridge, and the whole issue is with the sword. The die is cast."'

'Suetonius,' I whispered, gazing at him, and he smiled. He wanted me to know that he understood I was at a fork in the road. And he wanted to show me that it was in my power to choose my path. I had to take a gulp of wine, just to steady myself. Edgar was already on his feet.

'You missed out a great chunk, you know,' Edgar said. 'You missed the whole bit about the apparition and his trumpet.'

Lavelle clasped his hands together. 'Oh, how I *wish* the apparition would show me his trumpet!'

I burst into unruly laughter. Edgar's eyes were on me, round and raging. He let out a hard, angry growl, then turned and stormed off. I jumped up after him.

'Edgar!' I cried. 'Edgar, come back, it's just a joke! He just likes to joke!'

I chased my brother through the tavern, turning as I did to look back at Lavelle, who stared at me directly, grinning all the while.

The night was cold as we went outside. We were silvered by the Alpine moonlight. My brother spun around and faced me:

'Who is this fellow whom you have befriended?'

'It's just his humour. You mustn't be offended by him, Edgar—'

'*Mustn't be offended?*' my brother cried, so loudly you could hear his voice echoing in the street. 'He tears everything apart. He pours scorn on all that anyone counts on as being good.'

'He is amusing,' I said. 'His satire is such that he delights in—'

My brother pulled on his gloves, fast and angry. 'Satire, Benjamin? How drunk are you? Tell me, do you compare him to Alexander Pope or Mister Swift? He is a ruffian! A cruel ruffian—'

'He is not,' I protested, in a light, good-humoured way.

'And do you think this … cruelty will get us anywhere on our journey?' he asked.

'What cruelty?'

'You're drunk,' Edgar spat. 'That nonsense about culture being unhappiness, what utter drivel.' He nodded with great certainty. 'You will regret what has happened tonight, mark my words. We cannot afford any more mistakes.'

'Any more? What do you mean?'

Edgar held his arms by his side, his whole body rigid with tension.

'I told you in Paris that this matters to me. I told you that I know you don't take it seriously, but I do. And Mother does, and Father too. I am not going to allow you to let this ... *fool* make a fool of us! It's like Mother always says, you have to see things differently, you have to make *everything* a joke!'

I blinked in the moonlight. Was that what my mother said about me, her son, when my back was turned? I was stopped in that moment. I thought too of Augusta saying that my brother had said things about me behind my back, even if she had then immediately added she was teasing me. I realised then that we are not just our own thoughts. We are made of other people's thoughts about us, too, the ones they share with us, and the ones they don't.

'I'm going back inside,' I said quietly. If I had been drunk, I was no longer. 'Goodnight, Edgar.'

My brother bowed to me coldly, as to an unwelcome acquaintance. 'Goodnight, Benjamin,' he said. The two of us stood there, glaring at one another a moment more. Then my brother turned and walked away. I watched him slipping into the night.

I went back inside the tavern. Standing at the door, I could see the table where Lavelle remained seated, glass in hand: a cornucopia of food, wine, a dark hint of decadence, like the Caravaggios he had just reimagined, not as signs of achievement but of unhappiness. I walked slowly over to him. 'Did you have to be so terrible?' I asked.

'Yes,' he replied, smiling perfectly. 'Otherwise, how am I going to save you?' He gave a dark smile. 'When do you go south?' he asked then, as light as the air.

I was confused. 'South?' I repeated.

He was talking as if it was all nothing at all. 'Don't you want me to come south with you? Or are you afraid of what your brother will say?'

'I am not afraid of Edgar,' I said.

85

'Good,' he said. 'Good, Benjamin. It is very important in this life – the most important thing – for us not to be afraid.'

I was looking at him. I did not know what he meant. But I knew that I wanted him to show me.

PART TWO

SOUTH

*E*dgar insisted that I forbid Lavelle to travel south with us, and I refused. Then he insisted again, and I lied and said I would. But I knew already I would do anything to keep hold of my remarkable new friend. So instead, all I did was tell Lavelle to come at the last minute, when the Tourists' carriages were queuing to leave – there was always a queue. That way, Edgar would not be able to make a scene. He would fear the humiliation he felt the day after he had lost his temper in the street in Paris. I knew that this was a real betrayal of my brother, but I did it all the same. Edgar seemed relieved to arrive at the carriages and find Lavelle absent. He softened towards me, smiling, making a joke about how long it would take for all the carriages to clear. At the last moment, I wondered if Lavelle might, in fact, not come at all, but turn the trick onto me. Maybe he was lying in a room somewhere now, kicking his heels, smirking at what an idiot I was. I could hear a clock ticking, somewhere deep inside me. Would he come? Would he come? Desperately, I hoped so.

Edgar was talking about some pretty girls he had seen boarding a coach ahead of ours. I was not listening. I was craning my head around and around to see if there was any sign of Lavelle, but there was not. *Come on*, I wished silently to myself. The man who organised the coaches called us forwards. 'Come on,' Edgar said, aloud. It cracked my absorption. 'What?' 'Come on,' Edgar repeated. 'It's time to go.' That's when I saw my brother's face fall as he looked past me. I turned, and there, pushing his hair behind his ears, was Lavelle, bearing a small battered travelling case and a grin. I was so happy.

'Is this our coach?' he said. 'I thought you Bowen boys would have got something ...' he sniffed '... fancier.' Of course, Edgar and I had come without servants. The richer, aristocratic types might have a full supply of maids and valets. But here was Lavelle, looking every bit the pauper. Edgar's eyes ran him up and down. I held my breath, waiting for my brother to protest, but he did not shout or make a scene. Perhaps he found some small amusement in Lavelle's appearance – how he did not seem to be grand at all, and, in fact, looked rather threadbare. Or maybe one day he would be at a picture viewing or a card game in Venice or Verona, and any one of these people might suddenly remember him and question: 'Aren't you that chap in Aosta who ...?' Among the English, fear stalks even the most delicious moments. Instead, all he did was hiss at me under his breath, asking whether there had been some sort of conspiracy. I said, no, no, not at all. Lavelle had just turned up. But I was lying, of course. And Edgar probably knew it. If he did not, Lavelle's knowing eyes gave it away.

On the rare moments when my brother and I were alone in the next few days, he kept saying that he could not believe I had fallen under the spell of one so wrong-headed, so vain. And, yes, I knew that Lavelle was vain. In fact, Lavelle would be the first to admit it. Furthermore, he might say: 'Look at me, am I not beautiful?' (He was.) 'Am I not honest?' (He was.) 'To whom have I lied?' (To no one.)

'I tell the truth,' Lavelle sometimes said. 'That is what people like your brother cannot bear.'

Edgar called him severe, insubstantial, cruel, foolish, *aerial*. It was all true. He was delightfully, subversively, absolutely and brutally, aerial. He had appeared out of thin air, that day in Aosta. In London, my mother would have pronounced: '*One minute*, please, on the subject of theophany.' And either Edgar or I would have obliged, 'Theophany is the appearance of a divine being to a mere mortal, an apparition from nowhere, unexpected, unbidden, come to deliver a sacred message for the mortal to understand. In Greek mythology, there is the example of Zeus appearing to Semele, causing her to burst into flames …' Had Lavelle caused me to burst into flames? Is it embarrassing for me even to think that he might? He was made out of air, entirely, and I greedily sucked his being down into my lungs, every word he said, every condemnation he brought about the world, every smile, every angle of his face.

And so three of us went south together, Edgar cold with anger, Lavelle revelling in awkward silences, and me, simultaneously ally, hero and traitor. The chillier Edgar became, the more irreverent was Lavelle. If Edgar would rhapsodise on the beauty of some woman of society, Lavelle would flash his eyes to mine. 'Oh, yes, I know her very well,' he would say. 'She is a very great beauty, and everyone knows it, and she knows it, and that is all she has. That beauty.' This was outrage enough to Edgar, but of course Lavelle continued. 'But she has a flaw. She has nothing in her that you could call ...' He would pause momentarily, as if sifting through every shocking insult he knew and I would wait, my breath bated, to hear it. '*Kindness*,' he would say with a conspiratorial smile to me.

'Kindness?' Edgar would croak. Lavelle would keep looking at me.

'What else did you expect me to say, Mister Bowen?' he would respond, still grinning and staring straight at me.

'Well,' Edgar might croak, 'certainly not *kindness*!'

Whatever the conversation, Lavelle was always quicker, always deadlier. Edgar eulogised the friendship of Sir Gideon, perhaps as hope of regaining dignity after humiliation. 'Actually, I do know him after all,' Lavelle declared then, as if lightning-struck. 'My brother used to sodomise him when they were at school. Said he squealed like a Berkshire hog the whole way through.'

Edgar gasped, deeply shocked. I knew Lavelle did not have a brother. But then I saw Edgar's face confused and outplayed, becoming steadily angrier, and I explained: 'It's only a joke.'

'You are revolting!' Edgar cried at Lavelle, who preened beautifully.

'I know.'

'I don't believe a word of it,' from Edgar.

'Edgar,' I said, 'he is playing with you! Teasing you!'

They ignored me. 'No,' Lavelle insisted, 'it is true! My brother gave the poor boy's arse a mark of only three out of ten!'

Did I not see Edgar becoming more agitated, or did I just not care? It's hard to tell, judging your own actions, back through time, to know if what you did was thrillingly exciting or simply callous. Or, perhaps, a little of both.

'I admit that my brother did not say that,' Lavelle said. 'I think he said it was a Cumberland pig.'

When we left Verona for Vicenza, the mood became more tense. Our carriage rolled out of the city, into yellow flatlands beneath the last of the green mountains from which we had descended. We moved through glades of almond and olive trees. Farmers' heads, distant black dots, appeared to look up from fields as our coaches rumbled by, but they were not looking at us. They were only stretching their backs.

Lavelle had been chattering provocatively all morning and Edgar was stretched between politeness and irritation. Edgar said that he did not wish to stop to take luncheon, but would prefer to travel on through to Vicenza with as much speed as possible. We were already several hours into the journey and had several hours more ahead.

'No luncheon?' Lavelle cried. 'Isn't that a little bleak?'

Edgar sat back in his seat. 'I have a terrible headache. And I don't want to spend a second longer in this coach than I need to.'

Lavelle was watching my brother carefully. 'I understand,' he said, 'that your dear mother is a great admirer of Monsieur Voltaire.'

I felt a tension creep over me. What was he going to say? And simultaneously, a compulsion. What *was* he going to say? Edgar seemed bemused by the remark. He should have avoided replying – who knew better than Lavelle not to fall into the trap of answering questions you did not wish to answer? – but the opportunity to honour our mother was irresistible. We had been raised, after all, to honour her always.

'Of course,' he said. 'She is an intelligent woman.'

Lavelle gave a great, wide, sensual smirk. 'I am sure she is. But I do not know what that says about me, Mister Bowen. For I cannot stand Voltaire.' Some flicker of a crease passed across my brother's brow. 'In fact, I despise them all, all those Enlightenment types.'

'I … I am not sure I understand your joke,' Edgar said, almost sweetly. But sweetness was not really Lavelle's métier.

He frowned. '*Joke?*'

I felt alarm. I don't know why just then, but I did. 'Lavelle is full of jokes,' I said, and immediately I heard my own treachery.

'Of course, I joke and I joke,' Lavelle began with his jet-black twinkle, 'but that does not mean that people who praise Voltaire are not morons.' He flashed a beguiling smile. It took a second to realise what had just been implied about our mother.

Edgar reared up in his seat, boiling with rage. 'You seem *awfully* relaxed to hear such calumnies spoken, Benjamin.'

I hesitated – no, I prevaricated. 'What calumnies? It's just a *joke*!' I exclaimed. Then something cooler descended on my brother.

'Have you misrepresented yourself to your new friend? Have you not told him of your own erudition, Benjamin, your great love of learning? Have you not told him of how we all used to be at home, with Mother and all of our books and –' he said, very low '– little chats?'

There was truth in Edgar's questions. If nothing else, I had misrepresented who I had previously been to Lavelle. But there was a deep difference between Edgar and me now. Edgar still lived in the world of my mother. Learning was meaning. Enlightenment was daylight. But hadn't I belonged to that world once? Whatever rebellions I may have launched in my parents' house were tiny.

'We should play our favourite game.' Edgar's smile contained a darkness I'd never seen before. 'We should teach Mister Lavelle here the Minute Game.'

Lavelle was all bright amusement. 'A game? What game is this? I *love* games, Benjamin!'

Edgar's eyes were on me, hard, then. 'Oh, Mister Lavelle, did Benjamin tell you nothing of the Minute Game? Oh, he has been dissembling, perhaps, deceiving you.' He smiled at Lavelle, delighting in his fresh falseness. Then he glanced back at me, all irony. It surprised me to see him so … cynical. 'What kind of friend lies to his friend, eh, Benjamin?'

'Stop it, Edgar,' I said, 'you are making a fool of yourself.'

At this, my brother turned sharp. 'It is not me who is making a fool of himself!' He spat out a dismissive laugh.

Lavelle clapped his hands together. 'Oh, enough squabbling, gentlemen! Let's play.' He turned to look at me very directly. 'I *love* games.'

I felt such danger then, but from whom – Edgar or Lavelle?

'Wonderful,' my brother said. 'Benjamin, I challenge you to, in one minute, explain to us all –' he nodded to Lavelle, as if they were great friends, or at least, just uninterested acquaintances '– the great benefits of ... why, of the Enlightenment!'

'Stop it, Edgar. I shall not play.'

Lavelle was shaking his head. 'Is that the game? To recite all your historical and cultural facts in one minute, is that it?' He laughed. 'How marvellous! Like a parrot!' An image flashed into my mind: in Paris, the painted-gold birds, wheezing towards their deaths, poisoned and shot. Lavelle looked at me. He must have seen my reluctance. There was something like understanding in his eyes, something akin to softness. So then he turned to my brother. 'Well, Mister Bowen, if you are such a fan of this game, why don't *you* play it?' Edgar looked at Lavelle, momentarily reluctant, but then he seemed to reconsider. Maybe this would be his moment of triumph. Maybe he could ripen his mockery of me further in this delicious way. 'All right,' he said. 'The Enlightenment. In one minute.'

Lavelle clapped his hands. 'Oh, I am *so* enjoying this!'

Edgar cleared his throat. 'Our era of Enlightenment is the manifestation of the advances of the Renaissance, in bringing European civilisation to its apex, and the greatest flowering out of human understanding and knowledge yet.' At once I recognised the words, almost perfectly mimicking mine that night in Red Lion Square. His eyes – my brother's eyes – were flinty with anger. We had spent our entire lives dressed and schooled alike, eating together, sleeping in the same room, our futures planned so that we would never leave each other's side. But now we were breaking apart. I was so lost in this thought that I hardly noticed Lavelle had begun to speak.

'I don't think that it is demonstrably true, Mister Bowen, that ours is the greatest flowering of knowledge. What about the Muhammadan Golden Age, already five hundred years ago? That appears to have been a period of astonishingly complex knowledge. And we do not even begin to understand the knowledge of the Chinese civilisation, which appears very great and ancient indeed.'

My brother's eyes remained furiously on mine. Edgar was ignoring Lavelle. 'Tell him, Benjamin,' he said, with a pleasured snarl.

'Tell him what? I don't know what you mean,' I said, stalling again, but now in a different direction. Tell him that these were my words? Tell him that this was my game too? Tell him that my brother had turned against me, and that this was a wider game now, beyond the cheap currency of 'facts'? Edgar's eyes sparkled with victory. 'There's no interrupting, Mister Lavelle, no interrupting in the Minute Game!'

'That's not very conducive to intellectual rigour, no interrupting, no discussion,' Lavelle groaned, heaving with irony. 'But I suppose games have rules. So, gentlemen, play on!'

'Edgar, what are you doing?' I growled.

'I am telling the truth. What are *you* doing?' He glanced at Lavelle. 'Descartes laid the foundation for our Enlightenment ideals with the development of his rational way of thinking, breaking decisively with the dominance of the Church.' Impossibly, he recalled what I'd said word for word. He was trying to embarrass me, a private humiliation. 'This was the end of a long period of religious war in Europe in which conflicting churches had used their power to slaughter millions of Europeans. People no longer *tolerated* church dominance,' Edgar emphasised the word, I had not; he had changed its meaning. 'Locke's *Essay Concerning Human Understanding* was an important milestone. Do you remember that, Benjamin? Do you remember why I might say that?'

'Why?' Lavelle asked me, both of us, but neither of us answered. This essay had been of fundamental importance to our mother's educational choices for us. It was this essay which had created the path we were on.

'Of course, Locke has been much disputed,' Edgar continued. 'By Leibniz. And Spinoza disputed Descartes, but over time, these challenges led to a new way of thinking, in which the human mind, not the existence of God, was of paramount importance for civilisation. These advances led to the development of ideas of individual liberty, freedom of expression, and saw the end of theology as a basis for morality.' My brother took a breath. 'People have freed themselves from the Church.'

Lavelle sniffed. 'I am not sure that any of that is true.'

I turned to my new friend. 'What?'

'Well, Edgar's position is that people are freed from the Church, but isn't it truer that what people want is faith? Even if your mother raised you to be godless, most people want faith. Where kings have enforced enlightenment, there have been riots, so is it only the opinion of the elite that matters? Do ordinary people not get a say?'

My brother purred with pleasure at seeing the potential of a disagreement between Lavelle and me. 'But it was Voltaire, wasn't it, Benjamin,' Edgar said, 'who first argued that society must be based upon reason and not faith; that natural law must inform civil law, not religion; that society must be democratic and must protect the vulnerable, and that science be based on experiments and observation.'

Suddenly Lavelle burst out laughing. 'What rubbish!' he cried, highly amused.

Edgar turned to look at him, with open surprise. 'Rubbish?'

'Yes, you saying that Voltaire, the king of the Enlightenment, loves democracy and all that guff.'

Edgar puffed out his chest; his victory, moments ago, seemed quite squandered. 'It's true!'

'True?' Lavelle laughed again. 'Voltaire despises democracy and says the absolute monarch must be a "philosopher-king" – but an absolute monarch is a king who holds his dagger of freedom over the throats of his own people. Look at him. Oh, how he adopts the free thinker's pose whilst dancing for the money of the King of Prussia, a man whom Voltaire allows himself to think *very* enlightened but is the worst kind of despot. And we all know that King Frederick takes it in the arse.' He crooned with laughter and I did too – half groaning with shock that he said it at all – and Edgar shushed me, more immediately in panic than offence. 'And he is not the only one. Newton: in the arse. Spinoza: arse. Every person your mother ever admired: sodomites who liked it in the arse!'

Our laughter was like a thunderstorm pelting on a carriage roof. I could hear it raining down. 'And your mother teaches you Spinoza, but Voltaire hates the Jews. Voltaire would not have Spinoza in his damn house, I assure you! Your king of freedom and fairness hates Jews, the whole world knows it.'

The word 'Jew' alarmed my brother. Now Lavelle took on a calm, serene countenance and began to recite. '"You have surpassed all nations in impertinent fables, in bad conduct and in barbarism. You deserve to be punished, for this is your destiny."' His words had a surgical precision. 'Oh tell me, Mister Bowen, please, that you know who wrote that. Have you not read *One Must Take Sides*? Why, those words are by your very own king of freedom, Voltaire, and that nation of whom he wrote? Why, the Jews, of course.

'*Ha!*' Lavelle continued. 'There's your fucking Enlightenment. It forgives itself everything, nominates itself as its own hero and carries all its old bigotries, safely self-forgiven, within it. *Fuck Voltaire!*' he yelled. I almost fainted with excitement. '*Fuck* him! A Jew-hater who despises democracy and wiggles his wrinkly old behind in the hope that the King of Prussia might, for one fucking second, look away from the bulge in that handsome young dragoon's breeches. Ha!' he boomed – *again*. 'Fuck Voltaire, and fuck your Enlightenment!'

Edgar was silent. Such moments were delicious to Lavelle. 'Have I won this Minute Game?' he asked, all impossible cheek. 'It feels I have won this Minute Game.' He smiled gamely and winked at me. 'You never explained the rules of how to win but I am pretty sure I have done so, Mister Bowen.'

'I think you are the most hateful person,' Edgar spat at Lavelle, 'to not understand the goodness of these men and to sow such … such unpleasantness.'

'You find the truth unpleasant, Mister Bowen?'

Edgar groaned. 'These are merely cod-intellectual aspersions of the worst sort.' For a moment, there were tears in his eyes. I was shocked. 'There is a limit to—'

Lavelle did not miss his chance. 'To what? To enlightenment, Mister Bowen?'

It was a whip-crack of a put-down. Lavelle simmered brilliantly in his victory, and Edgar could do nothing but languish in defeat.

'You are a loathsome creature, Lavelle!' my brother shrieked, making a fool of himself just as his enemy had carefully planned. 'An absolute abhorrence!'

Lavelle clasped his hands behind his head and stretched his legs ostentatiously across the carriage between Edgar and I, forcing us apart.

'Oh, Mister Bowen, I think that is possibly the nicest thing you could have said to me.'

That night, we arrived in Vicenza, which is beautiful but dull. It is the city of the architect Palladio, whose ideas were so in fashion in London, and its new flat-fronted, restrained elegance was named neo-Palladian in his honour. Everywhere in Vicenza was stucco, and Doric columns, and perfect symmetries, now copied in the fashionable houses back at home. While Lavelle and I strolled around its quiet squares and empty cafés, in a certain glum mood, Edgar chose to stay in the inn where he and I had a room.

Finally, Lavelle and I sat outside a café with no one else in it, except for a resentful-looking waiter standing off to one side, and sipped a sweet, fizzy Prosecco wine, which should have gone to our heads but did not.

'Why do you provoke Edgar so?' I asked Lavelle. Above us, cicadas were droning loudly in the piazza's decorative trees.

Lavelle sniffed. 'Why not? He's easy prey.'

'Please, don't be so vile. He's my brother.'

'Oh, dear Benjamin, it is too late for you to protest, "He's my brother!" You have already made your choice.'

'What is that choice?' I asked.

He drew his face close to mine across the table and whispered: 'To slit your brother's throat for me.'

'Don't be so ridiculous!' I cried. 'He is still my brother, you know.'

He sat back in his chair and groaned. 'Oh, should we worship our brothers because of who they are? Should we worship anyone because of who they are? Dukes, scholars, popes, *Voltaire*?' A flicker of pleasure passed through me when he said that. 'I would rather kick them in the balls.' He lifted his glass to say cheers, but solely to himself. Then he looked at me more carefully. 'Did it not occur to you that I was protecting you?'

'Protecting *me*?'

'I knew your brother was playing some game designed to humiliate you. I let him play it for a while, let him think he was winning, and then ...' He mimicked a cat's claw, ready to strike.

I shook my head, sighing. 'Well, that's very good of you, but you don't have to provoke people all the time,' I said.

'I cannot tell how much I disagree with you, Benjamin, and I am shocked that you should say something. If someone is an idiot—'

'Edgar is not an idiot,' I said firmly.

'*Pfft*,' he grunted. 'Let's not argue about who is or who is not an idiot.' He raised his glass and drowned what was left of the Prosecco down his throat. 'No, hang on! Let's! Let's argue about who is an idiot! The whole damned world is an idiot. King George, Queen Charlotte, the pervert King of Prussia, the febrile Russian Tsarina, *Voltaire* and Rousseau, Daniel Defoe, Samuel Richardson, Samuel Johnson, and even poor old Isaac Newton, Socrates, Plato and Aristotle, and even Jesus Christ: every one of them is a gold-plated, first-rate moron!'

I laughed. He knew he could usually make me laugh. 'Do you not agree?' he asked.

'No, Horace. I don't agree.'

He feigned shock. 'You disagree with me? Then you must be an idiot too.'

I imitated a bow. 'So you said. I suppose you are the only one person who is not an idiot? Only you, in all the world, are not a moron?'

He did not react, but clicked his fingers for more wine. The waiter dawdled over and topped up our glasses. Lavelle took a sip of the Prosecco.

'I admit it,' he said. 'You are not an idiot. You are the most intriguing person I have ever met.'

I felt heat bloom across my forehead, a strange low panic at such unexpected words. My head buzzing, I pretended to listen to the crickets in the trees. There was the scent of the south on the night's soft breeze and I breathed it in, its drowsy effect.

'May I ask you a question, Benjamin?'

'What?'

'Why do you allow me to speak to Edgar in this way? Why don't you punch me on the nose, and tell me to stop?'

'I just have!' I protested.

'No, what you have done just now is make a meek complaint, but you will do nothing more about it. You made that complaint to look like you cared, but clearly you do not. So, I ask again: why do you allow me to speak to your brother so?'

'I want to hear you speak,' I said. 'It excites me.'

'Hmm,' he hummed, and took another sip of the wine. 'Then I am a philosopher and you the first acolyte at my school.' He raised his eyes upwards, in a comedic hopefulness. 'Does that make us Plato and Aristotle?'

'I thought you said they were idiots,' I said. 'I don't think we are like them, anyway. Plato didn't like to drink much.'

'What a churchy cunt.'

I laughed and raised my glass. 'So, what is the core tenet of your philosophy, then? In what do you believe?'

He paused, lifted his glass and swirled the wine around. 'I do not believe,' he said very dramatically. 'I *reject*.'

Maybe it was that febrile night, maybe the sweet popping Prosecco, maybe the vast droning orchestra of crickets in the trees, but that struck me as ridiculous. 'And what do you reject?' I asked, wanting to show that I was amused. But his mood was serious, his words measured out with care:

'Anything. Give me something, I will reject it. The Enlightenment. The Renaissance. Christianity, in all its foul guises. All your mother's philosophies.'

'You are fascinated by my mother!' I joked. 'Why?'

'Because I suspect she is a fraud.'

'How on earth is she *a fraud*?' I drawled the last two words.

'Your mother is very intelligent and very learned, and yet she makes you clap like a buffoon on a fairground for the attention of fools like Gideon Hervey. Why wouldn't she give you something ... better than that?' He put his hands together in mock prayer. 'All of Madame Bowen's fucking books. All of Edgar's fine friends. Edgar's predictable outrage at everything I say. Whatever else you wish. I shall reject it.'

He drew himself closer, looked me dead in the eye. 'It is the easiest and simplest of faiths. Rejectionism, I shall call it, when it has made me famous.' I knew that he was being facetious and yet there was something plausible about it too – that Lavelle, of all things, of all people, would inevitably end up a canonical philosopher. 'Because all a person ever needs to do is *to reject*. There is no sin, no forgiveness, no denial, no contrition, no priests to tell you what to do, no rules to learn, no teachers, no kings and no queens. If someone gives you a rule, reject it. If someone tells you that you must live this way, or that, reject it. Reject, reject, reject! It's the simplest of faiths and by far the most satisfying. You just reject, reject, reject!'

As he said the last line – our new, mystic catechism – in a queer singsong, I had a mouthful of fizzing wine. It was all I could do not to spit it out, laughing; so instead, I gulped it down.

Mother

We are continuing to have a marvellous time here on Tour and here, in Venice, I am sure Benjamin and I shall continue to prosper. Benjamin has made a curious friend named Lavelle, and I am making many good friends too. I am very confident that all will be well, but I will confess, Mother, that I am missing you and Father very much. Sometimes my heart feels a bit sick with it.

Yours,

Edgar

VENICE

$\mathcal{V}$enice, for those on Tour, quickly descends into an endless party. There were so many occasions that hosts sometimes struggled to find enough guests. The only thing worse than the wrong sort of person at one's soirée was no sort of person, so invitations were sent out to just about anyone. Hosts needed guests, meaning all guests had to do was make their presence in Venice known, write up cards of introduction and send them around the houses of those in the social whirl. And that's what Edgar did: he wrote out cards, changed the spelling of our name from Bowen to *Bouen*, to rhyme with Rouen, and sent them out to the aristocratic all and sundry. Of course, Lavelle and I thought this ridiculous. Lavelle teased Edgar mercilessly. The pretension – *Boo-wuhng* – was ludicrous. I mimicked that usher in Paris: BOW-WANG. BOW-WANG. But Edgar was not to be dissuaded. It impressed me in a strange way, how determined he was to succeed. And it was a success. Once he had appeared at one party, and then another, and had been introduced and became that most wonderful thing – *known* – that was it.

His breakthrough triumph was a very fancy invitation to a viewing of Canalettos at the home of the British Consul to the Doge. Edgar insisted that just he and I should attend. It was his idea that we should dress in our matching silver suits, with our whitest wigs. When we arrived, people turned. The announcer cried, '*Les messieurs Bouen!*' The room admired us, and Edgar bathed in the attention. I turned to look at my brother and in that moment saw how happy he was. I thought of him that day in Paris, on the Rue des Rosiers, screaming about how we would have to flee our shame. We had walked into the party, my mother's two halves, but now it felt to me that we were split asunder.

Cards came our way and Edgar made great play of how well we'd been 'known' in Paris. He told anyone who would listen that our friends had been named Hervey and Russell, and such. I watched the whole scene with disgust, my new rejectionist abhorrence. Edgar hissed that I could at least try to make an effort. Eventually, he more or less abandoned me, confidently talking to any august English person he could find. I started to think I was embarrassed for him but I was not: I was embarrassed for myself. After an excruciating hour, I left the party and turned towards a café where I knew Lavelle would be. I said to myself that this would be the last time: I couldn't go to one of these gatherings again. I walked into a triangular little square, where under potted olive trees I found him waiting for me, perfectly still, wonderfully handsome, eyes on me the moment I arrived.

'You escaped,' he said softly.

'Yes,' I replied.

Edgar was a great success at the party and, in days to come, many more invitations came his way. Soon he was knee-deep in new friends and had many occasions to be away from 'that fiend' and me. One might say I dropped him, but in Venice, he reciprocally dropped me. So, I spent more and more time alone with Lavelle, and it was delightful. I asked Lavelle if he could take rooms at our address, and he laughed. 'How should I pay for it?' he asked. 'With air, or with my arse?' I was scandalised, but in my determination to break away from the great seriousness of my background, I laughed and laughed, anxious to show how fully I appreciated his bawdy, shameful humour.

In those days I was content merely to be with him, in the shock of his intelligence. And in Venice, Lavelle revealed to me new sides of himself. He showed me his knowledge and curiosity for the world. It was charming, unexpected. I would never describe Lavelle as innocent – it makes me laugh even to use that word – but he was in that moment something pure.

He described Venice as the true light of Europe, far beyond Paris or London. Here, in its canals and islands, he said that there was something marvellous, something unlike anywhere else. He offered me potted histories of the city, and the great Republic that had grown up around the imaginative industriousness of its people.

As much as the things that every Tourist went to see – the Rialto Bridge or the Basilica of San Marco – he showed me how the city was formed from interconnecting islands, which had been rescued from marshland. He told me that in former times of great chaos, Venice had become a safe haven from the Dark Ages in Italy, and now the city had risen from the sea. The Venetians had become masters of irrigation and pumping water, so that they were then able to create the lanes and bridges that formed the city's spider's web of connections.

'You should like it here,' he said as the two of us clattered down a little side street, the heels of our shoes slipping on the wet, narrow embankment above a canal.

'I do,' I replied.

He laughed to himself, knowingly. 'It is a city of your folk. Merchants. Here more than anywhere, the bourgeoisie – held in such contempt in the London they alone made rich – are kings.'

In Venice I told him about our mother's guidebook, which she had lovingly created for us. It was replete with history quoted from various authors and its list of sights that must be seen: the Doge's Palace, the Basilica, the Cathedral of St Mark, which every Tourist went to visit. I thought he might laugh or demand to see the guidebook, but he did not. Instead, it seemed to inspire some competition in him to counter her. He said we had to take a gondola trip – *right now* – around the less salubrious parts of the city. We would go away from the famous and palatial south side towards the north, as far as Cannareggio. I asked him why. 'Isn't London the whole of the city, every grubby street, every muddy-footed urchin, every woman working on a street corner? Doesn't St Paul's Cathedral belong to them as much as to fucking Princess Augusta and Princess Elizabeth wiggling their podgy arses through the Hyde Park teashops? What is

London? London is every brick, every street, every face. The same is true of Venice. And we shall see it all.' He laughed to himself. 'We should write our own guidebook and send it to your mother, telling her the truth about all the places we are visiting, not the bilge she reads in travel guides and history books! What *would* she think of that?' Truly, I did not know.

The gondola, as instructed, took us into the scruffier parts of the city, until we reached the northernmost point, where the gondolier cried to us in Italian: 'Look, gentlemen, the *Ghetto*!' Men in long black coats stalked along the harbourside, inspecting stacked piles of products of every type, below which other men hauled crates up from small boats. I watched them, half fascinated, half frightened. 'They are Jews,' Lavelle said to me.

'I know,' I replied, and he nodded and said nothing more. Why should he? 'Venice must be a very tolerant place.'

The gondolier, we realised, understood a good deal of English, because he nodded approvingly of my comment. But such declarations – unexamined, unproven – irritated Lavelle.

'I hear quite the opposite is the truth. I hear that the Jewish population has dropped by two-thirds in a hundred years here in Venice.'

'*Peste!*' the gondolier said, which I guessed was the same word as French: the plague. It was widely reported that the Jewish population had been badly affected by the disease as it moved in waves back and forth across Italy. At this, Lavelle groaned – groaned *to reject*!

'I hear that ordinary Venetians like to pretend they are very good to Jews, but in fact, they are harsh and hostile to them. They claim it is the plague, but in fact it is violence, and the poor Jews give up in the end and go to live among the Muhammadans, who treat them much more fairly than our Holy Mother Church.' The gondolier had lost track of the English, but did his best to look very offended. 'I find that ordinary men and women are rarely anywhere near as tolerant as they claim to be,' Lavelle observed, with a sharp, derisive sniff.

I looked up at the black-cloaked men on the harbour, going about their business. I wanted Lavelle to know me, but how much was I willing to tell him? I remembered when Edgar had warned me in Paris to tell no one of what we learned about our mother's past. I had agreed then, but that was before I knew of the existence – the effect – of Horace Lavelle.

When we'd returned to the south of the city, we sat together on the steps of the Academy Bridge, sharing a paper wrap of fried sardines we had bought from a side-street window. 'So you are a virgin?' he said to me. There were no Tourists around. It was safe for us to speak English. His question caught my breath a little.

'I beg pardon?'

'You heard me, Benjamin. Do not pretend now.'

I felt a faint embarrassment, not so much to admit my innocence, but that I had to talk of it at all.

'Yes,' I said. 'Of course.'

He laughed, shaking his head. 'You are twenty-one, Benjamin. There is no "of course".'

I sighed unhappily, picked up a fried sardine and crunched it between my teeth. 'What is it like to be with a woman?'

He hummed to himself. 'You get excited. You kiss her and you touch her pussy. Sometimes, a girl will let you lick it.'

'Lick it?' I cried. There had been no mention of that on my mother's library shelves.

'Oh, yes, licking it is almost the best part. The girl will wriggle and roll if you lick it. You can change her if you lick it long enough.'

'Change her?' I laughed, shocked.

'Well, not change her personality or her beliefs, her views on Deism versus Theism, and such.' He was very happy that he was able to say that. And I, who came from a home created and mediated by an intelligent, learned woman, had never heard women spoken of in that way. I shifted in my seat on the steps, stupidly aroused.

'So are you ready to move on, Benjamin?'

'I don't think I should stand up for a moment, Lavelle,' I said sheepishly, and he laughed, took his hand and plunged it between my legs. He was searching for my erection, laughing still as I pushed his hand away.

'Get off!' I screamed. I was laughing now, too. 'Get off, Horace!'

The bag of sardines knocked to the ground and scattered down the steps in front of us.

As long as I could remember, Edgar and I had been a pair, but now a third had appeared in our lives – charming, ferocious, hunting, seductive. I allowed myself to be seduced, I offered myself up to him willingly. I had no regrets. But while I moved towards Lavelle, Edgar recoiled from him, repulsed. I am not sure which of us was being hunted, but it was only he who felt the attack. I felt the charm and the seduction.

Things began to change, because under this new pressure, they could not stay the same. Although my brother and I still shared rooms in Vicenza and Venice, and still travelled between cities in the same coach (but always together with Lavelle, applying his force), our separation became more and more profound. Edgar started going out very early, dressing whilst I was still asleep – or pretending to sleep. Lavelle liked to get up late. He was rarely at my door before late morning, and Edgar would be gone by then, off with his new friends. I would love to tell you, knowing what I know now, that I was sorry that Edgar and I were apart, but I was not. I was thrilled by my new life. It was not that I could not see what might go wrong. I did not care. I did not want to see.

As my brother fell in with this new set of friends, he sometimes did not even come back to the room at night. He would send a note saying that some friend (one was named Sir Percy Paget, which made Lavelle roar with laughter) was letting him stay in his suite. There, he would be tended to by servants and meet more fine people. Occasionally I did not see him for a day or even two, and Lavelle would joke, maybe he's dead in a ditch. I would tell him to be quiet, laughing to show how I enjoyed him scandalising me. But on and on it went, the unravelling of the bond between Edgar and me.

Lavelle and I never met where he was staying. He always gave me precise addresses of his lodgings and could, if requested, describe his accommodation in detail, but I was never once invited to visit. He just appeared at my door, every single morning, with the day ahead already planned, even if it comprised the two of us just drifting. Drifting and drifting, and falling forwards, too.

One day, he said that we should go out to the Lido, from where one could look back at the city itself. Here, during the Crusades, soldiers going off to kill for Christ camped out when the clever Venetians would not let them inside the city. Those good Christians had murdered their way across Germany. Venice liked Jesus, he said – but not that much. Having rowed there in a little galley with a handful of other visitors, all we found was a long slip of sand in the middle of the sea. It was empty except for the occasional clump of trees and sparse bushes. Dotted on the water, fishermen bobbed on boats, throwing nets into the Adriatic, but they were too far away to see us, or for us to see them, in any detail. The galley did not so much dock on the Lido as run aground, and we passengers helped each other out onto the beach, our expensive heels immediately swallowed by the sand. The men who brought us over on the galley kept shouting at us, '*Due ore! Due ore!*' That was what we had: two hours.

It was a warm day, and though Lavelle and I were not wearing wigs, it was still hot in our coats so we slipped them off and undid our cravats. All we had with us otherwise was a jug of water and a few oranges to eat. We walked a while along the Lido, away from the other Tourists, until we came to a crop of rocks that had formed a little cove. From there, one could see the city, glittering yet colourless across the bright, sunlit water. The two of us stood there looking at it, holding our coats under our arms. I let the jug of water hang from my hand. A warm and salty breeze was blowing softly over us. If we craned forwards, we could see down the long scooped-out line of sand. We were entirely alone.

'Can you swim?' he asked. I told him no. His wide, handsome grin opened across his face, and staring straight at me, he kicked off his shoes and dropped his coat down onto the rocks that edged above the water. Then he began to unbutton his shirt. 'I am going to teach you,' he said. He tore open his shirt and cast it aside across the rock. There he was before me, stripped to the waist, his body taut and beautiful. I felt my breath shorten. 'Come on,' he said. 'Get undressed.'

'Do you think we can?'

He looked around and shrugged. 'Who's going to stop us?'

Lavelle lifted up one leg and began to take off his stockings and then his breeches, pulling them down over one ankle, then the other. All the while, he kept looking at me and grinning, almost laughing. His hips were slim, his thighs long, his feet melted over the little rocks of the cove. I stared at his body, and finally at his cock, nestled in fair pubic hair. I could not think. I just stared at him. I was terrified – *terrified* – that my penis would get hard. I felt vulnerable; I knew I was going to end up looking ridiculous, humiliated. And yet, I wanted this.

'I don't know how to swim,' I muttered, in a low panic, perhaps hoping – against hope – that Lavelle would not make me go further. But, of course, Lavelle always drew me out to go further – always.

'It doesn't matter,' he said happily. He did not seem to notice – or even think about – his own nakedness before me. Was he truly so free? 'We can lurk in the water. It will feel good on our bodies.'

'You go in first,' I replied. 'Then I will undress.'

I knew that he could sense my nerves.

'Are you afraid to show yourself to me?' he asked. Well, there was the question, indeed. Boys like me are always afraid of showing ourselves. Nakedness among men is where the deepest shame of the sodomite lies, for his nakedness – emotional, physical – can only betray him, and betrayal can only destroy him.

With a great whoop of joy, Lavelle turned and raced straight into the water, splashing as he submerged. 'Oh, sweet Jesus, it's cold!' he yelled. 'Oh, sweet Jesus!' over and over again. He started swimming madly in a small circle, teeth chattering. 'I thought it was going to be warm!' he laughed again. 'I mean, come on in, it's lovely.'

There was still no one in sight. Putting my fingers to the buttons of my undershirt, I felt each ivory disc press into my skin. I pulled the shirt over my body. The hot sunshine hit my back and belly. Taking my boots off in turn, I heard Lavelle give another great whoop. He was standing chest-deep in the water, and then jumped forwards into a breaststroke. The pearly white flesh of his back and buttocks was swallowed under the surface, before he stood up again, sweeping his hands over his hair, splattering the air with diamantine droplets of water. I was barefoot, still in my breeches. 'Come on, get them off!' he yelled. 'Let's see the Bowen member!'

So I pulled down my breeches and finally stood naked on the shore. I felt the earth between my feet, unmediated by anything that might be called refined. The light breeze caught the hair on my thighs and belly. The sun was on my body, revealed to the world. Lavelle was looking at me, smiling and squinting in the brightness. Cupping my cock with my hand, I waded slowly across to Lavelle's side. 'Are you nervous?' he asked, his voice now low.

'Yes,' I said. He touched my elbow.

'Don't worry,' he said, 'there is no danger here.'

For a while, the two of us bobbed in the water, chilled beneath the surface, warmed above. I had never swum in the sea before. I had not imagined how it would feel, the buoyancy of saltwater, the pleasure beyond the fear of what was unknown. In the trees around the cove, birds chirruped. Lavelle made no attempt to teach me to swim after all. He pointed downwards into the water. 'There are fish!' I saw shadows dart and disappear. 'Look again,' he said. His joy, at such a simple thing, surprised me. It was not childlike, but rather it revealed an unexpected innocence. I looked down for the fish again. Instead, I saw the refraction of Lavelle's legs and feet.

He turned and swam a little way from me. I tried to follow him but something changed beneath the water. I fell slightly. My mouth went under the surface. Splash, a gulp. Swimming is a language either one speaks or does not. Swimmers do not understand how little or how much non-swimmers know of that language, and vice versa. Suddenly my face was underwater. Chaos overwhelmed me. I was submerged, splashing, and I was drowning. And then from nowhere, I felt a body against mine, warm and hard. I realised he was pulling me up from wherever I had fallen. Swallowing a great lungful of water, I flailed around, trying to stand up, yet still in his embrace.

'I'm drowning,' I yelped. There was saltwater burning my eyes, my nose, my throat.

'It's all right,' he said tenderly. 'Let me help you.' The front of his thighs were against my buttocks, his biceps holding my chest, the expanse of his nakedness, chest, belly, crotch on my skin, his hot breath on my neck. I turned slightly and broke our embrace. 'I am sorry, Benjamin,' he said, 'I forgot you could not swim.'

'I'm all right. It's all right.'

But he remained concerned. 'Forgive me,' he said softly. Forgive him? I had never thought he would be someone who might ask forgiveness.

Breaking waves, I moved to the edge of the water, but I stayed beneath the surface. I did not want to betray my erection. I felt ashamed, of my body and its desires. And ashamed of being almost twenty-two and such an innocent. Lavelle's gaze was on me.

'Don't be ashamed,' he said. Him saying the word – like he was my mind reader – quietened me. I watched him standing up, so that the water was only knee-high. Water cascaded from his skin. His penis, heavy and long, was dangling in mid-air, half-hard. 'If you learn one thing from me, boy, it is to never be ashamed of what you are. And you know what you must do to those who wish to make you feel ashamed?'

I was staring at his erection, then looked up at him. 'Reject, reject, reject?'

He put his hands on his naked hips and began to laugh. 'Precisely.' As he laughed, his penis grew harder. 'Show me yours,' he said. 'Show it to me. I want to see it. I want to see.'

My throat was tight; my stomach, empty except for a few segments of orange, ached. My head was reeling. I was a drunkard, spinning around, not knowing if I would be able to stop. I stood up slowly, the water rushing from my body, the whiteness of my half-Welsh skin more blinding than the sun itself. My cock was pointing straight up, as hard as it could be, simultaneously both weightless and immensely heavy – defying gravity's laws, it seemed to me. 'Benjamin!' he cried. 'You have a big one!'

'What?'

'It's fucking huge!'

Then he darted forward, to try to grab it. Now I laughed too, falling backwards, splashing into the water, then jumping to my feet again. The two of us wild with laughter, I realised the truth that I had been avoiding for weeks

I was in love with him. I was completely, rapturously, *recklessly*, in love with Horace Lavelle.

Piazza del Carmine di Siena.

Mother

This is Siena, a hateful place.

A longer letter will follow, explaining much about Benjamin and his infatuation with this awful Lavelle. He is a malevolent person!

I love you, Mother. I miss home more than I expected –

Edgar

SIENA

The weeks unfolded; the weather grew hotter. Increasingly, Lavelle mocked the idea that I had received something called an 'education'.

'What you have is a bunch of lies from a woman who wanted to conceal the truth from you, and a man – your father – who did not stop her. What else do you know? Nothing. You have never let your fingertip so much as touch the warm insides of a woman, so what have you learned that is even worth knowing?'

'Teach me about Beauty, then,' I said. 'Teach me about pleasure.'

Occasionally, when I saw Edgar, he railed again against my relationship with Lavelle. 'You will get yourself a bad name. Persons such as that, you must guard yourself from being so easily associated with them.' I knew what he was saying was true, but how could I explain the way I felt to him? I was wildly awake and thrillingly drunk. 'And Mother and Father worked hard and spent a lot of time and money to make us acceptable Englishmen. Do you think they made sacrifices so that you could debase and debauch yourself with dissolutes?' I let him talk. I did not stop him; I did not even pretend he was wrong. And I was in love. Gloriously, perilously, in love. For the most part, Edgar avoided me. And so I would fly back to Lavelle, and betray my family again and again.

'My brother says that my parents worked hard to have us accepted as Englishmen.'

'Forget your brother,' Lavelle said with a shivering command. 'You are better off without him.' Those sapphire-blue eyes were pressing down on me. 'You have me now.' Lavelle opened his arms upwards, like a messiah conjuring revelation before a crowd: 'Am I not an Englishman? Have I not accepted you?' I welcomed these moments. Like a heretic broken by the Inquisition, I felt comfort and relief in the act of my confession, and drew strength in the surety with which Lavelle presented himself as my saviour.

'We are on an incredible adventure, the two of us,' he said. 'A misadventure. A *folie à deux*. A madman's caper. Don't you want that?' he asked. 'Don't you want that?'

'Yes,' I said. 'Yes.'

One day, Lavelle and I decided to cover the whole of Siena in a few hours. It is a small place, historically but not humanly fascinating. We resorted quickly to larks, running around the seashell patterns of the Piazza del Campo. Lavelle caught my hand, and yanked me along, unafraid, always unafraid. The Italians stared at us, outraged, but we did not care. This was our misadventure. A grey-jowled priest tutted at us and hissed the word: *indecente!* Lavelle tore around and yelled at him with real venom: '*E tu,*

pederasta?' The priest looked shocked. No one had ever spoken the truth to him before. Then Lavelle guffawed, grabbed my hand and we ran off, our laughter patterning the air.

We wandered down the Passeggio. Lavelle pointed to a woman intently watching us. 'She is a whore,' he whispered. I looked at him, his eyes glowing marvellously and darkly. And the Italian woman smiled to herself and whispered mysteriously:

'*Finocchi.*'

The word means 'fennels'. I did not understand what she meant. Was she calling us fennels? Afterwards, Lavelle explained to me that when Italians burned sodomites at the stake, they would throw fennel bulbs into the fire. It covered the stench of the young men's flesh starting to melt, and the moisture in the bulb slowed down their deaths. He crossed himself. 'Hail Mary, full of grace, burn them sinners at the stake.'

We were standing in a narrow street, above which balconies hung as if in mid-air, and between them were strung washing lines. A low breeze moved through the dying light of the evening, and laundry danced slowly, so that the two of us were hidden by waves of shadow. All I knew in that moment was that I did not want to be burned alive in Italy any more than hanged in London. My confidence in his bravery faltered that day. Shame returned to me; the shame and danger of being open about who I was.

'Why must they burn sodomites?' I asked. Lavelle turned and stood in front of me, taller than me. In the half light, his golden aura was gone. He was now a shadow, a shape, above me.

'Maybe they deserve it,' he replied darkly. I could hardly see his face. He spoke with such harshness, it shocked me. I was horrified for a moment.

'Can you believe that?' I asked. 'Shouldn't we reject these … mores?'

He shrugged. 'What does it matter what I believe? They'll burn them all the same.' I realised then that his was not harshness, it was disgust at the reality of the world.

We were only in Siena a few days. On our last night there, Lavelle and I went to see a production of *La buona figliuola*, which had been a success across the Italian cities. I did not ask Edgar to come and he did not ask where I was going. Lavelle and I sat together in a small box I paid for, in a shadowy part of the theatre, with our cravats half-untied, wearing no wigs. My hair had started to grow and fell straight, black and shiny. My brother had already written to our mother to report on my dishevelled state. Lavelle laughed at everything I told him. We were far gone in the cups before we got to the opera. Throughout the music, Lavelle leaned forwards on the lip of the box, gazing at the singers who moved elegantly about the stage.

'I thought you cared nothing for the arts, Lavelle,' I said.

'I care nothing for *the* arts,' he replied, not taking his eyes from the stage. 'But this is Beauty, is it not? It is not me who rules that one thing is beautiful and another not.' Finally, he turned to look at me. 'Oh, I am sure those Canalettos you went to see were very pretty, but did the people you went with do anything more than gaze at them for a second and pronounce, "Hmm, very good"?'

I laughed. 'There was one of Westminster Abbey and some knights. Lady Howard swore blind that it was her Uncle Archibald third from the front.'

'There you go, then. That is the power of great, high-born minds for you. All that money spent on their education, and they would have been better off trained to muck out horses. I am sure their stable boys would have made more insightful art historians.'

The interval came, and the two of us stayed where we sat. Lavelle put his feet up on the edge of the box, crossing his legs at the ankles, so that below, one would have only seen his shoes floating in mid-air. We discussed the female parts, which were played by *castrati*, their high, pure voices eerie to English ears. In London, women were allowed to perform on stage, but in Rome, it was still banned by the Pope. Lavelle told me that most popes took *castrati* as lovers, in preference to women. I was not sure that this was true. When I said so, he shrugged to show he did not mind either way. 'We don't have to agree,' he said airily.

'Don't we?' I laughed. 'I thought you insisted on agreement!'

'No, *everybody else* insists on it!'

I remarked that the opera had the same story as Samuel Richardson's *Pamela*, which I had read a year before. At this he groaned audibly.

'What kind of Englishman are you?' he asked, arch and ironic. 'Englishmen are entirely uninterested in reading, everyone knows it! They cannot finish a newspaper article, let alone a novel. The English are far too stupid for that!'

'I am an Englishman and I am interested in books.'

'No,' Lavelle cried. 'You are half-Welsh and half-Dutch. You have no claim whatsoever on what the English know.'

'Then I declare myself an Englishman, just like you said I could, Horace.'

He groaned again. 'Please don't quote my nonsense back at me. If you are interested in literature, it is precisely a sign of your alien nature.'

His words were bracing. I tried not to show their effect on me. 'What about you then, Lavelle? Are you not an Irishman?'

'Oh, I am an entirely different beast, little Benjamin. I am an Englishman posing as an Irishman. The Anglo-Irish. Neither side likes us, but at least there are very many of us. We are a common enough breed. But half-Dutch-half-Welshmen, there are not so many of those. Truly, you are a rare flower. Like an orchid fetched from the Indies.'

'I am an alien on both sides, dexter and sinister,' I said, to amuse Lavelle.

'Alien and sinister indeed,' he said. 'I am not so sure about the dexter part!' He flung out a hand as if to tickle and I recoiled, laughing, confused.

'From which land do I come, then?' I asked to join in on the mischief.

'The Levant.' The tickling hand reached out again, and again I recoiled, laughing at his touch. 'Persia.' The hand; the recoil. 'Palestine. Yes, you are from Palestine come to spy on us for the Sultan in Constantinople, your *sensual* master.'

'You think I am an Arab?' I laughed.

'Yes!' he cried. 'Or maybe you are a Jew.' The hand still tickled, but I froze. I saw him recognise it at once.

The tickling stopped. 'Benjamin?' he asked. 'Benjamin, what is it?'

At the Ghetto, I wondered if I could tell him the truth about me. I wanted to share with him my deepest secrets. We were not even lovers, and yet here I was, stretching out my arms to say: here I am.

'My mother is a Jew,' I said. As soon as I spoke, I regretted it and began to gabble: 'Or rather she was a Jew, before she married my father. She was born a Jew in Amsterdam, and she came to England, to London, and she was married before, and then she married my father. We did not know.' I was panicking. 'Edgar and I, I mean, we did not know. We only found out in Paris. It's a long story.' I took a breath. 'It's a long story,' I said again, my throat clucking shut on the last word.

Lavelle was staring at me. 'Why have you told me this?' he asked, very gravely.

'I ...' I could not think. Why had I told him? To humiliate myself, to betray myself, to push him away? My panic had not abated, but bit at me, scratched and lunged. 'I want you to know me.' I blinked, afraid. And then, with my fears around me like a dog sniffing and snarling, he reached out his hand and caught my fingers, his skin against mine.

'Let's leave,' he said.

'What, Horace?'

'Come on, let's go.'

'But the performance is not over,' I said stupidly, like it mattered. I had not been taught that one could just leave if one wanted. 'The opera ...' I murmured.

He looked at me as those who find rules contemptible do. 'Oh, *fuck the opera!*'

Soon, we were tumbling out into the Siena night. The air was still warm and the streets filled with noise; the Italian language screeched and squawked on every corner. As we walked, I told him everything I knew: the wall of mystery that had surrounded my mother; how we had met our Cardoso cousin in Paris; how our mother's family was educated and cultured but poor; her first marriage, then her second, and how her family had cut her off; and lastly, how Edgar had told me never to speak of it to anyone. And here I was, telling him. When it was done, Lavelle let out a long, exhausted breath, although I had done all the talking.

'The first husband, this Solomon Fon—' he said.

'Fonseca.'

He shrugged. 'Whatever. Do you think your parents killed him?'

'*What?* No, of course not!'

He was pleased with his game. 'Maybe they did, Benjamin. Maybe they banged him over the head when he was sleeping and dumped his body in the Thames, taking it down to the river in the dead of night so they could be together.' He pulled a satirical face. 'Oh, how passionate.'

'Stop it,' I chided happily. 'I don't think so. My mother is not one for cudgels.'

He laughed. 'Not even one of her endless, worthy books?' He pretended to lift some heavy tome high in the air, then *thud*, brought it back down, as a blow. 'Whack!'

I laughed too. 'No, I don't think so!' It was all so ridiculous.

We reached a line of large orange trees and walked beneath it. The fruits were heavy and long past their best.

Still they rained down their aroma, sharp and florally sweet, but with the deathly sickliness of fruit starting to turn.

'Your parents lied to you your whole life,' he said.

'What do you mean?' I asked.

He sighed. 'What do *you* mean what do I mean? It is plain enough, isn't it? Your. Parents. Lied. To. You. What part was unclear?'

'No part.' It was true. I did know. Deception is a lie, and so is omission, and so is the creation of a world that only has one purpose: to dupe those who live in it.

'At least now you know the truth, Benjamin.'

'Do I?' I whispered.

'Not the truth of the past, perhaps,' he said, 'but the fact of it. And do you know what this means?'

'That we can no longer be friends?'

He looked first shocked and then annoyed.

'Do you fear I will reject you for your provenance?' he asked. Under the orange trees, a golden-haired demigod – *only demi?* I could hear him say – was laurelled by their thick green branches. He reached up to pick an orange. He held the fruit in the palm of his hand, his fingers pressing into the peel. A faint mist of sweet citrus oil dissipated into the air.

'Sir Gideon and all the rest would reject us,' I said.

He lifted the orange to his mouth, but did not bite into it, as I thought he might. He just held it there, breathing in its aroma, whilst revealing only his eyes, which stared at me. Then he handed me the orange. I took it in my hand.

'Fuck them,' he said. 'I never would, Benjamin. I will reject everything, but not you. And the thing of which you feel ashamed, I think you should feel proud.'

'Proud?' I asked, incredulous.

'Yes,' he said. 'Of course. When someone tells you to feel ashamed, feel proud. When someone calls you sodomite or Jew, raise your chin and look them in the eye and know that you are better than them. With their wives, and their children, and their friends in the country, and their pals in Parliament – you are worth one hundred of them.'

He looked up and began to recite, elegantly, without hesitation: '"Do not imagine that these most difficult problems can be thoroughly understood by any one of us. This is not the case. At times the truth shines so brilliantly that we perceive it as clear as day. Our nature and habit then draw a veil over our perception, and we return to a darkness almost as dense as before."' He turned to me and screwed up his mouth to one side, as if about to make a joke.

'Who is that?'

'Maimonides.' The great Arab-Jewish philosopher. He glanced at me, and his eyes were alive with dark mischief. 'One of your lot.' Then he burst into laughter and thumped me on the shoulder. Above us a row of nightbirds on a branch were singing in a line of call-and-response. I could never anticipate how Lavelle would respond to such things. Would he call it beautiful, or would he get out a slingshot and kill each bird? He closed his eyes, listening to their song. I watched him. With his eyes still closed, he began to speak: 'The Minute Game, shall we play it?'

'What?'

His eyes remained closed. 'One minute, on the history of the Jews in England. The Jews of England were a prosperous presence in the Middle Ages in England, having travelled to that mysterious, far-flung island after the Norman Conquest. But these were the days of the Crusades, and for the first time, Europeans, as one, agreed that they must hate the Jews. I believe it was the fond desire of the Pope himself that good Christians must murder Jews, and so it became their favourite pastime, the bullying, torturing, killing of and – more importantly – stealing from Jews. This continued until – I am not sure of the year – 1290, I think – when King Edward I ordered that the Jews must leave England. Edward I was a very devout man, one of the great kings of our country – the hammer of the Scots, the rapist of your own dear Welsh race – but he also owed a lot of money. So, to satisfy Holy Mother Church, he exiled the Jews in order to steal their money and pay off his debts.' Still with his eyes shut, like a ghost was speaking through him, he clapped his fingertips together lightly. 'Oh, the dignity of good Christians! Oh, the honour of the English Crown!

'For almost four hundred years, Jews were not allowed to set foot on English soil, but a century ago, Oliver Cromwell, England's greatest man – fuck Isaac Newton and Sir Francis bloody Bacon – wanting to investigate commercial possibilities, allowed them to return. And so the Spanish-speaking Jews who had fled to Amsterdam from the hands-clasped ministrations of those hate-eyed holy-joes Ferdinand and Isabella, were permitted to settle in some tiny quarter of London from which they were just about safe from provincial lynch mobs. How noble the English! How tolerant and fair! When I said that men and women are less tolerant than they like to think, I was of course talking about Englishmen!' He coughed to himself. 'And maybe the Spanish too.' He opened his eyes, staring at me very intently. 'Did you *really* never wonder how your Dutch mother spoke Spanish?'

He did not wait for an answer. 'Your mother has conspired to deceive you. She denied you her history, your own history. What Jews don't know about the truth of history is not worth knowing. They understand that the person who lives next door to them, and nods good day and asks after their children, will one day turn on them and drag them screaming through the street.' He closed one eye. 'And that's what your mother knows too. That's why she lied to you.'

His words were as heady as the orange's aroma. 'Do you mean I should forgive her lies?'

'Oh, no!' he said. 'The fact that your mother knows the truth of the world and still sought to deceive you is *unforgivable*. But your parents have deceived you in several ways, haven't they? You have things which should make you glad. You have great knowledge, you speak several languages, you have money enough to live freely. You should be able to live freely. Instead your father hopes to indenture you to his fucking shipping company for the rest of your life. Can you not just pay someone to run it for you, find some fellow – maybe low-born like your father – and give him a whole new life and chance, doing something he wishes? What is the point of money if it is not used to buy freedom? What is the point of money if it enslaves you to a life of drudgery? You might as well be King George the fucking Third, getting up every morning knowing exactly what kind of gilded day lies ahead of you, every minute and hour already prescribed, for the rest of your tedious bloody life! What fucking moron would want to be the King of England, enslaved from the moment of his birth?'

'Maybe I do wish to run the Company,' I said, even though back in London I had found the prospect unbearably boring.

He laughed dismissively. 'Why? Why do you wish to sit in an office all day until you keel over at seventy-two? You could be out walking on Hampstead Heath in the sunshine, you could be lying in bed with two whores whom you pay ten times their rate and tell to take a week off, and all the whores in London will throw flowers at your feet when you walk through St Giles.' He was laughing as he spoke. He was in love with his own scenario. Then he drew close. 'But seriously, Benjamin, *why* do you wish to run this company? Don't you want to be free? Don't you want to reject?' His eyes were gleaming with confidence and certainty. 'I tell you now: reject, reject, reject!'

I shook my head. 'What am I rejecting?'

'Whatever you decide. Reject your parents' dreams. They are their dreams, not yours. Reject their plans: going back to London, a society wedding, a lifetime in the trade they choose, in the house they bought. Whatever was given to you that you did not ask for, whatever rule was imposed on you that might limit you, reject it.'

'And what is left,' I asked, 'when everything has been rejected?'

His eyes glowed. 'Everything that you might actually want from your life.'

I had never felt such excitement, such hope as in that moment. 'Reject,' I said, and he nodded.

'Reject, reject, reject!' Lavelle thumped his fist into the air, and let out a great whoop.

'Reject, reject, reject!' I echoed. I was yelling too, and both of us started to jump around.

We went back to my *albergo*, and there we drank and laughed, and fell asleep together on my bed, in such deep friendship. At least, you might wish to call it friendship. During the night Lavelle and I moved together, so that in the half-light of dawn I found his face against my chest. I should have gently pushed him away, rolled him over to sleep alone, but I did not. I had not slept like that with another human being, not since earliest childhood, and it felt, to have that closeness, a true *terra nova*. We slept as one, the push-pull of our breathing matching up, forming a single rhythm. And when I awoke properly, I turned to face him and gazed at him for the longest time. Then his breathing changed, his eyes flickered awake, and I, in turn, quickly shut mine, pretending to be asleep.

Mother

I enclose an etching of Florence's Cathedral. You will
see the priests parade and this is very much how Italy
is – filled with priests. There are so many things to see
in Florence. I consult your guidebook every day. It
makes me feel close to you, Mother. Benjamin is thick
with this Lavelle all the time. I rarely see him. I make
company myself, but he does not seem to have time for
anyone but Lavelle. I ask him to write to you but he
refuses. I shall send a longer letter to try to explain
what has happened, and how sad I am feeling about it.

Your loving son,

Edgar

FLORENCE

$\mathcal{M}$y mother's guidebook had much to say about Florence and the city's centrality to the Renaissance. She told us about the rise of Florence as modern Europe's first truly mercantile city. She wrote of the Medici and the other great trading families, who rose from obscurity into astonishing wealth and power. And how this family – all those Lorenzos and Cosimos and Lucrezias – used their money to bring Leonardo and Michelangelo, and even Galileo, to the world. But when I told Lavelle this, he scoffed. 'Does she also tell you how, once it became politically expedient to, the Medici turned him over to the Pope too?' Around this time, I stopped reading the guidebook altogether. If he had told me to throw it on a fire, I would have. But he did not. In retrospect, I believe, perhaps he already knew he had won.

Lavelle asked what we would do on our first full day in Florence. He said that he was in a cheerful mood so I could choose whatever I wanted. I said I'd like to visit the Piazza della Signoria. I knew that this square was the centre of the city, lined with some of its most famous buildings. I still loved culture, I joked, which made him laugh, and spit: 'I knew you were a moron. I knew all along.'

The day was hot and the sun strong. All around us, other English Tourists, usually found twittering with their mix of delight and derision – *Oh, do look at that crenellation, it looks purely like it was hand-drawn, and, oh, do look at those peach sellers, they look quite like gypsies!* – were instead flagging. Men slipped off their wigs, their stubbled scalps glistening in the sunshine, and tried to fan themselves. Women in tight-lace corseting were piled on the edges of the square's famous statues, their great hooped dresses bunched up all around them, like sinking dinghies. *Oh, the heat! This infernal heat!*

Lavelle and I were hot too, of course. All he had to do was pull at his cravat, to show the contours of his neck, the line of his collarbone, brown now with sun, and loosen his hair from its knot to fall in curls around his collar, and he was transformed in quite another way. I would stare at his neck and understand what it felt to want someone – and more importantly, to know that you wanted someone.

After walking around the piazza, we sat down under the wide, classical arches of the Loggia dei Lanzi. Their shade offered relief from the punishing heat. Somewhere nearby, a French tour guide continued valiantly. A rag-bag of Tourists stood around him, sweat darkening their shirtfronts, make-up sliding off their cheeks and brows. They clicked their fingers at the wandering water-sellers, who were charging five times as much as the day before. 'Outrageous!' an Englishwoman cried loudly. '*Voleurs*,' from a pink-cheeked Frenchman. His pet dog was panting so hard, at any moment one expected its lungs to pop out.

'What idiots,' Lavelle whispered to me. 'They have more money in their back pocket than that water-seller will earn all year. They resent the ordinary person for their cleverness.'

'Because they feel cheated,' I said.

He shook his head. 'Because people like this don't like to be reminded of how stupid they are, and how vulnerable.'

'Vulnerable to whom?'

'To the mob,' he said, 'who might one day decide to rise up and slaughter them, burn down their houses and take their infants for slaves.'

I watched the Tourists paying up – yes, five times as much. The laws of supply and demand were in action. I stretched my legs out, in front of me, and looked down at my shoes. Our bodies were touching, along our arms and thighs. It was small contact but it delighted me. Gradually, I became aware that Lavelle had started listening closely to the guide.

'The Loggia,' the man was saying, 'was one of the first treasures of the Florentine Renaissance. Built in the 1380s, it was one of the first buildings in Europe to make explicit reference to Greek classical styles.' He indicated mysteriously at the columns, without explaining the reference. He now began to gesture around the Loggia, which was filled with famous statues. The group turned to look where he was pointing and saying: '*Perseus with the Head of Medusa.*'

I looked too, at the angelic youth in black bronze, with his stomach detailed with musculature. Helmeted to look like Apollo, he was entirely naked, holding aloft the Gorgon's head. 'This statue is famous,' the French guide was saying, 'for its casting process. Master Cellini forged the entire cast in stone, a single piece reversed, inside-out, and then poured the molten bronze into the cast in one go, a process which ran an enormous risk of failure, showing the artist's commitment to his art …' The tour guide droned on, barely aware of his own speech, saying things he had said many times before, every word exhausted and rehearsed. His listeners wilted in the heat, similarly exhausted. My attention drifted. I began talking about something, but slowly realised that Lavelle was not listening. Turning, I saw he was still watching the guide, the way a cat studies a bird.

'Horace?' I said, but he did not break his gaze.

'Hypocrites,' he hissed. 'Look at them all, these hypocrites. The guide pretends he cares, the group pretend they care, but not one of them does. Look at the statue. Look at its beauty. Look at Perseus's beauty, the sheer contemptuous victory on his face as he kills Medusa, the extraordinary technique in achieving the ripple and bend of his musculature, even the defeated, heavenless blankness on the dead Medusa's face, her head held aloft, the blood – cast in bronze – dripping to the ground, her hanging voicebox – look at the majesty of every inch of this statue. And now look at these blockhead oxen staring up at it, *daring* to imagine they understand. They might as well be staring at a hay bale in a field. It would arouse the same amount of feeling in them. But now they can go back to London and say, "Oh, we saw *Perseus with the Head of Medusa* and it was *sublime*!"' Uncertain, I laughed because I was not sure what else to do. But then he spat: 'I would like to stab them all.'

His words stopped me. Only moments before, I had felt joyful, and now ... 'Horace,' I began, understanding that something had changed, 'it doesn't matter.' He was restless in his seat. There was a sense that something was about to happen. 'Leave it, Horace. Whatever it is, it doesn't matter.'

He slowly turned his head to look at me.

'But it does matter, Benjamin,' he said. 'Nothing matters more than ...' His voice trailed off – it seemed to shiver down to nothing on the air.

'Than what?' I asked. He closed his eyes.

'Than speaking truth to liars. To hypocrites.' He opened his eyes, rose to his feet, not looking at me again.

'Horace, what are you doing?' I cried. I caught his arm. He shook me off.

'I am going to tell the truth to liars.' He went to move then stopped again. 'Hey, you, idiot!' he yelled in French towards the guide, across the heads of the crowd. 'Hey, you! You fool!'

People started turning towards us, hearing that word *fou* on the air. 'Hey! Liar! Fool!'

I had seen him satirical before, seen him savage. But I had never quite seen him like this before, shuddering with rage. The guide, used perhaps to the interruptions of onlookers, turned, exquisitely bored. 'Monsieur has something to say?'

Lavelle laughed, black and hard as jet. 'Oh, "monsieur"?' He flung a hand at Perseus. 'Are you going to say nothing of what everyone is thinking … *monsieur*?'

The guide sighed. 'Which is?'

'This beautiful boy has no clothes on. We can see his cock.' He used the word *bitte*. 'Ladies,' he cried at no one in particular, 'do you know what a cock looks like? Take a good look. You might need some idea of what your wedding night will bring.'

One or two of the young ladies, sitting down in the heat, smirked at his shamelessness. Another leaned forwards to take a closer look. A man, seeing the ladies' knowing glances, cried, 'Sir, where is your honour?'

He was talking as much to the ladies as to Lavelle, of course.

'Lavelle,' I whispered, just wanting him to stop. 'Come away.'

The guide for his part continued to look more bored than angry. 'What is your point *exactly*, monsieur?' he asked, trying to wither, and so to silence.

'What everyone is thinking is this: did Master Cellini make this boy so beautiful because he wanted to fuck him? Or perhaps he wanted to be fucked by him?'

At once, there were gasps and cries of 'Monsieur, stop!' and 'Monsieur, the ladies!'

'Stop it, Lavelle,' I whispered. But he would not stop.

'Come on,' Lavelle was crying. 'All this false erudition, all this posing of we-are-so-refined-we-hardly-noticed-his-cock-in-our-faces—'

I had the most awful feeling that he was revealing nothing, that he was simply making a fool of himself.

'Lavelle,' I repeated. 'Come away …'

I wanted him to hear that I cared for him, that I wanted to save him. I gently tugged at his sleeve but again he shook me off. He rendered me so pathetic, not through caustic words, but by ignoring what I was asking of him. He was shouting now, madly. 'Go on, tell them,' he continued, 'that the Greeks, and those copyist Roman and Renaissance fellows, preferred small penises. They regarded large ones as a symbol of foolishness and barbarism.' He bowed now as an actor in his own performance, that of the helpful guide with adoring audience, but this was not a game to him. He bowed to show his utter contempt for them, his loathing. Rising from his bow, Lavelle began to speak, loudly, to an unadoring audience:

'From Aristophanes himself: "If you do these things I tell you, and bend your efforts to them, you will always have a shining breast, a bright skin, big shoulders, a minute tongue, a big rump and a small prick. But if you follow the practices of today, for a start you'll have –"' he inhaled before delivering his quoted list slowly – '"a pale skin, small shoulders, a skinny chest, a big tongue, a small rump, a big prick and a long-winded decree."'

He laughed out loud, and hearing him laugh that way, like a madman, crushed me. He had always been so strong, so inventively clear about the world. He had always seemed so invincible. But madmen are not invincible. They are vulnerable. They need care and love. They need someone to take their hand and to tell them that everything is going to be all right, even if it won't be. On he went: 'But who wouldn't rather ride a big-cocked barbarian than to have poor Perseus's tiny tinkle jabbing away at your entrance?'

The guide finally snapped. 'Monsieur, *enough*!' he bellowed. A man with a heart-shaped beauty spot stuck up his fists like some caricature of a pugilist, ready to box an exotic creature from the Indies, which I saw then that Lavelle almost was. Something shifted imperceptibly in those few seconds. Eyes fixed on Lavelle, the lunatic, the crowd began to glow with amused, steely contempt. People started to snigger. Oh, dear, he is one of *those*.

'Lavelle –' I began, touching his arm again, as tenderly as I could. I didn't want him to seem the fool. Or rather, I didn't want him to feel like one. Still, I wanted to offer some kind of protection. Until that moment, I'd thought him the one person in the world who would never need protecting. I watched his shape, his humanness, a shadow in the sunlight of the square. He needed me, as much as I needed him perhaps, but in a different way.

Could he hear my thoughts? Did my insights reveal themselves to him? Maybe they did, for immediately he tore away, pelting through the crowd. I watched him go. All the time we'd been together, I had never fully committed to Lavelle's worldview. I had been playing in the shallows of his revolutionary nature, laughing at his jokes, enjoying his attention. But now I understood that in any revolution, there comes a time either to commit, or flee. I could have turned away then, but I did not doubt or hesitate. I went after him.

He came to a dead stop before another great statue and just stared up at it. I halted just behind him, not quite at his side. I was breathing hard – more through panic than exertion – I could feel the sweat under my coat, in the heat of the day. Yet there was no sheen on his brow, and his breathing was steady.

'Horace,' I whispered. 'Speak to me. Tell me why you are so upset. I don't understand.'

'I don't want you to understand me,' he murmured. His eyes were so focused on the statue. 'Understanding people is overrated.'

'I want to understand what *this* is!' I cried but then I relented, shaking my head. 'It feels like a kind of delirium.'

He just kept staring up. He did not respond. I felt so nervous watching him that it took me several seconds to look up too. When I did, I saw a huge green bronze posed extraordinarily above us: a figure of a woman, both haunted-looking and frightening in her power, holding a knife high above her veiled head. Beneath her squatted a much more powerful form of a man. The sword was gilded, although most of the gold was gone now. The woman's hand tore at the man's hair. He was entirely in her grasp. She was about to cut off the man's head. Their faces communicated everything in that moment: the darkness of her certainty in what she knew she must do, and his sheer terror, as he anticipated his annihilation. Lavelle was staring up at it intensely. 'Judith and Holofernes,' I said. 'Do you know the story?'

'The woman who takes revenge on the man who would be her rapist,' he said flatly.

This was not the version Edgar and I had been told by our mother. 'No. On learning that the General intended to destroy her city, she tricked her way into his tent and killed him. She is a heroine.'

He laughed, a dim, dark laugh. 'For Christ's sake, Benjamin, there is no heroism in cutting off your rapist's head.'

Why was he talking about rape? This was not the version our mother had told us at all. 'What is there, then?' I asked because I did not know what else to say.

He took a low, growling breath. 'There is justice.'

He began walking forwards, in slow steps. If I had not known better, I would have believed he had been drinking, but not a drop had passed our lips. He was breathing, even and hard, so that the whole of his body rose and fell in an exhausted rhythm. I followed him; of course I did. We said nothing, but soon we were standing before the statue of David. If Perseus had been a beauty, then David was truly a boy-angel. People were crowded around, gazing up at this perfection. To one side, a group of older men stood, talking in portentous, intellectual Italian, looking up at the statue. As with *Perseus and the Head of Medusa*, they talked about form and line. They talked about how they should interpret Goliath's absence. And what about the *contrapposto*?

Without warning, Lavelle leapt up onto the statue, three times his height, all smooth white marble, as if to climb it. He clambered against a long, elegant leg, but his chest was barely above its knee. The sheer size of the statue resisted Lavelle's advances, but still he clung to the stone, like a man to a shipwreck.

'This city is full of death!' he was yelling, pathetically half slipping from the statue as he did. 'This city is a history of death. All the fennels burned, all the heretics killed, all the wealth accumulated whilst the people in the city starved, all the books burned – and you all stand here, pretending, *pretending* that all you fucking love is art! It's horseshit! Horseshit! Look at you all, you fucking hypocrites! I wish you all dead! *I wish you all dead!*'

Steadying himself, he again started clambering up the boy's body, as if to try to sit astride his shoulders, but he still did not manage it.

'My God, Horace!' I cried. He was hanging off the statue's upturned arm, the hand of which was held close to his mouth. Lavelle tried to get his feet to purchase on the sloping thighs, but started to slip and fell hard, crashing onto the stone floor of the Loggia.

'For Christ's sake, Horace!' I screamed, running to him. At once, I saw the wound on his forehead, pinkly raw. He rolled onto his back, starting to laugh wildly – out of control. But as soon as I went to help him up, he kicked out at me, making me jump back.

'Get off me!' he screamed, scrambling to his feet. Across his forehead the scraped skin looked stingingly red-raw. He wiped it with his coat sleeve and a little blood smeared into the fabric.

'You've hurt yourself.'

He launched at me, not to strike me, but to push me away, to resist my help. People around us were staring. Someone was saying over and over again in Italian: *pazzo*. Everyone was gawping. Suddenly his mania had vanished, and all that was left was humiliation. He looked at me sadly, sorrowfully. His eyes were filled with tears. I held out my hand to him.

'Come on,' I whispered, 'let's go.'

He was still looking into my eyes.

'I am not the mad one,' he whispered. 'They are. *They are.*' I saw then that whatever had been in him these last moments had entirely gone. He trusted me again. He took my hand and I pulled him up, and we began to walk away. As we did so, the French and the Italians pushed at us, yelling insults, telling us never to come back. But in their impotent outrage, somehow I saw that Lavelle still, alone, spoke the truth about the world.

We drifted, exhausted, through the city towards the River Arno, until we found ourselves sitting on a wharf in front of the Uffizi, between the Vecchio and Rubaconte bridges. We did not talk for a long time. It was by then late afternoon, and the Tuscan heat had abated somewhat. We sat in the shade of a lemon tree, heavy with fruit: the scent of sherbet was all around us.

'What possessed you?' I asked him eventually.

'I despise hypocrites more than any other.'

I laughed, but so bleakly. 'I thought that you despise everyone equally, Lavelle.'

He held his eyes on the ground for a moment. 'You told me the truth of who you are,' he said, seemingly apropos of nothing. 'You told me about your mother and her lies.'

I did not understand. 'So?'

He took a pause. 'I have lied to you too.'

'About what, Horace?'

'About everything. About who I am.'

I wondered what was to follow.

'Who are you, Horace?' I stopped. 'Is your name not really Horace?'

'Yes, unfortunately,' he said. 'I was not born in Ireland. I was born in London. And my family didn't send me here. There are no "them". No disappointed parents. No deflowered maids. I am not in any peerage.'

'Oh,' I said. 'I see. Why have you lied?'

'I could not tell you the truth.' He breathed out and I heard the fibrous emotion, the trapped tears, in his chest and throat. 'I am too ashamed of the truth.'

'*You*, ashamed? You are the most unashamed person I have ever met.'

He looked at me. I saw the ghostliness in his eyes. 'I play games, Benjamin, you know that. Everything. For. Ironic. Effect. I told you, I *love* games.'

I sighed. 'So what is the truth, Lavelle?'

'I am an orphan. I do not know much of my origin, except that I was low-born. I was found one morning, a baby, in the street on Bride Lane, off Ludgate Circus.'

'My God,' I said, 'that's hardly ten minutes from my house.'

He hummed a little at such a curiosity.

'My room is not far,' he said. 'Shall we go there? I don't want to talk here. I don't want anyone to see me like this.'

I'd always assumed Lavelle's lodgings would be modest. He never had much money, as far as I could tell. I paid for most of the things that we did together. How he paid for everything else was a mystery. But it had never occurred to me just how modest his lodgings might be. In Florence, he was housed in a hot and coffin-like attic off the Via Tripoli, a dingy part of town. The room was brown and threadbare, almost empty of anything comfortable – just a bed and a stick chair. Without even a cupboard, his clothes were *everywhere*. There was no balcony; the window barely opened at all.

'How do you sleep here?' I asked. 'It's so hot.' He replied that he had not slept here – not often, anyway. Then where did he sleep, I wondered but did not ask. The two of us sat down on the bed, which was merely a thin mattress on a raised wooden buttress. We had already removed our coats and now we kicked off our shoes, too. I had tried to wash the blood out of his coat sleeve, but he told me to stop. He could get another coat, he said, but I looked around the shabby room. How could he buy new coats if he could only afford to stay in places like this? I wondered at him coming south with us from Aosta. He had travelled across Italy in a coach paid for by us. He had never paid for a meal, but neither had he ever complained that he was hungry. I never once stopped to wonder if it was just because he had no money.

'You were saying that you were found in the street as a baby. Who found you?'

'An Irishman.' He looked up at me, in this small, tender way. 'That is why I say Ireland when people ask where I'm from. I understand something of the place, though I have never been. He was Anglo-Irish, from Dublin. So we didn't talk Gaelic at home. He was a scholar.'

'What kind of scholar was he?' I asked.

He shrugged. 'Does it matter? He had his own money. The greatest of blessings: independent wealth. Classics, I suppose. He read Latin and Greek and knew every line of Cicero and Plato. He named me after the Roman poet. So I really am just a literary reference, a classical illusion, a claim at ... merit. Shall I quote you some Horace,

Benjamin?' I did not say yes. '"We are but dust and shadow." How very fucking true.' He sighed. 'Yes, the man was a scholar, as erudite as they come. He liked Petrarch, Boccaccio, and liked nothing more of an evening than to sit with friends and recite whole chunks of the *Decameron* from memory. The fucking *Decameron*. I hate the fucking *Decameron*. "Nothing is so indecent that it cannot be said to another person if the proper words are used to convey it." What a filthy lie – plenty of things are too indecent to speak of. What kind of privileged moron thinks up such shit?' He was imperceptibly nodding, then suddenly drew a deep breath. 'He had this huge library, over two floors of his house. We were made to sleep in it as children, on the bare floor.'

We? I did not ask. 'That is why you can quote almost anything. Maimonides, Spinoza, Aristophanes, whatever else.'

He shrugged. 'There was nothing to do but read, and if we did not learn, we got beaten. For our own illumination, he used to say.'

'Were you never allowed out?' I asked. I heard the judgement in my voice.

'Were *you*?' he spat. But then he relented. He tilted his body slightly backwards on the bed, as if it were a relaxed, louche sort. But in fact, he was moving his head further back so that we were no longer looking at one another. 'There were several boys,' he said. 'The scholar took a number of us in. Lucan and Juvenal, we all had some stupid name.'

And so he revealed himself, and I began to understand. I thought of our childhood in Red Lion Square and how Edgar and I had been its creations. What unhappiness was in Lavelle's past that had made him this way? Was I now standing at the pool of his origin, from whence all his anger came?

'If you were unhappy, why didn't you run away?'

'I did not know that I could leave. Do you see? Do you see why I speak to you the way that I do? Why I want you to know you can leave *anything* behind, you can find your own truth? I did not know that I could leave that life – no one ever told me it was possible – but I could. I was just like you before you met me – not under lock and key, but merely made to feel afraid.'

He had opened the shutters on my life and let the daylight in, revealing my weaknesses and cowardice, my failure to question the lessons I'd been given. But I had never imagined that he had done so because he saw his own experience reflected in mine.

He continued: 'When our boyish bodies began to change, his friends would come. He would make us perform for them. Do you understand?' I did not fully, and yet on some vague level, I did realise what he was saying – horribly, I did. 'I became a man – physically, I mean – when I was thirteen, and as soon as I and the other boys did, he set us to pleasuring these friends of his, all scholars and aesthetes too. That was why he took us in to begin with. We were there to be trained – we literally slept on the floor of a library, but he trained us, too, to do things for these men. We were orphans from the street. No one was looking for us. Children can be left to die, to freeze in the street, be murdered or spirited away to slavery. Who cares? No one cares in London. So we did the things that those men wanted, 'But –' he continued, with great seriousness '– I was very beautiful, and men like that want to defile beautiful things. They pretend they love beauty, that they admire and appreciate it when they see it. But they saw it in me, and all they wanted was to despoil it, to ruin it, to render it diminished.'

I was so moved and so unready for his words. 'You are not diminished, Horace,' I said gently. He shrugged as if perhaps I might be right, but I might just as easily be wrong.

'We had to sit with these men and talk about Tacitus or Spinoza, and then, when we could smell the stench of wine on their mouths, take them to a room.' He gave a bleak laugh. 'I can always get hard, no matter what, and so those men liked me best of all. I would fuck them, until their toes were curling. Do you understand now, Benjamin? I grew up in a brothel for men who wanted to pretend that they were good whilst they secretly did bad things, men who wanted to bring beauty into the world whilst they raped children. And if they paid a little more, the child they raped would have to sweetly tell them that they loved them. "I love you." Those three disgusting words.'

'How did it end?'

'One day, when I was eighteen or so, after all those years, the scholar told me to leave. He told me I was too old now. In Greek love, he said, the boy must learn from the man, and the *erastes* – his grand word for the pederast – must not sully himself with another man. A boy is beautiful and pure, but a grown man is not.' He blinked for a moment. Did I see the pinkness of tears in his eyes? If so, it was gone as fast as it arrived. 'I was too old. I remember staring at this man, the closest thing I have known to ... not to a father perhaps, but at least someone who cared whether I existed in the world. I was stunned, realising in that moment that all I had ever been to him was an actor who could, for a while, perform a role to satisfy the perversions of his coterie; perversions they could justify with their pretensions. In short, men who rape little boys don't want to rape eighteen-year-olds.'

The whole of his existence was laid out before me: the child abandoned, the child taken in, consumed and deceived by a revolting inversion of what it is to be loved, then discarded. And in front of me I saw that same child, still desperate for love, who had constructed a fabulously resistant armour that kept love out. 'Did you just leave?' I asked softly.

'After a fashion,' he laughed grimly. 'I started punching him, until I was in such a blind fury, that I honestly cannot remember what happened. Next I can recall, I was standing in Farringdon Street, my knuckles raw and a bag of money with me.' Finally, he sat up and looked straight at me. 'Do you see now how I make money?' he asked.

Finally, I did. 'You sell yourself.'

He hesitated. 'Sometimes I steal. If I go to a party somewhere, and sit with a fine lady or engage in conversation with an ageing gentleman, I will flirt, and then, when they are not looking, put my hand in their bag. You never know what you might find. Or I'll make my way into someone's room, find their trunk, open it, steal a coat. When first I met you, I wondered what I could take from you.'

'Why did you not take anything?'

His eyes flicked to mine and he shrugged, looking like some ordinary boy telling some ordinary truth.

'I just liked you.' He laughed a little. 'Isn't it terrible? I liked you too much to steal from you.'

I blinked slowly. The heat of the day had sunk into my bones. I felt sweat in the dark places of my body, trickling cold across my skin. I knew that he was done, had told me everything he wanted to. He had revealed his origin story: how this magnificent, malevolent creation sitting next to me came into being. I put my arm around him, in comfort, and let my head fall against his.

'What a pair we are,' I said.

He laughed gently, happily, and we sat there like that for perhaps a minute. Then he turned his face towards mine, and somehow – I don't really know how – I realised that he was about to kiss me. We had never kissed before. I had *never* been kissed by anyone before. That day, I had been there for him, tried to protect him – and now he was going to kiss me.

'Horace, you don't have to,' I said, pulling away slightly. I did not want to think that this was another transaction. His eyes burned into me. His mouth moved slowly around mine, then he leaned forward and kissed me anyway.

'I want to,' he said, the skin of our lips still brushing. 'You don't know how much I want to, Benjamin.'

When I think of what unfolded in the following minutes, images pass in my memory as a blur. Our mouths, open and warm. Our bodies, peeling backward into the shape of birds with their wings pinned behind, from which our clothes stripped themselves away. We were Apollo and

Mars, the two rippling figures I'd torn from the pages of a stolen book, long ago. Or perhaps, we were two clumsy boys, trying to kick off our breeches, without breaking our kisses. Soon, his body was on top of mine, naked and warm, his penis hard like mine, his hands on my biceps, touching the skin on the side of my body, his legs between mine, pushing my body upward, spitting in his palm, and asking if I was ready.

'I don't know,' I said. 'Will it hurt?' He did not answer.

'I cannot let someone inside me,' he said. 'I ... I just cannot.' It did not matter. It was just a few, intense, electric seconds, until our bodies were convulsing and we were blinded, our semen shooting from our cocks, our minds wiped clean.

A man ejaculates and then there is silence. In his body, in his head, in the room around him. For that brief, billowing moment after sex, man experiences absolute silence. He has erased himself from his own existence. He cannot think, he cannot hear. And then slowly – or is it quickly, too quickly? – that feeling passes, and he begins to piece the world together again, a swirling mass around his head, gradually coming back into a recognisable shape. He is his performed self again, for good, and for ill.

I turned, and he was lying next to me, gazing at me directly, his eyes shining with – did I dare think it? – love. And when I returned his gaze, he blinked and looked away. Until that moment I had assumed that he might have come to heal, to change me. But maybe we came to heal and change each other. I reached forwards and kissed him softly on the lips, and he smiled a small, sweet smile. I hadn't known such happiness even existed.

In the morning, he kissed me at his bedroom door and said he would see me later. We hung there a second longer, as if neither one wanted the other to leave. I yearned to stay connected to him for as long as possible, but in the end, I knew I had to return to my lodgings. I walked alone, dawdling in the morning sun, back towards the *albergo* at which Edgar and I were staying. When I arrived, my brother was seated, bolt upright, at a small tray-table on which had been served a selection of bread, ham, cheese and olives. Edgar did not like olives. Usually, he ate ham with great gusto, but today the food was hardly touched. I bid him good morning quietly as I walked into the centre of the room. He sat there, frigid with hostility – and for all the world, he could have been our mother.

'Is it true that you were fighting at the Uffizi yesterday?' he asked. He did not look at me.

'No,' I said.

He turned briskly, stiff with annoyance. 'I was told by Sir Percy Paget himself that you were *seen*.'

I was confused for a moment. 'You believe Percy Paget over me?' I asked.

'*Sir* Percy!' I laughed at the foolishness of the correction, but this only made Edgar angrier. 'Is it *true*?' he shouted.

'No.' I could see Edgar watching me. 'It was in the Loggia dei Lanzi and it was not me fighting. It was Lavelle, and in truth, it was not even a fight. It wasn't even vaguely a fight.'

'Oh, Benjamin!' Edgar groaned, letting go of his anger and replacing it with concern. 'Don't you see how dangerous this has become? Don't you see how you are going to harm yourself?' He was watching me with our mother's determination. I had to look away. But then something in him changed: he softened. He grabbed my arm playfully, and suddenly he was that sweet innocent who had spoken dreamily of the Tour in our shared bedroom on Red Lion Square. Who had looked forward to new friends and pretty girls, lovely parties and happy endings. 'Look,' he said, in a tone that searched for reason, 'why don't you just come away with me? We can leave in the morning first thing, just up and go to Lucca. Or to Pisa or Arezzo. We can just forget about everything. We can just carry on.'

Truly, I saw that he was being sincere. He thought that this was a perfectly sensible thing for us to do. I cannot say that it did not touch me – even after everything I had done to hurt him, he still wanted to be a brother to me. But Edgar did not understand – how could he even begin to? He could not know the way I now felt. 'What about Lavelle?' I asked. 'I cannot leave Lavelle.'

He sighed, not angrily – despairingly. 'You *can*, Benjamin. You can leave him.'

Even the thought of it was like a knife at my throat. 'No,' I said. 'No, I'm sorry, Edgar, I can't.'

'Benjamin—'

'No, Edgar!' I howled, and then added more quietly, 'I'm sorry, Edgar. I will not leave Lavelle. I cannot ...' My brother's jaw set, in just the way our mother's did. We were silent a few seconds. When he finally spoke, it was with a dark disappointment.

'When we reach Rome, Benjamin, you and I should take separate rooms. If you will not give up Lavelle, we should stay away from each other. I cannot watch you harm yourself.' He looked at me briefly, and I saw in him then the last vestige of our old shared bond. '*Please*, Benjamin, please reconsider.'

But I think both of us already knew that I would not.

Veduta del Foro Romano

Darling Mother —

This engraving is of the ancient Forum in Rome.
Remnants of the old world are everywhere in the city,
but sometimes I struggle to see the value of being here.
Mother, I know you will think it strange to hear me say
that. I have made friends – Benjamin does not seek out
my company at all – and still I long for home. I go to
parties, but feel like I am fading. How can that be? I
read your guidebook every day, yet often find myself at
a loss of what to do. Some days, I wake and wish I
were in London, and this trip had all been but a dream.
If only I could see you, Mother, I think I would feel
better, but do not worry about me. Please do not worry.
I am just being silly, perhaps. Today I will go out and
see Rome, Mother! Rome!

Edgar

ROME

A sadness and an excitement hangs over those arriving in Rome. Rome is the heart of the Tour, its point of light. But for many it is also the Tour's closing breaths. A few move onwards to the southern Italian cities – Palermo or Naples – as Edgar and I would. The adventurous, of which we were not part, went to the Turkish lands in Greece. But for most, after Rome the Tourists would be returning to England to lives that were waiting to begin.

I felt a different terror at the prospect of the Tour's finale. I was not ready for anything to end. I felt as if in all the years I had been alive, I had been just a breathless body. Lavelle had come and, metaphorically and literally, given me the kiss of life. His breath was in my lungs now. His breath was making me live. I did not want anything that was waiting for me in London.

In Rome, my distance from Edgar became an ocean. Now and then, he would call on me at the room I kept. When he visited, he spoke coldly, dealing only in facts. He asked nothing of Lavelle, and he never arrived unannounced. Without the issue ever being addressed explicitly, I understood that this ensured he would never need to encounter Lavelle at my lodgings. Now that Lavelle did not need to torment Edgar, now that he possessed me, he did not fight this. Have fun, he would cry, knowingly.

I asked my brother if our mother knew we were separated and he did not answer, replying only that there was money enough to pay for two rooms. He preferred to talk of the new world in which he moved. He was now very close to this Sir Percy Paget, who had tattled on the scene Lavelle had made in Florence. Through him, Edgar had met all sorts of English titles. He had earned access to the greatest parties in the city, at the palatial homes of Orsini and Barberini, Borghese and all: the very highest in Roman society. He told me that he was paying court to a woman whose uncle was very high up in the Scottish peerage. I knew where the truth lay, even if Edgar did not. Augusta Anson had already revealed it to me. These young women were never going to marry Edgar. They thought us inferior, vulgar, tedious. They would permit his presence until such time as there was no longer any amusement in it. When I told Lavelle of Edgar's romantic ambitions, he laughed mercilessly. 'Has he told them yet that he is the son of a Welsh bog-dweller and a foreign Jewess? I don't think Welsh-Jewish boat-rowers will cut much ice with the fucking Duke of Argyll!'

Lavelle toyed with our deepest secret, made light of it, almost made me believe it was nothing but a joke – if we wanted it to be. Eventually, Edgar announced he was leaving Rome for a week. A minor Colonna princess, alleged to be very licentious, had invited a group of young Englishmen out to a country palace. Lavelle said that he had heard the princess had a taste for British virginities. 'Maybe she'll stick a finger inside him,' he said, 'just to check if the chicken is done.'

I would love to say how in Rome, I saw all the wonders of the ancient world. I would love to tell you that Lavelle and I obsessively inspected the ruins that emerged from the modern city, like toadstools on a tree, as detailed by my mother in the guidebook she had written and which Edgar now kept himself, with me no longer worthy of looking at its sacred pages. But in truth, the map that I studied was that of my lover's body.

The education I received in Rome was physical – visceral, sexual – nothing to do with culture. I gave myself entirely, compulsively, to this new field of study: Lavelle's desire, and mine; his pleasure and mine, which became ours. He was the eternal city whose geographer I had become. As I did so, the rest of existence fell away. It was now the end of summer. Every day, I closed the shutters to keep out the world. In those weeks, we had no need of it, its tedious details, its ballet of fools, except perhaps as the lightest, most remote entertainment. We were the cleverest boys in the world. We were *certain* of that.

Lavelle kept asking me if I had written to my mother. Did I not want to write to her? I heard an edge of mockery in his tone. 'Don't,' I would say. 'Leave my mother alone!' I was laughing as I said it, but still I was unsure. Why did he care? Because he had no mother? Because of what he believed she was like, as a person, a parent? 'I think it would be funny,' he said, the sort of thing he said when he wanted to obscure his real motivations. In the end, I wrote a letter to her just to stop him pestering me about it. 'What are you going to tell her? We haven't done any-thing but fuck!' he said scornfully. So I lied about seeing the Coloseum, pretending I wrote the letter while sitting in the midday shade offered by the Arch of Constantine. I never sat among the ghosts of the ancients at the roofless Forum. And I barely noticed the Trevi Fountain tinkle, even if I told my mother it was 'truly a masterpiece of the last century'. 'Have you told her how often you have my cock in your mouth?' Lavelle asked. 'Have you told her how my semen feels when we are walking in the street and it trickles out of you, warm on your inside leg?' He laughed as he lay sprawled on my bed, whilst I, naked, sat on a chair at a desk, scratching out my lies. I laughed aloud, happy to hear his terrorising, happy to be its audi-ence, and just plainly happy. I had found the person who explained everything, and he wanted me.

During sex, our bodies melded into one, two forms touch-ing each other, kisses on soft skin, lips meeting. We opened our eyes and looked at each other in the moment. And afterwards, we would lie together, my mouth against his chest, his leg folded across mine, our breath warm and shared. All those years with Herr Hof, all those books we read, those *things* we learned – they now seemed so worthless. And yet when Lavelle quoted obscure philosophers, they felt essential. He could see through the stench of their pretension to what remained beautiful.

We – the Virgin and the Catamite – grew around each other so that anything else no longer seemed to exist. For me, sex itself was a revelation – the intimacy, its power, the way it absorbed loneliness and offered completion. For him, sex had used to be a performance, a slavery and a mask. But coming to the same bed, two boys, two men, naked before each other, we were suddenly on the same journey.

Were we transformed? I wanted to ask him: are we transformed now? All these years later, I imagine his eyes on mine, his mischievous, handsome grin spreading, his head tilting back on my pillow, the rise and fall of his chest as he sighed and said, 'Kiss me.' I imagine it now because it was the single most thrilling experience of my life. I say that without regret. I say it absolutely in honour of what I felt, during what seemed like infinite days.

'What do you want for your life?' he asked me once, as we lay in our bed, the sheets tangled around our bodies. It was midday outside and our room was stifling hot. We complained about the heat and yet, as new lovers, we did not move. Now, bright, white rays of light flooded under the shutters and spun out hazy webs of palest gold along the floor. We were lying next to each other, his arm around my back, both facing upwards. His hand idly cupped my bare shoulder, and a finger drew circles on my skin.

'What do you mean?'

He laughed. 'What do you mean what do I mean? What else can I mean? What do you want your life to be?'

I stopped to think. 'I don't want to run the Company,' I said. 'I don't want what my parents have prescribed for me.'

'Ha!' He laughed again. 'That's what you *don't* want, but what *do* you want?'

'I don't know,' I replied, but I was not sure, even then, if I was telling him the truth. In fact, I was beginning to see precisely what – or rather who, of course – I wanted for my life. 'I want to be happy,' I said eventually.

We spent our days in those sweat-stained sheets and only went out in the evening. I wanted the world to see him at my side, his beauty and his strangeness, and to see those things reflected onto me, shining golden on my skin. So, eventually we had to let the world back in. Our limbs aching with sex, our bellies empty with exertion, we tumbled out into the chaos of the lamp-lit Roman streets, in search of an extension of our togetherness.

Rome is a city of whores, and so it is a city of whoremongers, too. Choking on the burning stench of the oil that lit the lamps, a parade of flesh moved this way and that: girls who looked like Botticelli angels, and their mothers who looked like anatomical plates depicting advanced syphilis; runaway slaves, armed with a knife to cut the throat of anyone who tried to steal their bodies again; and boys, boys everywhere. Beautiful boys, ugly boys, willowy boys, fat boys, boys for every possible taste, and around them men. Cardinals grabbing at their crotches. Tourists checking how much money they had in their purses. In doorways, figures writhed, kissing and carousing. On street corners, prostitutes haggled out deals with a toughness that would have made even my father, master of hard-won deals, blush the colour of a boiled lobster.

Lavelle and I perched ourselves at any place where we could get a drink, and sipped at glasses of the wormwood or almond liqueurs the Italians profess to like. 'That is the reality of our world,' he said. 'Fuck Voltaire.' The first night he'd said that had also been the night he had first fought with Edgar. I had loved it then, and loved it now. 'Fuck Voltaire. Fuck Petrarch. Those women are our truth-tellers and should be our heroes too.' I did not believe every word he said; lovers don't need to. What they need is the other's existence, in their full, known magnificence. And so here we were, amid all the din and filth and chaos, and I was in high spirits. It was him. It was being with him, touching him, hearing his words, bathing in his reflected brilliance that made me so very, very happy in a city of whores. He looked at me and said: 'We are lucky, you know. To have found each other. We are two halves.' I had never told him what our mother had called Edgar and me, and how a part of me had always suspected – or rejected – the notion that I was incomplete or insufficient on my own. But when Lavelle said it about us, it was like music started playing, a private concert that existed only for us. It was true: we were the genuine 'two halves', who had somehow found each other across the vastness and unpredictability of the universe. Or, at least, that was how it felt then, in Rome.

One morning, I awoke early, my head still tender with the excesses of the night. Lavelle lay next to me, facing me directly, fast asleep and breathing deeply. I watched him for a moment, sleeping peacefully, his face close to mine. I knew that he trusted me. Had he ever trusted anyone before? My penis was hard at waking – but I did not move to rouse him. I wanted to let him sleep.

I slipped from the bed, and walked in a circle around the room to stretch my legs. My erection faded as I walked to the shutters, opening them slightly to peek outside. Already the sun was hot, glancing over my skin in a long, yellow line. Down in the street, the insistent cries of market traders and hawkers rang out in a raucous chorus: lemons, broccoli, *cavoli*, *melanzaaaneee!* This was Rome in the morning, swaying its hips.

'Hello.'

I turned back from the window to look over at him. He was rubbing his eyes, groaning as the first twitch of his hangover made itself known. But he was still so beautiful, and I felt so blissfully fortunate and complete. Love was calling us forward, daring us to speak. I knew it then. Step forward, love cries! You are alive, so grasp the moment!

'You asked me what I wanted from my life, Lavelle. Well,' I took a deep breath, 'well, I want this.'

He regarded me for a moment.

'Do you, now? Well, how are we going to *get* this? How are we going to live this life? Rooms like this cost money. Amaretto in the evening costs money. Food costs money. Even money probably costs money.'

'I don't know,' I whispered.

'Don't worry,' he said. 'Clever and beautiful boys can live on air.' Before I met him, it had never even occurred to me that I might be clever or beautiful.

'I am in love with you,' I said. 'And I want this, forever. I want you, forever.'

His blue eyes settled on me. Momentarily, a smile hovered on his lips. But then the corners of his mouth began to turn upwards, and his smile slowly transformed into a smirk. There was a second of silence, where the only sounds were the voices from the street below – the vegetable sellers: *Cavoli! Melanzane! Cavoli! Melanzane!* I saw him gazing at me in amazement.

I wish I could say that he rose from the bed, walked towards me and held me and said: it is you who has understood me, it is you who has solved the mystery. I wish I could say that he said the words to me: I love you. But he turned around and let his face fall into the bed, pretending to return to sleep.

I told Horace Lavelle that I loved him, and he said nothing back.

ISOLA SACRA
(A HOLY ISLE)

I waited for his next move as I tried to make sense of what had happened. I love you. 'Three disgusting words.' All these weeks, across Italy, I had watched Lavelle play with Edgar – taunt and humiliate him – and – yes, I admit it – I had done so approvingly. Had he now turned his merciless gaze on me? I could not bring myself to believe it. And yet, waiting for him to open his eyes and look at me, to show me something of what he felt, I could not come up with a better explanation.

Eventually, Lavelle awoke, making great play of how tired he was. He said nothing about my 'disgusting words', instead declaring that he wanted to go on an adventure. I watched his hard, lean chest and stomach, the lines of his thighs and the curve of his penis. 'I am tired of Rome.' He said it with his old performance tone.

'How can one tire of Rome?' I asked, turning away from him and looking back out at the light and activity of the street below. My voice sounded a shadow of itself. Did he hear the way it had been stripped of purpose? And if he did, was he afraid, or did he feel his objective had been achieved? To gain the advantage, my golden lover waved a carefree hand. I felt its motion in the air, drawing me back to face him.

'One can tire of anything,' he said, meaningfully.

He moved closer and loomed above me. I could hear him breathing, a steady tide washing over a shore. 'Anything.' Lavelle always had the skill to identify vulnerability and choose that moment to land the lump hammer down on a tender heart once more. Suddenly, he smiled puckishly. 'I think we should go to see the ruins at Ostia Antica. Then we should go to Isola Sacra on a row-boat.'

I shrugged. 'Why?'

'You were the one who wanted to see the classical civilisation. Well, is there not a large heap of it at Ostia Antica? And it might be amusing, for they say there is all sorts available at Isola Sacra.' His eyes wandered around the room, fixing on the unmade bed with the sheets thrown back. He looked at it for what seemed a very long time.

'Are you going to say something?' I asked.

He creased his brow, deeply, to show the impossibility of what I asked. 'About what, Benjamin?'

He was staring at me directly: a challenge, an invitation to combat. But I did not want to play the games he loved. I would lose. I would always lose to Lavelle.

It was another blistering Italian day, but people had begun to talk of autumn. *Autunno, autunno*: soon it will be cold. English Tourists had timed their arrival this far south so that they could head home before the advent of mist and drizzle. We hired a carriage which quickly moved us out of the commotion and filth of Rome and into parched and yellowed countryside. We travelled along the curve of the Tiber, the water on one side and on the other, fields dotted with saffron-coloured melons or in a sea of wheat, another with aubergine plants – a canvas of pale green pricked with dark purple jewels. We two remained silent except that now and then, Lavelle would say something cruel about Edgar and his friends, and what they would be doing that day. I did not laugh, but neither did I protest. It would be hypocritical for me to start objecting now. Instead, I kept my eyes fixed on those fields, intent on not giving him the satisfaction of amusing or offending me. I started to wonder, why was I here? What was I doing? And I should have asked: what was *he* planning?

The carriage turned off the river road to head south for Ostia Antica. Soon, we were queuing with all the other sightseers who also claimed to be bored of Rome. Ostia Antica had been the port for Ancient Rome. It had once been one of the largest cities in the Empire, but, the guide continued, as St Augustine had noted, fell into disrepair long before the barbarians came. Lavelle said he'd heard that lepers lived here, and that one could see little groups of beggars among the ruins. There had lately been a great craze for archaeological excavation across Italy, but it had not yet reached Ostia Antica. Columns stuck straight out of the earth, hinting at antique temples (or maybe marketplaces) beneath. Mysterious steps leading nowhere and broken villa walls appeared like the backs of whales arching out of oceans of red-yellow earth. Here and there, almond and pomegranate trees grew among the rubble of the past. For years, the masons of Rome had been thieving from the site to build new *palazzi*. Sometimes, if there was an earthquake, ancient buildings would be hurled up, and masons would return as soon as it was deemed passably safe to purloin more stone.

We walked through the past, resolutely not talking about how things had altered between us in such a short time. I felt like my belly had been cut open and we were committed to sightsee, politely skirting the matter of my guts spilling out along the ground.

'What do you think of it?' he asked eventually, in an uninterested way.

'I cannot help but think of all these people who lived here once,' I said.

He looked at me, his eyes mysteriously ambivalent.

'They are all dead now,' he replied. And I thought: yes, I know, precisely.

My head aswim, I said I wanted to return to our carriage. *It's hot. I'm tired.* The driver took us back towards the Tiber, and Lavelle said we still had to go to Isola Sacra. I did not want to go, but he directed the driver to take us to the quay from which one could hire boats that cross the river to the island. It was named holy because the Romans buried their dead there. 'You see the graves, see the graves,' the driver kept saying in practised scraps of English. A menacing glimmer passed over Lavelle's eyes. It reminded me of the day he went berserk in the Loggia dei Lanzi – that day of revelations in Florence.

As we approached the river bank, Lavelle became increasingly distracted, his eyes searching for something unknown. His irritation had not abated. The river water was a dark greenish-blue, its boats little flecks of white. The carriage rattled to a stop at the shabby quayside where groups of young Quality were waiting for transport. I asked him if we were going to join them. He laughed under his breath as his eyes scanned further down the line of boats towards the men and boys who worked them.

'Horace,' I said. 'Horace, I just want to know—'

He looked at me, his eyes alert to danger, and then turned away again.

'What, Benjamin?' he asked. 'What do you want to know?'

Only then did I understand that *I* was the danger.

'I don't mind if you don't love me back,' I said, though it was a thoroughly black lie. 'But don't ...' My throat closed with emotion, threatening to betray me. 'You don't have to hurt me because I said I love you.'

'Don't make a fool of yourself,' he said, before adding, 'Or of me.' He blinked. I saw the tightness around his mouth. All the while, he avoided my gaze. 'Do you want some real sport?' he asked then, changing tack without a second's pause.

'What?' I asked.

'Some real sport?' I sensed the apprehension, or maybe it was bitterness – the acrid vapour trail on his breath. 'Not all this talk about ...'

He did not say 'love'. *No*, I began to say. *I don't want to.* But he grabbed my hand before I could answer and yanked me out of the carriage, down onto the quayside.

He pulled me towards the point which he had been looking at earlier. I yelled at him to stop, but his hand was on mine like a vice. Suddenly, I knew that this was not the same crazed act as at the Loggia. He was about to show me – perhaps, if I'm being kind, if I look back now and really twist my vision enough to save my sanity – what a stupid, innocent boy in love needed to see.

Two lads, wearing bright white tunics over dark breeches tucked into boots, were watching us intently. Sensing their gaze, Lavelle shifted his direction towards them. They were handsome and lean. Their boots were caked in dried river mud. One was around eighteen or nineteen, the other nearer fifteen. Perfectly for Lavelle, they were simultaneously immaculate and filthy. The lads' eyes and smiles settled on us, with the hard greed to which travellers become accustomed. I turned to look at Lavelle, and saw that his eyes were suffused with desire.

'Horace!' I cried but he did not turn back. 'Horace, I don't want to!' Of course I could have moved away, stumbled back to the carriage and waited. I could have thumped him in the head and screamed, *why would you do this to me?* Lavelle turned and stared at me, his eyes searing my flesh:

'Do you want to know the truth of me or not? Do you really want to understand?' *Did I?* I wondered. Of course I did. But at what cost? Any cost, perhaps. That's why I always – from that very first day in Aosta – followed him when he strode away. And I did it again now.

The two 'brothers' pointed down to a little boat with a bright blue sail on which a huge black cross had been painted. They rowed us to a patch of rock some distance away, where we could see other visitors disembarking, and tied the boat to a makeshift jetty, long since rotted into black honeycomb by the saltwater. We did not leave the boat – all that followed took place on the rocking tide.

Out of sight from any prying eyes, the lads lifted their tunics and pulled down their breeches to expose their penises – the older one's was hard, the younger one's flaccid. I could hardly breathe on seeing them, but Lavelle's eyes were on fire. He was no longer looking at me. Oh, he knew I was there. He knew I was seeing the scene, but he no longer needed to look at me. He knew that I was already defeated. The older brother with the hard cock was indicating what would follow next. A moment later, he and Lavelle were lying under a baked sheet of tarred canvas, both of them remaining clothed. Once underneath, the older brother whispered, *aspetta! Wait!* There was a moment of silence, and then a low, carnal grunt. From whom, I did not know.

The sheet began to move in a steady rhythm. I looked away but I could still hear the sheet rustling, that rhythm quickening. Two breaths began to speed up, Lavelle murmured something, whispering to a lover that was not me. Eventually I heard a long, deep groan and then another. I froze to hear them, froze in my heart's deepest places. All the while, the younger brother stared at me resentfully while tugging at his own irrevocably soft penis. I kept looking away, at the artless glitter of the sun on the Tiber.

As we were rowed back to shore, Lavelle sat in the boat with his arms stretched victoriously across its width. At the dock, he paid the two lads, who complained it was not enough even as Lavelle shooed them away, like flies in the heat. We walked back to the carriage with them crying after us: '*Signori! Signori!*' It was a pathetic moment on this most pathetic of days.

On the carriage ride back to Rome, I was silent, and Lavelle did not have it in him to make anything better. He was never nice, never kind. I saw another side of Lavelle then, self-satisfied in his savage beauty. The sun had made his pink-gold skin even darker. Freckles had patterned his nose. His lips had dried and frayed, but had not become uglier.

When I still said nothing, he began his loud and dark performance. 'Oh, my Benjamin! What an innocent you are. You should have gone away with your brother to the Romagna in hopes that the virgin daughters of England might remove their gloves long enough for you to brush your fingertips along the inside of their forearms. Why shoot inside hearty Italian whores when you could have played *canasta* with the fucking Marchioness of Bute?' His joke sounded cruel because he meant it to.

I continued to say nothing. My silence was a form of power I hadn't realised I possessed until then. But now I saw it. Those small acts of rebellion on Red Lion Square – I had had it then, not replying to my mother's requests for agreement. I just had not been able to name what it was – what resources I had inside me. The longer I remained mute, the more he became irritated. 'If you feel shame, it is of your own doing. You want to be free, but look, freedom revolts you. At the first opportunity, you talk of love, you talk of forever. Why talk of those things? They are lies! The sodomite knows more than any other that love is a lie, a delusion!'

Finally, I found my voice. 'Does the sodomite know that,' I asked, 'or the boy locked in a pervert's cellar who is so disgusted with himself that he now calls love itself disgusting?' His eyes widened. 'I know now what you are, Horace. You use glamour to conceal how damaged you are, but I see through your theatre. I see that broken boy inside.'

He groaned, genuinely revolted. 'My freedom revolts you,' he said again, casting around for some retort.

'You are repeating yourself,' I snapped.

He did not like it. He faltered once more. 'But I am a living revolution, Benjamin. It is you who does not have the *guts* to live in a truly free way, but instead makes declarations of love like a heroine in a *cheap* novelette! I reject hypocrisy!'

'Reject, reject, reject?'

'Precisely.'

I burst into laughter. The satire was all mine now. 'Do you know what your problem is?' I asked. 'All you do is to rant about hypocrites and boast that you are going to slit their throats! How fine for your morality.'

His back straightened. 'I shall reject,' he spat.

I laughed dismissively a second time. 'And what is left after all this rejection, Horace? What is left, apart from your vanity?' He recoiled at my words. 'Look at Ostia Antica. When everything has been torn down, what is left? I have the measure of you,' I said. 'You ask all your questions, but you have no answers. No *real* answers. You talk about hypocrisy and revolution, but it amounts to not a jot.'

'I shall reject!' he insisted, snarling. 'I shall reject whatever tired, safe little world you wish to draw me into. Love. A fake marriage. You wish to trap me. Shall we live in a house somewhere with a dog, and when one of us tires of the other, creep off to some dark lane or heathland to find a hole to fill, and creep back, saying nothing? A cosy companionable marriage like that of your parents, or do they still fuck each other every night to hide their regrets? I shall reject.'

'You shall reject the possibility of love?'

'Yes,' he said, with the conviction of a priest torturing a heretic. 'Yes!' I fell silent again, not in a show of power but in final defeat. 'Yes!' he said a third time. 'I shall reject even love!'

I felt like I had been hit by a carriage crossing the street. But I took a breath, and asked him the only question that remained. 'And when you've rejected love, Lavelle, what's left?'

He was too clever – or maybe too afraid – to answer that.

Back in my room, I sent down to the *albergo* kitchen for food and wine. Lavelle lay on the bed in a prowling silence. Bread, cheese and salami arrived. He took an end of bread and tore at it with his teeth. He slurped some wine from a pewter cup, winced and still said nothing.

'Shall we go out?' I asked. I did not want to go out with him. I did not want to stay there, either. And I did not want him to leave.

He snorted. I had seen him cruel before, seen him unkind. But previously, I had been the audience for his bile-black humour, not the object of its attack.

'I know what you want.'

'What?' I asked. He filled his cup with wine and drank it down hard, wiping his mouth on the back of his sleeve. Red wine stained the silk a permanent purple; he did not care; there are always other shirts to acquire, other fools to steal from. In one fluid movement, Lavelle moved forwards and kissed me. And for a second, I let him – felt his tongue enter my mouth, a warm intruder – and then I pulled away. I was not suddenly revolted by him. Despite what I'd witnessed on the boat, I did not think of him as my assailant. I was hungry for his touch. Soon his mouth was on my neck. His lips were soft on my skin. We were kissing and, at once, I realised it was probably for the last time. How horrible. How necessary.

He began to pull down my breeches and turn me on the bed. He ripped open his shirt and I heard an ivory button bounce across the room. I felt the leanness of his body against my back, his erect penis sliding over my skin. A second later, he was inside, slamming against me, fast and hard. It lasted only thirty seconds, no more than that, and then it was over.

Afterwards, he lay against my back for the longest time. Where our skin was bare, I could feel the beads of our sweat blending. After a couple of minutes, he whispered my name. I pretended to have fallen asleep. 'Benjamin?' he said again, but I lay perfectly still. I felt his fingers on my shoulders. Their tips moved slightly over my skin. I felt the tenderness of their touch. *Where is the evidence that I was ever loved*, the broken-hearted person whispers. *Here it is*, the slightest touch whispers back.

'Benjamin?' he repeated for a third time. And yet I still did not reply. In that moment, I hoped my silence cut him like a wound.

Eventually, we passed into sleep. Through the night, we moved together, so that I woke once and found his face intimate against my chest: our bodies knew either everything or nothing. I should have gently pushed him away, rolled him over to sleep alone. Instead, I moved my arm upwards to the one pillow. Without waking, he moved closer to me, letting out a contented sigh. I drifted back to sleep while the push-pull of our chests formed a breath.

I was woken by a loud knocking at the bedroom door. The light under the shutters was different now, honeyed. Hours had passed. The banging at the door continued. And then a voice from outside. 'Benjamin! Open up, Benjamin!'

I shook Lavelle, who was snoring.

'What is it?' he asked softly, and in his voice, I realised that he had momentarily forgotten what had happened between us.

'Open up, Benjamin! Open up!'

'It's Edgar,' I whispered.

'Shit,' Lavelle said, twisting in the sheets. There was nothing in the scene that would not suggest fucking. Edgar started kicking the door. I slipped from the bed.

'Open up, Benjamin!'

As I unlatched the bedroom door, Edgar burst in, his black cape fluttering bat-like behind him. Thankfully, he was alone. He saw Lavelle, pulling on his clothes, and me naked, and smelled the room – the reek of sex. Edgar flew at Lavelle, yelling about scandal, about shame, raining fists on my lover's bare shoulders and chest. Lavelle, still hardly awake, crumpled beneath him. I yelled at Edgar to stop, and lunged forwards, ripping at his shoulders to pull him away. The three of us stood there, frozen. Lavelle and Edgar were glaring at each other, both bristling with fury, their months of mutual hatred now in full display.

'You should go,' I said, pointing to the door. It took Lavelle a moment to realise that I was talking to him.

'What?' he cried. The truth was this: I was glad to see my brother.

'I'm sorry, Horace,' I said. 'You should go.'

I looked at him and saw the confusion in his eyes. 'Do you mean for now?' I said nothing, and then he asked, more loudly: 'Or do you mean forever?'

'You should just leave, Horace.'

Something changed in him. He raised his chin, let his beautiful eyes pour coldly over me. Then he paused, looked at me nakedly for a moment. His gaze held on mine, and I saw truth in the emotion in his eyes. I saw their glassy uncertainty, fading hope – an acknowledgement, at last, of what we had meant to each other. I knew then that I had been *something* to him, even if he could not say the words, and I saw how if I had said again, 'I love you,' it would have meant everything to him. I don't know if he could have ever said it back to me – maybe he was just too damaged – but I could see that he was waiting for me to repeat it. But I did not. It was too hard, there was too much risk involved, to say it again. I decided to protect myself. You can't defend the damaged person forever – eventually, you have to defend yourself.

'You should go,' I said quietly. A wave of hurt washed over him, fleetingly, and then something harder appeared in his eyes. He stared at me with such hatred.

'You're nothing to me,' he spat. 'You are just the same as all the others. I should have known what you are. How small you are, intellectually –' he hissed in dismissal '– and in every way.'

He turned sharply and left, slamming the door. The room shook. I blinked, and he was gone. Everything terrible and everything wonderful was gone. He had changed me, taken me apart and put me back together again as a new person who understood what he wanted his life to be. Or, perhaps, he had simply shown me what I had always wanted to be. And now, was all that gone too?

Numb, I looked back at my brother, who had not even taken off his cape.

'It is true,' he said, 'you are subject to scandal. You have gone too far, been too brazen. People are not blind, Benjamin. I don't think the scandal is fatal, but this has to end now.'

I felt exhausted then – exhausted by my family, exhausted by Lavelle, exhausted by desire and sensuality and fun, things I had once craved, exhausted by engaging with the world. I put my face in my hands.

'I have been brought to such a place, Edgar. I am afraid to admit how low I have been brought.' My brother's mood changed, to one of quieter concern. He put his hand on my shoulder. My hands dropped from my eyes, and I looked directly at my brother. 'I feel like I have been ... destroyed.'

'No,' he murmured. 'You are not destroyed, Benjamin. We are here. Together. Who knows anything, really?'

'What?' I whispered.

He smiled kindly, my brother from whom I had so willingly divorced.

'You are still my brother, Benjamin, I still love you.' I felt a wave of relief pass over me. 'We will go south,' Edgar was saying, taking charge. 'We will put all of this behind us. It's nothing, really. Just the silliest kind of talk. We shall go to Naples and we will have the best of times. We shall be brothers again.' Then he embraced me, pulling me against his body, until I fell limp in his arms and wept. It did not occur to me at the time quite what Edgar was giving up: his successful new life in Rome. It was only later that I came to see what he had been prepared to sacrifice for me.

Oh, Mother —

This fine hand-coloured engraving is of the fire fields of Monte Vesuvio, of which Pliny the Younger wrote about the death of his legendary uncle. Naples is full of the rage for uncovering the site of that great eruption – all we Tourists go to see it, for it is to see the Roman world truly as it was, in situ. It is very fearful to be so close to such a thing as a volcano – for Englishmen, at least. Do you see how the fire consumes the fields, as if they were paper? Can you imagine how it would be to burn the world so? Benjamin and I are in great spirits (and wholly reconciled) and all is recovered! I am so happy with events, and for your two halves to be reunited. Now I feel that we are invincible and nothing – no one – can harm us.

Soon we will be home and you will embrace us and <u>I cannot wait</u>, Mother!

All my love,

Edgar

NAPLES

To the English mind, Naples is another universe, in a way that Bologna or Florence are not. Seven centuries before, it was part of the Arab world and, as many before that, of the Greek. The waters around the south of Italy are said to be still tyrannised by Barbary pirates, whose abduction of whole villages into slavery yet fevers European imaginations. Edgar and I were going to sail home directly from Naples, stopping only at Gibraltar and Lisbon. My brother prattled on about our marvellous, connected future: of friends, of weekend shoots and riding in the country, balls and trips *pique-nique* to the Park, the lovely English girls who would accept our suits.

We took a few days out of the city so that we could traipse over the so-called 'fire fields' under the volcano Monte Vesuvio, where palaces had been revealed beneath the ash. A guide explained that the ancient city of Pompeii had been destroyed, and scholars were busy corroborating the literary evidence for the event. He said that the whole thing had been described by Pliny, but only recently had it become known that this was the actual site of the city. Edgar observed that our mother had read Pliny. 'Huh!' the guide harrumphed. Later, Edgar sent a letter to her with an engraving on that very subject. The guide explained that it was over a hundred years since the first discoveries, but now in our golden age – when men were after enlightenment 'so very, very much' – excavation had accelerated. We looked at some frescoes, in which men and women cavorted carnally. The guide told us primly that the local priest would soon come to cover them, as Ancient Romans had been extremely iniquitous. Had we read Suetonius as well as Pliny? 'Huh!' he harrumphed once again. There was a faint whiff of disbelief that Englishmen might have read *anything*.

Many invitations came in the early days in Naples, and often these were from friends Edgar had met elsewhere, in Venice or Rome perhaps. Every evening there would be a party at a villa, or a concert at the Basilica Santa Restituta, and Edgar would urge me to appreciate the opportunities laid before us. *Yes, we have met good people in Naples*, he wrote to our mother. *We have been such a grand success. We have made you proud, Mother.*

Perhaps I would walk obediently into my future and be a good person after all, I thought bleakly.

But here is the truth. I thought of Lavelle all the time. As a madman obsesses over the fractures of his past, so did I mine. I felt his absence trembling in my flesh, along the muscles and nerves of my body. I felt it in the pressure in my throat and the weight of my tongue in my mouth. My fingers and my legs seemed to ache with his vanishing.

And I was back where I started. Oh, my brother was acting with the best of intentions, but I could only see that what Lavelle and I had been together had departed – a puff of smoke. One morning, just around dawn, I thought I heard his voice calling in the street outside our room: 'Benjamin! Benjamin!' I was in bed, half asleep. 'Benjamin! Benjamin, I have come back!' Rising, I crept to the window, Edgar sleeping soundly, my feet bare against the early-morning cool of the stone floor, just in case he was there, come for me, entreating me to run away in the night. Down in the shadows of the street there was a clatter of movement. My chest tightened. I pulled back the shutters and went out onto the small balcony. 'Horace?' I whispered. 'Horace?' A cat, alerted by my voice, meowed and slunk away. No one was there.

I waited for a note to arrive from him, telling me where he was, that he was there in Naples, the address of his *albergo*, telling me what time to come to him, but there was nothing. I thought of him, the golden god who stood with the sun behind his head. I remembered the tilt of his chin, how his opened cravat revealed the muscles in his neck; his laughter, both the kind that was hard, and the one that was soft and reserved for private moments together. I remembered his body against mine, his weight upon me, the brush of his hands along my stomach, his lips kissing the most sensitive parts of my neck. And then I felt fear as I realised he was never going to write to me to tell me how to find him, because he did not want me to find him. I was nothing to him, just as he had said – his last words to me.

Sometimes I walked around the city on my own, to get away from Edgar's well-meaning, rediscovered hopefulness. In the streets around Santa Lucia, I saw dark-eyed street boys beckoning me down alleyways. At the port, young men gathered in flocks to sell themselves to sailors. What would it be like to go with them to some sweaty room, to lie on my back and let them slide inside me as Lavelle had? If I closed my eyes in some dark, shuttered place, with them above me in shadow, could I imagine that they were him?

Once, I encountered a man of forty or so, sitting in a gaudy *calèche*. He was handsome and dark, rugged from years spent sitting in the sun. His face had a square-jawed symmetry, and his mahogany eyes did not falter. 'You want me to ride you, *signore*?' he asked in French, holding the reins up as if to demonstrate. 'You want me you ride, *signore*?' he repeated in faltering English. '*Vous me comprenez, signore*?' he whispered conspiratorially. 'I will ride you *so* good, I ride you, *signore*. I ride you hard. Like woman. Ride you good. Make you feel like a woman.'

His eyes were all over me, licking his lips. He wanted money, I knew, but he wanted to fuck me too. I could see his hunger, first for the money, then for me. I turned and pushed out into the city. '*Signore!*' the *calèche* driver was calling behind me. 'Good price! Good price, *signore*!' In Naples, I had hoped to get better. Gradually, as the weeks unfolded, I realised I was getting worse.

As those last weeks in Italy passed, we became aware that our daily slew of invitations had reduced from flood to a trickle. Edgar wondered aloud whether my scandal had pursued us. He worried about what had happened in Paris. We could not afford another defeat. We had to go back to London with all our connections in place. Soon we would be going home, he said. We wanted to play the game well now. No mistakes.

All Saints' Day was very quiet in Naples for those on Tour, as all Neapolitans went to visit the graves of their parents and children. It was the first of November: the first vaguely cold day we had encountered in Italy. Churches were open only to service-goers. The massed bell-ringing across the crowded city only highlighted the exclusion of Protestant English visitors, and we hadn't been invited to join any party. I talked of roaring fires in an English winter, the way the leaves would be turning on the trees outside the window in Red Lion Square, and listed all the things that we should eat when we got back. Edgar licked his lips at lamb chops and apple pie. 'Oh, and custard, and good English gravy too!'

After midday, we found an *osteria* where people lunch-eoned under pale-green olive trees. Eating outside was a last act of resistance against the onset of winter. Our meal of fried fish, salad and bread gave little comfort against an unexpected chill. My brother sat biting his nails – something he had never done before. He wondered why we were not receiving invitations, and how we might start to be invited again. While we were being served very strong, small coffees, Edgar leapt to his feet without warning and peered like a hunting dog across the garden's expanse.

'*Gideon! Gideon!*'

On the other side of the *osteria* was Sir Gideon Hervey. He was with a very finely-dressed group of

Englishmen picking through their food in a bored way. Augusta Anson was not with them. 'Gideon! Gideon!' Edgar repeated.

Sir Gideon began to glance around to see who was calling his name. My brother was immediately on his feet, pushing through the garden's empty tables. 'Gideon! Gideon!'

Upon seeing Edgar, Sir Gideon's face was paralysed with revulsion. He reared up, held out his hands, as if he were about to be attacked in the street by a beggar. Instinctually I rose to my feet. Nausea swept through me. Lavelle had somehow scrubbed these people's *realness* from my mind. They had become ogres in his revolution – ludicrous grotesques. But here he was, Sir Gideon, glossily spectacular, unshakeable in his self-belief.

'Mister Bowen, do you mind not abusing me in public?' Edgar came to a confused stop. 'And do you mind avoiding this familiarity? You should call me *Sir* Gideon, as any person of Quality would know.'

I saw the knowing glances of the other diners and realised what was about to happen: the Cut. The rules of 'the Cut' are universally understood. When one is cut, by a refusal of a friend to acknowledge one, or a turning of the back as one approaches, it is an act of scorn, of absolute rejection. It is stripped of all forgiveness: one can neither forgive being cut, nor can one forgive those cut. And once one person cuts, another will follow, and another, and another. Social conformity is a fever that men are only too eager to catch, no matter if it kills them.

'What do you mean, Gideon?' Edgar asked.

A lady diner called out derisively: 'Didn't you hear, man, it's *Sir* Gideon?'

Edgar looked at her helplessly. 'But we were friends in Paris, and now—'

Now the 'Sir' himself spoke up. 'Friends? Good grief. I would hardly describe us as friends.' Sir Gideon turned to his companions. 'One knows how Paris is, of course, full of those desperately seeking inclusion.' His tone was that of the sort of ice that traps swimmers under its surface.

'Come away, Edgar,' I whispered. My brother's pride flared.

'No, Gideon, we were friends and now—'

Sir Gideon turned his nose, as though coming upon the corpse of a dead dog.

'But, Mister Bowen, you had no business being my friend. You should never have dared to foist yourself upon me.'

Edgar reared up. 'What can you mean, Gideon?'

The woman half-screamed: '*Sir* Gideon, man!'

My brother's confusion was swirling around him. I looked into his eyes, the same colour as my own. But his dark irises seemed drained of anything at all. They appeared curdled, opaque. He blinked. I saw him trying to comprehend what this moment could mean.

'If I have done something to offend you, sir,' he went to bow, and everyone looked both amused and appalled, 'then I – I apologise.'

'Offend me?' Sir Gideon pretended to protest. 'I am not offended. What have I to be offended at? What I am asking is that you *go away*. That's quite a different thing!'

The lady who had repeatedly reminded Edgar about Sir Gideon's title lifted her fingers, wrapped in duck-egg-blue silk gloves, to her lips, and giggled maliciously. A man at her side added loudly: 'Why don't these *parvenus* ever know when it is time to leave, when it is time for them to run along back to their dirty little shops?'

I thought of what Lavelle would do. He would have had some remark ready that would tear them down and expose their posturing.

'Why am I cut?' Edgar whispered. Sir Gideon lifted his silk handkerchief to his nose, to ward off the stink of those who do not know better. '*Why* am I cut?' Edgar insisted. '*Why?*'

'Information has been revealed about you,' Sir Gideon said, with a sigh that heavily denoted tedium. 'Someone has spoken out against you.'

'Information?' Edgar stammered in panic. 'What information?' Sir Gideon did not reply. 'Who is my enemy?' Edgar asked, his voice cracking. 'Who speaks against me?'

I felt the breeze through the garden's olive trees. The breeze knew the answer long before I did. But then I heard it, the truth, and I knew – I knew the answer.

'A wretch named Lavelle is your enemy, sir,' Sir Gideon said. 'It is he who has spread all round Rome that the famous *arrivistes, les Bouens* –' he said it like la Boleyn, with her head on the chopping block '– are *Jews*!'

The word danced on the air mystically. A low, deep grunt slipped from my brother's chest. 'It is one thing to have to put up with the attentions of the middling sort, and to have to tolerate *sodomites* –' Sir Gideon flicked his kerchief disdainfully in my direction '– but quite another to be expected to consort with *Jews*!'

I felt an appalling nausea rising to my gorge – all those exquisite, aristo English faces grinning and grimacing. In that single moment, our mother's project had unravelled, and its failure had become explicit.

'Come away, Edgar …' I repeated. I knew he could hear my confusion. 'They're not worth it. They are dogs. Don't you see? Moronic, aristocratic dogs.'

One or two of the men, who moments before had sniggered at our humiliation, got to their feet, outraged: 'I say! Blackguard!' They did not expect to be spoken to precisely as they would speak to others.

Edgar grabbed at Sir Gideon's sleeve.

'We are not Jews! We are not!'

Sir Gideon was shouting for him to release him immediately.

'Stop it, Edgar!' I cried.

'Tell them, Benjamin! *Tell them!* Tell them that we are not Jews!'

But I could not – I would not – I did not want to – tell them. I had been searching for the truth of who I was, even back in London, and now we were here, and he was asking me to deny it. But I felt then that I had moved past denying the truth. So I remained silent. My brother hung there for a moment, dazed and humiliated. Then, without a word, he bolted from the scene, pushed chairs this way and that across the garden of the *osteria*.

As I chased after him, all I could hear was the precise, gleeful mockery of Hervey and his friends. I said at the beginning that there is no fairness in the English, but I see now that maybe I was wrong. There is a morality to the cruelty of English people: they believe that those who possess the correct lineage and money have the right to wield them lethally against those who do not. There was not a quiver of humanity or a suggestion of an alternative viewpoint in the way that Sir Gideon and his entourage behaved. They had acted as they needed to in order to preserve the precious status quo. We were their quarry. And in their world, those they killed deserved what they got, precisely because it was *they* who had done the killing.

I marvelled at Lavelle. How absolute he was in his revenge. Cruelty is like a chess game, played with a cool, long vengefulness, and now Lavelle's heartless, clever Queen had effortlessly tapped Edgar's plodding King off the board. My brother was running down a narrow lane, his wooden heels echoing loudly against the cobbles. His shoe caught, and he stumbled to the ground, allowing me to reach him.

As my brother clambered to his feet, I saw that his breeches were torn at the knee and his stockings were smeared with wheel oil from the cobbles. His wig had half come off his head, his pale cheeks red with upset and exertion. 'Let's just go home,' I said, hoping to return the mercy – the brotherhood – he had given me in Rome. 'Let's just go back to London. None of this matters, Edgar, none of it.'

'What are you talking about, Benjamin? Nothing matters *apart* from this. This is why we came here. To make ourselves the equals of those people, the good people; to have friends back in London; to complete the journey that our parents have devised for us!' He was all inward confusion. 'How did Lavelle know?' His eyes were searching my face. Did he see my horror, my guilt? '*You* told him,' he said, in disbelief. 'Oh, my God, Benjamin, *you* told him. Was there no part of you, from your arse upwards, that you did not give him?'

'I told the truth. For once in our family, Edgar, someone told the truth.'

My brother groaned so hard, it sounded like a scream. 'Oh, fuck the truth, Benjamin! *Fuck the truth!* The truth doesn't matter any more.' Then he growled, angry. 'It is you who has done this to me! To us!' He launched himself at me and struck me hard in the face. I reeled backwards, landing with a thump. Looking up, I watched my brother's eyes run wildly along the ground, taking in what I had said. Then he started to kick me, throw more punches, trying to expunge his anguished rage and disappointment. Finally exhausted, he fell away, and I slowly moved my arms from my head. Edgar lifted his gaze, staring into the mid distance, his face collapsing as defeat eclipsed fury. 'Do you know why I hated Lavelle?' he asked.

'Because he wanted you to hate him.'

Edgar gave a small, bitter laugh. '*Unlike you*, we aren't all his, you know! We don't all feel as Lavelle commands us! Do you know why I hated Lavelle? I hated him because he was the worst of you,' Edgar said. 'He was clever – you are clever, cleverer than me – but he threw his cleverness away on nothing, and now you want to do the same. He was ironic – I know I am not ironic – but you are, and you used that irony not to perceive truth but to attack the world. I hated him because I knew from the start that he would steal you away from us, from Mother, Father and I – and he did. But what I hated most of all was that *you* made it so easy for him. You gave yourself to him, and I saw there was nothing I could do to win you back. I asked you over and over to pull away from him but you could not. You wanted whatever he served you, and look where we are, Benjamin. Look how he has devastated us. You revealed to a monster things that were not safe for you to reveal. I knew from the very start, from that awful journey out of Aosta down to Vicenza, that if you let him, this man would destroy us. For once, it seems I was the clever one after all. And so I hated him, but I should have hated you, because it is you who has betrayed us.' He became quieter, looking at me so gravely. 'Whatever follows, you have created, Benjamin. Do you hear me? Whatever follows, *you* have created!'

He took a great, raw, tearful breath, and then ran off, leaving me on the ground. The heels of his shoes clattered on the cobbles, echoing against Naples' old buildings. I started to stand – but my brother was already gone. I did not rush to follow him, as I had with Lavelle in Florence. Instead, I waited. I let him run away. It was a terrible mistake.

I shouted my brother's name through the brightly coloured lanes around the Spaccanapoli, still desolate on All Saints' Day. Running footsteps echoed in the alleys and up steep walls of houses that almost touched. The sound of good heels on cobbles rings out so loud, and it was a sound that haunted me for long afterwards. I eventually ran after him but it was too late, I had lost him. I wandered, turning in those lanes, calling him still, until I could shout no more.

Exhausted, I sloped back to the *albergo* to await his return. The day passed and grew darker. The *albergo* owner told me – as best as we could understand one another – that my brother had already been back to the room. I had been wandering around Naples, searching for him, when he had been here. I checked the room for clues of where he might have gone. I noticed that our mother's guidebook, which he had brought with him from Rome, was gone.

I lay down on my bed but did not sleep. The gloaming passed into twilight and on into night. I lit a candle and waited. The candle ran down to the wick. Then, from nowhere, there was sudden commotion, a thumping at my latched door. Outside, the *albergo* owner's wife stood with two strangers. All three of them were shouting and pointing, and began pulling at my shirt, indicating that I should go with them. They jabbered as one, and at odds with each another. The only word I could discern from their torrent was *fratello*. Brother. The word wormed its way into me, and though I did not understand, I gave myself up to their chaos.

We ran through the lamp-lit Neapolitan night, down from Santa Chiara towards the Golden Castle and on to the little square harbour beneath it, with narrow pebble beaches. The water was black, except for men holding torches that illuminated a body caught on fishermen's poles. On gently skittering waves swirled pages of a book – the same size as our mother's guidebook – and with every second, each page moved further away from its neighbour, as if it was now refusing to cohere and exist any more. Edgar must have gone back to the room, found the guide-book, like a sacred text, and brought it here to destroy, as he had come here to destroy himself.

Neapolitans, excited and appalled, started to gather around, marvelling at the sight. This is what I meant when I said it was too late. And this is what Edgar meant when he said that whatever followed would be my fault. I began to take breathless steps through the crowd.

I began to shout my brother's name. As I got nearer, the Neapolitans parted, as bit-part players do in a theatre scene, instinctively recognising that I was one of the leads.

His head was bare, his short black hair wet and matted. I let out a quick breath, and then another, and another, feeling my throat shut tight. I took a few steps forward. I blinked. The world blurred momentarily; a tear caught, then dissipated. Around me, I could hear people chattering in urgent Italian. 'Edgar?' I whispered. 'Edgar?' But I knew that my brother was dead.

PART THREE

THE SEA

$\mathcal{S}$ailing back to London, I was lost: lost in grief for my brother's death, and sadness for the way our relationship had deteriorated in the last months; lost in my regret at turning Lavelle away; lost because of all he had shown that was so different from what I had been raised to see; lost because I knew that, even amid the devastation of reckoning with Edgar's death, my body still yearned for Lavelle. It was shameful. I knew it was. But recognising your shame changes nothing of your desire: it burns it deep into your soul.

Each morning I awoke with the lurch of the waves. I would turn my head in bed to one side, expecting to see Lavelle, before realising that I was alone. Only then did I remember the truth. My brother had taken his life. I had written to my parents of Edgar's death, saying that he had drowned, but I offered no more information beyond that. I carried the events of the last day of his life with me everywhere. The memory of Edgar's words, that whatever happened next would be my responsibility, was seared into my mind. If we had honoured the intentions with which this Grand Tour had been conceived, we *might* all these months have been the best friends of Sir Gideon Hervey and Augusta Anson. Certainly Edgar would still be alive, travelling home alongside me.

I found a small Protestant church in the city and here the son of two aliens was buried, his brother the sole witness. I did not tell the priest that my brother was a suicide. Edgar was lowered into his grave, and dry Italian soil was cast upon the cheap little coffin. I watched numbly as he disappeared into the greedy mouth of earth. Somewhere above, a flock of seagulls reeled and cawed and a salt wind blew in. I could feel it, warm and southern, on my lips. Maybe I could have taken a boat to Sicily or Malta after all, and from there moved on to Tunis, and travelled across the Sahara to some remarkable place, like Timbuktu or the land of the Ethiopians. But the priest was at my side, whispering to me in poor French. 'Sir, the service finished. The time is here to pay.' His voice was brutal, but as I turned to him, he was smiling like the Lamb himself.

I handed him fifteen ducats. He lowered his eyes flirtatiously, like an actress at her last performance as an ingénue. 'Twenty, sir.'

'We agreed fifteen.'

He smiled again. His teeth were the most perfect ivory I had ever seen. 'I heard the Royal Guard looks for fast burials. They say an Englishman drowned himself yesterday. Is it this body?'

His pious eyes rested on me as his docile smile turned thin and coercive. He did not *want* to inform the authorities. He did not *want* to think of my brother going to Hell. I gave him the money.

Open water was punctuated by occasional stops. Our voyage broke first at Gibraltar. There, British naval officers in blue best-coats and white stockings prowled the port, hungry for diversion. After that, we stopped at Lisbon for two days. I drifted around the city, which had been destroyed a decade before by an earthquake so huge it had been felt in London. Almost every house, church and palace was reduced to rubble. My mother had read aloud to us from a newspaper story of the great loss of the palace of Ribeira. Oh, the vast libraries – oh, the collections of Titian and Rubens smashed to nothing, just ruined scraps of canvas and frame. Ten years later, the people of Lisbon still hung around in tents and shelters with the eyes of those tired of surviving. My mother never once told us how many tens of thousands had perished, how many more still suffered. I wondered if she would grasp the depth of the human tragedy now that *her* son was dead.

At sea, I said nothing of my brother's death to my fellow passengers. I did not want a Lancashire colliery owner's wife to claim they understood because her own dear sister died of smallpox when she was fifteen, or that a Cheapside lawyer commiserated having lost four babies so young. I wished them no ill, but I was afraid of others sharing their stories of loss. If they asked for introductions, I was terse and my responses obfuscatory, which led my fellow passengers to imagine I was very grand. And I saw the ludicrousness of the situation; my desire to stand apart made them yearn for my company all the more and, believing I was a *bona fide* member of the Quality, they sent more and more requests.

I thought of lovely Augusta. Would she find me funny or appalling now I had perfected the art of being so impervious – or imperious – to others? Would she shake her fan and offer me a kiss, now that I was so deadened inside? Weren't we now a most excellent match, both so heartless, both so cruel?

LONDON

It was eight months since Edgar and I had left for Paris. When our ship docked at Southampton, England was soundless under an early snow. It was almost dark when the shout went out, 'Land-ho!', and people rushed to see home. North of the town, a patch of low hills glowed luminously white. As we alighted, a thick fog descended on the shabby little port. I hired a private carriage to take me back to London – I could not bear to travel in a shared coach, with strangers. I wanted to be alone, to stare out of the window and think – not to make polite conversation. I had enough money left, just about.

Reeling through the English countryside, the trees at the sides of the roads threw scary silhouettes. We only stopped at staging posts, where crooked-teethed men came to offer me a cup of wine, or a sheep's-bladder of water, or half a pork pie. I wished them away but they did not go. On the second night, I was shaken awake by the carriage abruptly stopping. Blinking, I gazed out into the nocturnal sparseness of an anonymous heath scraped over with snow. The driver, sitting above me, said,

'This is Streatham, sir.' I leaned out of the carriage window – a cold wind fluttered across my face. It was just shadow against shadow – black, open country. The driver laughed and pointed ahead. 'Look down there, that's London.' I turned my head in the other direction. There in the distance, countless distant lights furnished the dark. It should have felt like I was home.

Arriving at the Thames, I saw boys of six, seven and eight down at the water's edge, breaking up the ice as best they could. Every year, several of them fell through and froze to death, but every year, new boys replaced them. I asked the driver if he could go on without me and wait at my home. I wanted to breathe the cold air and let the ice settle me before I faced my parents again. The driver waited for me to descend, and then cried to the horses and pulled away.

Even on a deep-winter night, London Bridge was heaving with market stalls, people coming in and out of the houses and taverns that lined its sides. The bridge had been salted so that business was not interrupted – the most important thing of all. The north side of the river, London itself, was muted by the snow. The people moved slowly, hoping not to slip. The city had receded into warm, noisy taverns, behind townhouse doors, leaving the streets to the most unfortunate for the wind to blow around. Whores working the north side whistled and grunted at gin-soaked men staggering past. I watched them turning and turning in the snow flutters and the dark. This was a London I had hardly seen before I went on Tour. In part, my mother had kept my and Edgar's eyes from seeing it, but in truth, I would not have been able to see the reality of the world as it showed itself to me. It was Lavelle who had taught me to see that reality.

The bells of St Andrew Holborn rang out, but as I walked past its open doors, there was not a single soul inside. Suddenly, I was struck by a fresh dread. What if my parents had not received my letter? What if my father had replied telling me to stay put on the Continent, not to come home? Never tell your mother, never reveal your shame. What if they had sent that letter, but it had been lost, intercepted, held for ransom, sunk on a barge that did not make it across the Channel? In those closing moments of my journey, I felt overwhelmed that this had not been the hardest part. That lay ahead of me: facing my parents, their sense of loss, and how I would ever really explain what happened to Edgar and me in Italy.

At the edge of Chancery Lane on Holborn, drunks were exchanging curses. One of them, a woman, threw a punch at a man – who threw one straight back and split open her nose. Others began to pile in, slipping and sliding in the crimson-splattered snow. A bloodied phoenix, the woman rose from where she had fallen and flew at the man, clutching his head in her hands and banging it hard against a brick wall. The man's howl was so loud it made everyone recoil. Just for a moment, my eyes connected with the woman's. We looked at each other, and I saw in her a mix of pride and shame. I thought then of Lavelle, and scurried across the road, picking through the filthy melted slurry towards home.

Turning into Red Lion Square, I saw the carriage was waiting by my parents' house. I thanked the driver, who had already unloaded my – and Edgar's – trunks. I pulled the bell and waited for the footman to open up. He bowed and murmured, 'Master Benjamin.' I entered the hallway and kicked the snow off my shoes, slipped off my cape and handed it over. I asked where my parents were. My father was dining alone in the drawing room.

'And my mother?'

The footman cast his eyes downwards. 'Madam doesn't come down to dinner much these days,' he said. And so I understood: they knew.

I went up the first flight of stairs to the drawing room, but hesitated at the door. The handle was cold to my touch. Then, breathing in, I pushed the door open. The room was immediately warm, and a fire was roaring. There, I took in the scene captured for that moment, and clear still in my mind. Silent in candlelight, my father hung over a bowl of soup. The spoon at his lips, he was not dressed. He wore a skullcap rather than a wig. Perhaps, with my mother not joining him, he felt no obligation to. He had a dressing gown over his shirt and breeches. How old he looked, how vulnerable. I had never thought of him that way before. William Bowen was in his fifties – an age by which plenty of Londoners are already dead. But nothing about my father had ever suggested physical weakness. He was strong. He was tough.

I shut the door and my father looked up. Saying nothing, he stood and moved to embrace me. And when we were close – and even that closeness surprised me – I heard him whisper: 'My son.' Perhaps I had expected him to shout, or to issue me with reproaches. He did not. He held me for a long time. His breathing was raw, fibrous with emotion.

'Have you eaten, son?' he asked, letting me go, and I said no. I had not even realised that I was hungry. The bell was rung. A new maid, a pretty thing I had not seen before, appeared and got a good look at me. The staff would soon be talking. In the time it took for soup, bread and cold meat to be brought, for my father to pour me a glass of wine, I noticed that there was no mourning black anywhere. 'I did not know if the house would be hung with black.'

My father shrugged. 'For whose benefit, Benjamin? No one comes here.'

I nodded. I had not forgotten the cloistered nature of that house – I remembered it brightly – but I had forgotten its totality, the completeness of our isolation. It was as if my parents had placed a plague quarantine on the dwelling – and in doing so, also on us children. Looking around the room, I noticed the mirrors were covered with cloth. 'That was your mother's request,' my father said. 'It is an old custom, I believe.' Our eyes met briefly and his searched mine for the first time. 'She just said she wanted to do it, because of ... well, you know.' Did I know? A Jewish custom perhaps, but my father did not know what I had discovered. I nodded, saying nothing.

We began to talk about all that had happened in Italy. I avoided much truth. Could I invite my father to imagine the black-hearted wonder of Horace Lavelle? Or the social viciousness of Augusta Anson or Sir Gideon Hervey, precisely the sort of people he had fantasised would become our new friends? Instead I told of a tragedy. I described how Edgar had gone out, and how I had been alerted in our room at the *albergo* and led to a shocking scene by the harbour. I had no explanations, I said.

My father growled to himself, 'It must have been an accident. That must be the reason.' He glanced at me then, waiting for me to dare to contradict him. I did not.

Hours passed into a deep, snowy night. Flakes whipped at the window on gusts of wind. My mother did not appear. She must have heard my voice – the voice of her surviving child – through the floorboards, but still she did not come. When it was long past midnight and the room had become cold with the snow outside, my father went to a basket of dry logs and tossed one onto the fire, so that crackling flames were thrown out. 'At least there is you,' my father said.

'Me?'

He spoke into the fire. 'To inherit, I mean. The Company must have an heir if it is to have a future. That was always our plan.'

A wave of dread passed over me. This was, then, the truth. The plan, which should have been in tatters, was still in place. Nothing had changed about their intentions, except that Edgar was dead. Everything else was the same. 'There is something I must tell you,' my father said, suddenly strangely cheerful. 'I am building a house.'

It seemed so incongruous. 'A *house*, Father?'

'Yes, I have bought some land, in the open fields at Bloomsbury.'

'But why?'

'Why?' he snapped. He seemed aggrieved that I should even ask. 'I thought it was a good project for you and Edgar to undertake, to lead on, as the family transforms.'

He spoke of Edgar in the present tense. 'But Edgar is dead,' I said, confused. 'Has nothing changed? Are we to pretend that everything is not changed?'

My father shot to his feet. I stood up to meet him, but he punched me hard in the cheek. I stumbled backwards across the room and crashed, dazed, to the floor. It flew back to me then: the secret I had kept of my father's violence, the time I had seen him turn a debtor's face to bloody pulp when I was a boy. He stood above me, hunched over, as if ready to punch me again. 'Apologise,' he growled. I said nothing for a moment, still stunned. '*Apologise!*'

'I'm sorry!'

My father let out a cluck of a breath, with tears inside. Then he glanced down at the floor. 'I'm sorry too, Benjamin.'

But neither one of us seemed sorry, not truly.

The morning after I returned, I lay supine for a long time on waking. As before, I woke without remembering everything that had happened – but this time my moment of realisation came more rapidly. I was in the same bed in which I had always slept, in the same room, in the same house. And yet things were now so very different: Edgar was gone, and Lavelle existed. I felt I understood the world. I knew of what unhappiness it was capable. And then, waking more fully, I realised I had been dreaming of Lavelle, at the Lido again, but this time my mother and father had been sitting on the rocks of the cove. Edgar was there too, and they were all pointing and laughing at the two of us, two naked boys with hard cocks, covering ourselves out of shame. It was Edgar laughing the hardest, the most mockingly, as if he had played a trick on me. In dying and compelling me back to this life, he had got his revenge for all my treachery. At least, it had seemed that way in the dream.

I gazed up at the fissured plaster in my bedroom ceiling. The same fractured map I had studied before we went away – tracing the arc of our voyage, one side of Europe to the other – whilst Edgar had chattered on, excitedly and full of hope. Our room might look as it had before we left, but it is grief's nature to change how everything feels whilst leaving every brick, tile, picture, cup in the same position.

Though it was not late, my father had long since gone to the office. Business continues. I went to the mean greenish mirror in the corner of the room – this had been covered too – and pulled off the black cloth. I checked my face for a bruise and was thankful when I saw there was none. Having dressed and taken breakfast alone, I prepared myself to visit my mother. Knocking, hearing her quietly say, 'Enter,' I found her sitting perfectly still on the edge of her bed, staring outwards. A heavy, black lace shrouded her head and shoulders, falling over a dress of simple black satin. Her eyes ran across me frigidly. She made no move to open her arms for me. She sat stock-still, her eyes deep, cold pools. I went to her bedside and stood before her. Still she did not stand up or offer me her cheek.

'Mother, will you not let me kiss you?' I could see how she shifted upon hearing my words, my voice. I counted out the seconds of silence, and with every second that passed, my body seemed to blaze a little bit more. 'Mother, shall we have tea together?' I said. She did not answer. 'I can ring the bell for the maid.'

She took a careful breath. I could not tell what it contained, but it did not bode well. 'I thought you two looked the same, Benjamin, but now I see that you do not.' Still, she made no move towards me and instead sat back, recoiling from the possibility of my touch. 'You were like angels in my mind, and now I see you here, Benjamin, and nothing in you seems good.'

I cricked my neck, to accommodate the force of her words. 'I never said I was an angel, Mother. I never wanted to be one.'

Her eyes flared. 'What is wrong with angels, please?'

I wondered how Lavelle would reply. Something about virgins, flea-bitten wings, and stains on white dresses. 'There is nothing wrong with them. I never said there was. I just said I never wanted to be one. An angel. I am just a man, Mother.'

Did the word 'man' surprise her? That's what I was, what my brother had been too. 'Edgar was an angel,' she said sharply. 'He was always so sweet.' The last word turned to a whisper in her mouth, and I understood then how people transform the dead into saints. We were silent a moment longer, until she asked, 'Why was your father shouting last night?'

An image of her flashed through me then. She was standing on the floor above, knowing I had returned, listening to her husband shouting, and thinking, good, *good*. 'Nothing,' I said. 'It was nothing.' Her jaw clenched.

Just as I had seen her in Edgar when he was angry with me in Italy, I saw Edgar in her now. She looked down at the floor, briefly, letting her silence scald me. 'Are you angry with me, Mother?'

She fidgeted, then folded her hands in her lap, before looking up at me with fierce eyes, which threatened more blows. 'I told you to take care of one another, and did you?' she said, her voice hollow and raw. 'Was this taking care, Benjamin? Was it? You made an oath to look after one another, and look what has happened! Did you *honour* this oath?'

'Mother—'

'Of course I am angry! These days, I am nothing but anger!' She looked around the room and then, suddenly, sharply, back at me. I saw her ice, that bitter wrath. 'Who was this Lavelle person?' she asked.

'What?'

'Who was this Lavelle about whom Edgar wrote to me?'

I hesitated before her. 'He – he was my friend.'

The word 'friend' made something in my mother flinch. 'Edgar said that he was a very terrible influence on you. Your brother –' she gulped, holding back tears '– wrote to tell me of all your lovely English friends. All the very best families. Why could you not make friends with those people, I should ask?'

'I did.'

'Edgar said, no, you did not. Said you did not even try. Said you gave yourself up to irreverence!' She spluttered on the word. 'Malevolent! That was the word Edgar used about this Lavelle. He said that he made you forget all about our plan.'

'I never forgot, Mother.'

'Then why did you not make friends with all these fine gentlemen, I should like to know, all the wonderful people whom Edgar befriended so easily?'

'I tried but—'

'But *what*?' she spat angrily. 'But what, Benjamin?'

'They could see what we were, Mother,' I said.

She turned more fully to look at me. 'What does this mean, Benjamin, please? Don't use English to be obscure!'

'It means that they would not accept us as Englishmen, as their peers. They knew what we truly were, that we were not like them.'

'I do not understand, Benjamin. Edgar wrote to me to say these were excellent friends with very proud names.' She sounded so Dutch; I had forgotten how Dutch she sounded when she was angry. 'He sounds a very sinful person, this Lavelle.'

'He was my friend, Mother, and neither he nor I are to blame for Edgar dying.'

She rose to her feet so that we were standing close to one another, as perhaps we would have if she had embraced me when I first entered.

'I know what is this,' she said, her English mangling with anger. 'I know you have stopped yourself from being accepted. I know. Out of some spite or fear, yes, I know this! You seek to disobey me, to upset me and disappoint me. Well, look what has happened with your games—'

I did not want her to speak like this. 'Mother, please.'

Her eyes were on me so very hard. 'I just don't believe that there is no blame,' she said. 'There is *always* blame.'

That seemed such a bleak thing to say, so inhumane. But then I thought about my experience of the world in the last year. Where was blame not laid? 'I don't know what you are suggesting, Mother,' I said pathetically.

'Tell me the truth, Benjamin.' She paused. 'Did this Lavelle kill Edgar?'

'What?' I cried. 'What? No, of course not! Mother, I swear to you, no. No one killed Edgar. He killed himself.'

Maybe this was the first time she considered this. My father would have concealed her from any hurt. After all, he lived to make her happy. Her eyes went round, then shrank.

'How can you say ...?' Her shock turned back to anger. 'Why do you lie about this, Benjamin?'

Now my anger was rising too. 'He drowned himself, Mother! He drowned himself …'

'No,' she said, shaking her head, glaring at me. 'Not my beautiful Edgar! Stop saying this, please!'

We stood there, our faces hot with emotion, our chests rising and falling. We said nothing for a long time, she contemplating her son's suicide, me dazed not just by the blow, but by the moment, too.

'For a long time,' she eventually began, 'I thought that this man Lavelle, he must be the Devil—'

I wanted to laugh. Horribly, I started to. I was ashamed that I should, but it burst out of me, a kind of spiteful convulsion. I wondered if it was true. Maybe Lavelle had been the Devil. After all, don't they say that the Devil is a charming man? Lavelle was diabolical in every sense of the word, from the worst to the best, the repulsive to the exquisite. God hated the Devil because he spoke the truth. Man fears the Devil because he means to do him harm. Truth-tellers can be harm-doers too.

My mother was watching me. I saw her horror and her hurt that I should have been laughing at this, the worst, the most painful time of her life.

'I just want to understand,' she said.

'I don't know that I could explain, Mother,' I said. 'At least not in a way that you could understand. Lavelle showed me another way to be.'

'Another way? How could you not want the way your father and I have devised? We were going to give you the world.'

Her eyes were so earnest. She absolutely believed in what she had just said. I almost felt sorry for her. And I would have done, if not for all the damage they, with the best of intentions, had caused.

'I just don't know if I want what I have been given.'

At this, my mother changed. She hated me now for what I had said. She wanted to punish me. She moved to the chest against one wall. From the top drawer, she pulled a cachet of cards and flung them at me. As they showered to the ground, I saw that they were letters from Europe – his whole record of the last year of his, of our, life.

I leaned down and gathered them up one by one, only able to catch glimpses of my brother's words. From Paris: 'We have your precious guidebook and it "guides" us everywhere. We have met some marvellous people ...' From Venice: 'Benjamin has made a curious friend named Lavelle ... I will confess, Mother, that I am missing you and Father very much. Sometimes my heart feels a bit sick with it ...' 'Mother – this is Siena, a hateful place. I miss home more than I expected ... He is a malevolent person.' From Florence: 'He does not seem to have time for anyone but Lavelle. I ask him to write to you but he refuses.' And from Rome: 'I am fading. How can that be? I read your guidebook every day, yet often find myself at a loss of what to do. Some days, I wake and wish I were in London, and this trip had all been but a dream.' And lastly, his letter from Naples, when he thought us reunited and was so full of hope again. The picture of the volcano at Vesuvius. None of us had known then of the inferno about to consume us.

Peeling through them, I saw that this was not actually my history. It was Edgar's history of him and me. A narrative had been created, a version of events that I recognised as being true to him, but not to me. But even as I saw how he described my friendship with Lavelle in terms meant to harm me, I saw too how vulnerable Edgar was, how hard the whole journey had been on him, how frail his mind had become.

Throughout our travels in Italy, I had felt his censorship, railed that he was trying to stifle and control me, laughed at his foolishness. Now I saw that, in his own rather inarticulate way, he'd been trying to find a way to say that he missed me, that he felt alone, that he needed me, his brother, to help navigate a world in which we were strangers. I had been too selfish, too self-involved, too … *exultant*, to see it. I had not understood, or wanted to understand, or chosen to understand, that he might need me. None of it felt good to read. None of it made anything seem better – quite the reverse.

I looked up at my mother, and she had her hand outstretched, waiting for me to return the letters. They were the holy relics of a martyr, more sacred than any empty treatise, any stupid book. 'Give me my son,' she whispered. 'Give me back my son.' But, of course, I could not.

Our house, previously so full of talk and laughter, of family life, became a cold, silent place. Dinner at six was a thing of the past. The Minute Game was never mentioned. No one quoted Voltaire. My father and I never acknowledged that he had struck me or that, perhaps, I had deserved it. November turned to December and then January, a new year but one without hope. I had lost Lavelle. Edgar was dead. Nothing had changed and everything was ruined. January slipped into February, and rain replaced the snow. I began to wake, remembering even in my sleep what had come to pass. In that house on Red Lion Square, we came to understand that grief was a long, jagged journey. How long, though, we could not have begun to imagine. Some nights, I would take a carriage to Hyde Park, where I would wait in the darkness for hungry mouths and hands to appear. For one desirous, blinded moment, I could pay to forget Lavelle, forget Edgar and forget my mother's hate.

My mother and I rarely saw each other after that first morning. She preferred to stay in a separate bedroom she had started to keep, away from my father. Difficult days passed into disturbed, haunted months. Beginning in the shipping office, I accepted my new life without pleasure or meaning. Every day was more boring than the last, filled with meetings with creditors and debtors, management accounts, debriefs with clerks and secretaries. Clocks ticked slowly, days dragged by, and I accepted it as a prisoner with a jail sentence. Meanwhile, my father and I pushed on with the building of the new house. In those years, and several before that, London had started to look different. Its rapacious spread, out towards Islington, Paddington, Chelsea and Camden Town, was defined by a new era of architecture: very different to the Dutch style of Red Lion Square, its long, flat, elegant neo-Palladian lines invoked the Italian style we had seen on the Tour.

A bewildering array of new, smart addresses appeared. Hanover Square, Grosvenor Square, Manchester Square, Portland Square, Fitzroy Square and Bedford Square all came into being, as if by the wave of a magician's wand. Our area, to the north of the city, changed as rapidly as any. The fields and meadows beyond the old Foundling Gate started to be paved over completely. Bloomsbury, once a perilous bog filled with the decomposed bodies of the dead, was fast becoming a genteel place for the rich and fashionable, an elegant new city away from the clamouring stench of the old.

My father and I met with various architects. He told them that we wanted a grand project. But tasteful, I added. All the houses in Bloomsbury look the same, so how do we stand out – and yet not stand out? This is the English conundrum, I see now. One architect made the observation that when you build the house that out-does all the others, the one that is the same, but not the same, is better. We rode with that same architect out to Hampstead Heath to see the country house at Kenwood which Robert Adam was redesigning for the Earl of Mansfield. As soon as I laid eyes on it, I understood what the project could be.

One day, I met my father at the building site to assess the progress of our new home. Time had passed. It was now autumn again, ten months since I had returned from Italy. We met in the late afternoon, the sky above us a polished pale grey, a mirror of the new London styles. As I approached, five minutes after our appointed time, I could hear my father's voice, his Welsh accent more pronounced as he began booming. 'You cannot be late in life,' he said. 'The businessman's life must be lived by the clock.' What a joyless way to live your life, a voice murmured in my head. To whom did that voice belong? But, of course, this was my life. And whose fault is that, the voice asked.

We walked around the site together. The brick walls were now up three floors. We twisted among the cane and rope of the scaffolding. The work was good but my father could not stop himself from spending a little time speaking Welsh to some of the labourers. When I'd been younger, I had felt some unknown – mysteriously communicated – shame to hear my father's native tongue. Now I heard it differently: it was harsh, yes, yet run through with music. There was an ease with his own language that I did not always hear when he spoke English.

Afterwards, we perched on a foundation buttress at ground level. We were facing west, and late-afternoon sunbeams – no heat in them, it was too late in the year for that – broke through the grey clouds. My father closed his eyes briefly. I watched the patterns of the sun on his face, the light bleaching out its jowly lines. I saw my father as timeless again, a man almost beyond age. Once he had been a poor boy in Wales. The scraps he had told us of his childhood: tramping up wet hill-sides in the rain, hearing the chapel harmonium playing on the chilly air; the absolute absence of any material possessions; the strange summer when the fever came and took away his mother and his sisters and he sold everything to come to London to make his fortune. This boy born of nothing, who set out to reinvent himself and largely succeeded, was now the man building a grand new house in the most fashionable part of London. I thought of his ability to refuse his predeter-mined future – one of poverty and obscurity in poor, obscure Wales – and, indeed, his life now. What was it that made him not see that his sons might want that too? Perhaps it was a part of that determination that won him success.

'What do you think of the building works?' I asked, shaking off my thoughts. My father turned and looked at me.

'I think it is to schedule,' he said, in his matter-of-fact way. I laughed a little. My father did not mind that; he knew who he was.

'But do you like it, Father? Do you think it beautiful?'

He sniffed. 'I don't think about such things. I think only what it means that people like us should have a house like this. I will trust your opinion when it is finished. Like I once trusted your mother's.'

His use of the word 'once' affected me much more than I might have imagined. The truth of the death of my parents' love pressed on me. My father seemed to see some shift in me, seemed able to discern my upset. 'Benjamin,' he asked, 'is something wrong?'

I felt such a pressure on my chest, like a hand placed hard against the breastbone, chasing the breath from my lungs. 'Father, may I ask you something … something sensitive?'

He seemed uneasy. 'Sensitive? I'm not sure.'

'You don't have to answer, Father, if you don't wish to.' I looked at him and he did not refuse my going any further. 'When did you realise you were in love with Mother?'

It was never knowable how my father would react to things. In many ways, he was a steady, predictable person, but his temper rose quickly. His fists had been on my face and on the faces of others too. People don't forget the hands that hit them; a child doesn't forget his father committing violence against another any more than he forgets how the father draws him into keeping it secret. But he smiled, lost in a sudden memory.

My mother, he began, had told him – back when Solomon Fonseca was alive and my father was his employee – how she dreamed of skating on the Thames, but that for quite a few years, the river did not freeze. When the river froze over, she had heard, Londoners would go down onto the gleaming ice, like thousands of turning birds. Then one year, the river froze hard. Ships were halted mid-stream, unable to move.

'To my surprise,' my father said, 'your mother asked me if I could go skating with her. She had no one else to go with – Solomon was a sickly sort of person and did not want to risk a chill. We walked together to Thames Street. They lived on Cheapside then, so the walk was not far, five or ten minutes, no more.'

'Did Mother used to go out and about in the street like that?' I could not remember the last time she had even left the house. My mother had very occasionally spoken to Edgar and I of Amsterdam as a city of skaters on frozen canals, but she had never told us that she had been one of those who skated across the Thames.

My father's eyes shifted to mine. 'Sometimes,' he responded. He continued with his story. 'Down by the river, I could see the figures on the ice, some stumbling, some gliding. Suddenly, I felt nervous.'

'That you might fall?' I asked.

He gave a half-nod.

'But also that your mother might see me fall. I was a young man then, and I was proud. Your mother must have sensed this. She looked at me – and I had not spoken a word – and said that she would teach me how to skate.'

So my mother taught my father how to stay upright, though it was she, in all the hoops and petticoats of her dress, who should have worried about falling. In those days, people didn't wear skates. They just took their chances to slip and slide. Now and then, he would fall and she would catch him before he hit the ice, and they laughed, touching for the first time. As they began cautiously to spin and dance, his hands would be at her corseted waist, her fingers reaching for his. Even through gloves, their touch was real. Eventually, they made it to the other side, all the way to Southwark. There, where the ice was thick enough to hold those ships hostage, circus troupes gathered – the freaks grimacing and hollering whilst people gathered around to point and laugh. Some spectators threw things at them: snowballs, food, spare change. 'Your mother thought this cruel – she said it was not right – and it struck me then, her kindness and her care. She is a very serious person, a very intelligent person, I knew that already. But her kindness ... I had not expected that. I don't know. She has always been so kind to me.' Something blew through me, a feeling of regret. Had I not seen this quality in my mother? Had I been too harsh on her?

'In those days,' he continued, 'no one worried about these things. But she told me she abhorred cruelty. She did not agree with the trade in slaves. I had never heard *anyone* complain about slavery in London. No white person, at least. She was the first. She was like no one I had ever encountered before, the most remarkable person I ever met in my life.' He sighed happily, love's light still in his eyes. 'That has never changed.'

Eventually, they had clambered ashore. It was she who slipped now, and he held out his hand to steady her on the icy steps up to the wharf. 'We walked back across London Bridge, the two of us. All the traders were outside their houses on the side of the bridge. There was the smell of caramel in the air, and your mother asked me what the name of toffee apples was in English. She did not know. She said the name in French – I do not remember it, Benjamin.' *Pommes d'amour*, I did not say, afraid that my education might shame my father's shortcomings. 'I wanted to buy her one. I slapped my pockets – I had had some money, but I must have dropped it on the ice and not noticed! What a calamity. Your mother fixed me with that knowing stare of hers, with that small smile she wears on her lips. "I have money for myself," she said, and brought her purse from inside her coat. She went up to the trader who handed her the steaming, sticky apples. Your mother was gazing at me with her beautiful eyes, there on London Bridge, and handed me a toffee apple. I remember so clearly thinking, *Who is this person? From where did this incredible person come?* I had not known before then that such women might exist.'

His voice faded to nothing, the memory like a jewel in his life. And my father, gruff, frightening, sober, had just offered to me the simplest, loveliest portrait of love. And in hearing his story I felt so keenly the way love had withdrawn itself from my life. I too had encountered a remarkable person – unlike any other I had ever met – but he had left me.

'How long was this before Solomon Fonseca's death?' I asked my father, breaking his reverie and my regret.

'What's that?' he growled, pretending not to have heard. He got to his feet. I did not ask the question again. I did not have to. 'Not long, I suppose,' he said. And then he walked away.

That evening, I took a hackney cab out to the village of Hoxton, now just about joined to the eastern sprawl of the city. People of fashion do not go to Hoxton. Only certain sorts of people go that far east. But in a world that only mentions the word 'sodomite' alongside the instruction 'Kill the', the knowledge of places you can go is like a black-magic spell. Share it wisely and only with those you can absolutely trust: your own kind.

The places where someone like me could knock on a door and be welcomed inside is information that is transmitted fleetingly, secretively – the sodomite version of a Freemason's handshake. Perhaps, after an encounter with a stranger in an unlit alley, someone might whisper, 'Sometimes I go to this address ... There is a place where we could meet ... In Hoxton ... I'll give you the address and the sign you'll need in order to know which door it is ...' But you do not arrange to meet there, because men like us cannot risk falling in love when falling in love can be fatal.

The carriage set me down on the end of the road to Hackney, far outside the city. From here, I marched, head down, through the empty, unlit streets. Here and there, a body – or bodies – churned in the darkness, then stopped as I walked past, both daring and, surely, afraid to be challenged. I walked on. Voices whispered, and then receded, enveloped by the night.

I found the address I had been given. Halfway down, precisely as it had been described, I saw a blank, lilac-coloured sign outside. 'Why blank?' I'd asked. 'Because who would put a sign on the door of a business which caters to those who need to be invisible?' 'And why lilac?' The man simply stared at me, not sure if I was innocent, or dishonest.

I knocked at the door and a heavily barred shutter was slung back. An eye was at the door. Inside, I could hear faint laughter and the sound of raucous fiddle playing. A man's voice asked, 'Yes? What?'

'I am like you,' I murmured. The eye swivelled around to look me up and down. Then it gave a great, camp cry.

'You don't look anything like me, dearie! The very *thought* of it!'

I hesitated. 'I mean, I am the sort of man you might want to come here.'

'Oh, no, duck,' the eye chortled. 'I like more what is described as a "handsome" man.' A pause. 'No offence.' The eye did not blink but just kept staring out at me. I thought I should leave, scurry away, but at the last moment said:

'I have money.'

'Well, dearie,' cooed the eye. 'Why didn't you say so before?'

The shutter slammed closed and the door was unbolted. Inside, the man with such high standards was revealed, short and portly, his bald head unwigged. 'You go upstairs, dearie,' he said, 'there's a boy at the top, but you can't fuck him. He has the pox.' He laughed again. I went up the stairs and stood outside a door that was very slightly ajar. Beyond, I heard a gaggle of men's voices, laughing, talking. The air was thick with pipe smoke. I could smell sweat and sex. My nerves bit me. I put my hand on the door and pushed it fully open. In a room twenty feet by twenty, and spilling up into a stairwell, there stood so many men, a crush of hungry bodies. I saw men dressed and half-undressed. Men who wore make-up and women's clothes. Men with their arms around other men, with their mouths on their cheeks, necks, mouths. They were young men and old men, hard-eyed men and innocent lambs. Fat men, thin men, tall and short men. Every possible kind of man.

The pox-boy – who was not a boy, but probably a man of around thirty – slapped me on the arm. 'Oi,' he went, 'a threepenny bit, if you please. This ain't all free.' *A threepenny bit,* I thought. Half a day's wages for most men in London. I looked out at the men, who seemed, as one, to turn to look at me. They were staring openly, weighing me up: my beauty, my lack of it, what was good and special about me, and what was ugly and worthless. Then, it felt, they began to look away. One, then another, then another. The world looks away: you are not its centre after all.

I began to push through the fleshy mass. I felt a hand touch my buttocks, fingers dancing over the muscle. I turned around and found myself facing a white-haired man grinning at me, his teeth black and gapped. I smiled and twisted away; he touched my buttocks again. I turned back to him and whispered: 'I'm sorry.' 'Don't be sorry,' he replied tartly. 'Just fuck me.' My breath caught hard and I pulled away. I changed direction, walking straight into a circle of six or seven men all facing one corner of the room. Then I saw what they saw: a man seated in a chair. Between his legs was another man, entirely naked, with his head in the man's lap and the man's penis in his mouth. The man who was having his cock sucked was enjoying having an audience, like a king in his court and we his loyal subjects, silent in awe. Only then did I notice two or three of the spectators had their penises in their hands. Others were looking on as if it was all too boring. Then I heard a groan, a rocking grunt, and the man with the penis in his mouth stood up and turned to the half-a-dozen onlookers. Semen spurted out of his convulsing body, splattering over the floorboards. All but one of us jumped back to avoid the spray getting on our shoes. The remaining man fell to his knees to try to catch it on his protruding tongue. I had been across Europe. I had been Lavelle's other half. I thought I had seen it all. I thought I had heard it all, and yet here we were, we men, gaping at this orgiastic display. I did not know if this was Heaven or Hell.

The cock-sucker came back to his senses, naked before strangers. The madness of his desire – his hunger – had passed. His embarrassment and humiliation could now return, the crushing weight of shame every sodomite knows, in which he was raised every day of his life. He scrabbled towards a little seat against the wall where his clothes lay neatly folded. A man's orgasm is both his motivation and his shame; they are precisely the same thing.

I went with a tall and masculine-looking man up to a tiny room high in the attics. The room was dirty and spartan, with just a bedroll on the floor and a small chest of drawers with a jug and bowl on top, presumably to wash oneself with after. 'Do you want to leave the door open?' the man asked.

'Open?' I echoed, not understanding.

'In case someone wants to watch? Do you want to be watched?'

I shook my head. I felt such a foolish innocent. '*No*, I don't want to be watched.' He grinned at me, said, 'Good.'

His smile was suddenly, luminously, beautiful. He turned from me and locked the door. We looked at each other for a second and our uncertainties receded. I stepped forwards and kissed him. It was soft and tender, that surprising moment of connection with a stranger. We moved down onto the bedroll, slowly removing our clothes. He was much older than me, forty or forty-five perhaps. His body was still broad and hard – a man's body. His chest and stomach were tufted with sparse hair, his shoulders muscular. I touched his penis; it was getting harder and warm in my hand, and he groaned softly.

'What's your name?' I asked. He moaned at my touch but he did not answer. 'What's your name?'

'Shh,' he went. 'No names.'

Soon we were lying down, and he drew my body on top of his, both of us naked. He pulled back from the kiss and looked far into my eyes. In his deep, older voice, he said to me, 'I want you to fuck me.'

I was shocked. I had never fucked someone before. 'Don't you want to …?' I asked. His eyes glowed no.

'I want you to give me what my wife cannot. I want you to fuck me hard and put your seed inside me.'

Lovers are performers. They perform the roles they are prescribed, and that they prescribe themselves. Now, I performed as a man. Lying on his back, he pulled his legs apart and up into the air, to show his hole to me – what should be a comic moment but is, instead, one of breathtaking intimacy. How can two human beings who don't even know each other's names be more intimate than this? I raised up on my knees at the altar of his body, my erection held in one hand, my other holding one of his thighs. I touched my penis against his hole. He spat into his palm, then rubbed the spit over the end of my penis and pressed it onto his body. 'All right,' he said. I pushed and his body tensed, and then relaxed, and he looked so happy to feel me. But what I desired was not even considered, by neither him, nor me.

I fucked the man and all the while he kept his eyes shut and his mouth open, whispering, 'That's good … So good. Fuck me … That's good …' I was inside him and watching him, and even as I stayed hard, I floated somewhere high above my own head, floated up to the ceiling of that little room and gazed down at this man who did not even want to tell me his name. And as I drifted above him, I pictured him in a small house somewhere, off Cheapside or Ludgate Hill or somewhere in the Lambeth countryside. I pictured his mild homely wife (or maybe she was fierce and intellectual) and a gaggle of children (or maybe a nursery of empty cots and a graveyard full of infants).

Who are we all? I wondered in that moment. What world did we – and our parents, and their parents, and every king and pope and peasant in a field – construct to bring us here, to this fearful, merely fleeting, free moment? Did any of us know what we were doing? (*Yes, Lavelle would whisper, yes, we knew.*) Did we give it even a moment's real thought? (*Why pretend we did not? We all know the truth, no matter what we profess now.*) People can be happy, I wanted to yell, and they can help other people be happy too. So why have we committed the world to such blame, loneliness and misery? (*Are you thinking of me, Benjamin? Are you always – on some level – thinking of me?*)

And then – still inside the man, still performing my lover's role – maybe I said, 'That's good,' too, when it was not good, when it was awful and lonely and frightening. I pictured this man with the life he might have, and his wife with the life she thought she had, and their lives together – which resulted in him coming to this place, to find a nameless man to fuck him – and I felt only horror. I did not want any of this. I did not want, twenty years hence, to have to make up a story in my Bloomsbury palace to my society wife claiming that I had to go out on business. I did not want to kiss my children's heads to say goodnight so that I could come out here, for this moment of pleasure and truth – a moment constructed solely for the purpose of enabling a life full of lies.

So I lied like lovers should: '*Oh, that's good, you look so handsome, so beautiful ...*' Then the man grabbed his hard penis – not to jerk it but to stop his semen from shooting out all over his own belly. He failed, and his skin was suddenly patterned with liquid pearl. His head rocked back, he took a deep breath, and I knew that he wanted it to be over. He wanted our intimacy done. To let the lies resume. *Shh, no names.* I knew I was not going to ejaculate, so instead I grunted loudly and pushed my penis deeply inside him, to pretend that I had. I could see from the pleasure on his face that he bought the lie. I let him. My life was before me, and it was the life of this man.

With a sudden urgency, I knew it was a life I did not want. It was a life that for me would have been like perpetual drowning. *Reject, reject, reject!*

Running the Company and finding a pleasant wife I could deceive. *Reject, reject, reject!*

A life that was someone else's dream, and not mine. *Reject, reject, reject!*

Lavelle had been right. Other people's dreams are no basis for a life. We must seek as hard as we can, as a matter of emergency, to find our own dreams, our own lives.

My father insisted our Bloomsbury palace be called Bowen House. It was all I could do to stop him having the name chiselled into the lintel above the front door. He decided that there had to be a great society party – a debut – to launch me, the grand new house and our entwined future in the world. I felt only dread at the prospect. I would be back at one of those awful parties in Paris, still trying to find aristocrats who would deign to speak to me, yet this time it would be my own event. Without my knowledge, a woman named Jennings was taken on, who provided advice to those arranging great social events. Jennings asked whether we were hoping to be 'lavish' or 'discreet'. 'Lavish,' my father said. 'Discreet,' I said, and my father looked angry. 'Lavish,' he repeated.

It was agreed that my father would not be present for the debut. It was he who suggested it, though Jennings agreed much too eagerly. She nodded emphatically and said the idea was 'splendid ... well-judged'. It was embarrassing that she so clearly felt that my father did not belong at such an occasion. I was angry that she should not hide her social contempt – towards the man who was paying for the entire thing, and paying her too! – but I noted that my father did not resist. My father was not even English, so the contempt of one race for another made my blood cold in my veins. But this was England, and each of us understood our place. Of course, there was a deeper irony underneath: it was my parents who wanted all this, wanted me to leave them behind and become a 'better' person than them. It was me who realised that their dream was not possible. And yet here I was, continuing the charade.

The day of the party arrived too quickly. I had hardly time to think. Every level of life at Bowen House was at some form of fever pitch. Chocolatiers in St James's were sent to for the finest assortments, elaborate fruit arrangements adorned the hallway and the skins of apples and lemons were carefully pricked with needles so that their sherbet scent perfumed the air. It only made me want to puke. The whole day, I was rigid with shock. I felt like someone who had awoken inside his own coffin.

The grand ballroom we had built on the first floor was to be the setting for my entrance into society. The room – seventy feet by forty-five and opening out onto a great balcony – was ruled large enough to accommodate our guests. Jennings had said it was necessary to purchase at least six hundred blooms. Musicians were to be hired, of course, but even since my return the fashion had changed. A large ensemble, consisting of string and woodwind players, was now the done thing. The style of music, the so-called classical style, had to be pretty and evocative. No lugubrious religiosity. No more contrapuntal considerations of the soul. These days, people wanted to dance. I wondered at the parties we had attended in Paris where no one danced at all. Things would have to change, even in Paris. Jennings explained what was 'in' and what was 'out', and my father listened to her patiently, simultaneously observant and bored.

'What if no one comes?' I asked, out of sheer, unhappy malice.

'Beg pardon?' she snapped.

'What if no one comes?'

'Oh,' she cried, 'they will come. You make enough noise, enough fuss, and they will come!'

Newly recruited cooks spent two days preparing moulded mousses of salmon and champagne, neat little cutlets tied with paper bows, and pastry baskets filled with gleaming, candied fruits. I tried to eat some, but the sugar seemed to stick to my lips and to the roof of my mouth. They were overpoweringly cloying and made me feel nauseous. Jennings sent out for several crates of champagne and uncut ice to keep it cold. I had a new suit for the occasion made from expensive silk in vertical stripes of white-gold and silver-blue. I had an excellent white wig and a coiffeur came to brush it out and powder it into a soft bluish grey. Jennings said she believed my face should be powdered, but my lips unpainted and no beauty spot. She wanted me to be as pale as possible. The artificial look was very in that year. Better not to show an inch of natural skin. 'A silvered Apollo!' she declared, but I know I am no such thing. I am thin and dark – not ugly, but certainly no Apollo. She tied my cravat herself and placed it with a diamond pin, and when I complained that I could hardly breathe, she shook her head. 'Good, it must be tight! Cravats are most attractive when they are tight.' The most attractive cravat I had ever seen hadn't even been done up properly, and it showed plenty of natural skin.

Eight o'clock arrived, and I had to go and take my place at the doorway to the ballroom to receive the attendees. My father had left at seven-thirty – gone in good time to hide himself away at Red Lion Square. Did he dine with my mother that night, knowing that I was safely out of the house? Did they delight in the knowledge that they had defeated me enough to get me to this point, rescued from the wreckage of their dreams? Or did she remain sequestered in her bedroom, alone with her griefs and accusations?

A trickle of guests were announced, the names decidedly unimpressive. Then more people came. I felt a deep sense that I wished to be away from there, that I had woken up and realised all of this was a fantasy. The room began to fill. There were conversations all around, delivered with great, theatrical animation. There was some dancing when the first ladies arrived, and I danced too, without joy, without sensuality. We formed into large battalions – men on one side, women on the other – arranged as if to commence war. We did *contredanses* with their complex rules that everyone knew. We paraded and turned and stuck our noses in the air and took dainty, over-practised steps. The new music played, all stagey, whimsical levity. As each dance ended, everyone applauded the musicians and each other, lightly tapping fingertips into cool, gloved palms. Good people were performing their roles: who could be the most *distingué*, and who the most *soigné*. My nausea had not quit me. But the object of disgust was not them; it was myself.

Jennings came to my side, and asked me why I was not making conversation. 'Make conversation!' she urged. 'Be a success! You only need to be ambitious to be a social success!' *Oh*, I thought, *is that all you need to be?* I went up to one group and introduced myself as their host. We had never met before. There were shallow bows all around.

'I am surprised,' one fellow was saying, looking me dead in the eye, 'that it is as nice as it is. There is *some* taste here.'

Another offered, in a voice very nearly well-meant, 'I expect that you had to find some sort of person to tell you how to do it. The building, I mean. The architrave, and such.' I talked about the architect in an erudite manner. As I talked, they stared at me blankly, as one does at a menagerie rhinoceros – a remarkable beast and nothing else. When I could say no more, they nodded briskly, 'Very good,' and turned away.

At half past nine, there was something of a commotion as a party of new arrivals entered. People turned and a buzz of excitement passed around the room, which meant someone of very good Quality must have appeared. Jennings flocked to my side and whispered, 'Who is it?' People were announced: a Pelham, a Granville and a Cavendish. These were the top drawer, as good Quality as could have been hoped for. Jennings looked as pleased as punch. 'It's a miracle such folk have come *here*,' she said. 'You must make an excellent impression.'

I looked up at the entrance and saw the men there, dressed in the most impeccable way. Each of them was staring above the heads of the little people, managing to look simultaneously amused and unimpressed. Out of earshot, I saw them exchange comments to each other, which – I could tell from the pinch of their lips and the roll of their eyes – were not kind. Oh, I was used to cruelty – *his* cruelty, the most jaw-droppingly exquisite of all – but that had been run through with humour and style. What were these powdered cadavers in the best velvets and silks to do with that, with their cold savageries designed for spite and nothing else? Jennings tapped my shoulder and hissed, 'Go on, *speak!*'

And so, every step I took getting heavier, I went up to the three young, fine men and bowed and told them who I was, which they evidently thought amusing. 'You have come to us to introduce yourself?' the first man said. 'How very … *egalitarian* of you, Mister Bowen.'

'How delightful to be compelled to be introduced to you, Mister Bowen,' another said. 'Is there champagne?'

In my panic, I did not remember which one was a Pelham and which a Cavendish and Granville.

'What an effortful party!' said the third man. 'You really have gone to a *great deal* of effort.' He sniffed. 'And it shows.'

They each had a nosegay tied to their waistband. One – the Pelham, I think – lifted his now.

'Is it true that your father came from nothing … in *Wales*?'

'Yes,' I said.

'Well,' he continued, 'some excellent persons are Welsh these days. The Earl of Pembroke, for example. He's a first-rate fellow. Does your father know him?'

I saw another of them suppress a smile. 'I do not think that Harry Pembroke is all that Welsh, you know. I was two years beneath him at Eton.' The man proceeded to make a series of squawks and yelps and everyone laughed. 'His wife is Georgie Marlborough's sister, you know.'

'What, old cross-eyed Bessie?'

'Yes, indeed. She's great friends with the Queen now—'

'Is she? *Quelle grimpeuse!* Those German conversation lessons her mother insisted upon have paid off!'

Again, black-beaked laughter. *Grimper*: to climb. They were insulting this woman, but of course, in truth, they were insulting me.

'This is all very modern, don't you think?' a possible Pelham said. 'Very enlightened.'

'Enlightened?' I asked.

He smiled, a little awkwardly. 'For us all to be here –' he dropped his voice conspiratorially '– in such a … *meritocracy.*'

What black magic made me turn away from them in that moment? It was hot in that room and my eyes were burning. I had had enough. I was still in someone else's dream, and that dream was a nonsense. I suddenly knew that I could not go on.

'Well, really!' cried the Pelham, outraged that someone as low as me could reject their company. Was Jennings standing somewhere, hand to her throat, crying, 'Mister Bowen! *Mister Bowen!*'? I would reject her, too.

I put my fingers to my cravat and pulled at it. Its diamond pin shot out, flying down onto the floor. It was then I saw a figure in the doorway, watching me. Wearing a coat of gold silk brocade, his cravat was undone, his unadorned skin glowed, his flaxen head was uncovered, his sapphire-blue eyes were shining on me, filled with amused mischief. I had wondered at what devilish strength had entered me, and now I knew. I said his name, like it was part of the dark spell: 'Horace ...'

With his hair swept back from his face, his hands on his hips, he seemed like a man made of gold. He was looking straight at me, laughing. At once, I felt it throughout my body: my desire, my fear, my joy, my anger, my relief. I blinked slowly. My heart was thudding in my chest. Blood was pounding in my throat. He kept smiling.

I walked towards him. He spread his hands wide to display himself, and his smile grew into a grin, almost into a delicious dark laugh. 'Have you forgotten me already?' he asked. I felt my chest falling short of breath. My eyelids flickered, my tongue swelling in my mouth.

'How did you know?' I asked.

'All of London knows about this party. It was you who forgot to send me an invitation. Are you enjoying the company of your disgusting new hypocrite friends here? Or would you like me to get a musket and shoot them all dead?'

'What did you say?' I whispered.

He arched an eyebrow. 'Shoot. Them. All. Dead.'

I was numb, astonished, happy, afraid. 'Do you remember,' I began carefully, 'the first night we met, that you said that you had come to save me? Do you remember from what you were going to save me?'

He nodded. His grin had not left him. How beautiful he looked, the handsome gilded man, with his hand outstretched towards me.

'From your fate,' he said, a beat on each word. 'From your upbringing. And from the world.'

I put my hand in his, feeling it warm and strong. His fingers closed around mine, and he pulled me away from my own party. It was as if he were winged – the real Apollo – and we were flying, out into the freshness of the night. And all I could hear behind me was Jennings shouting, 'Mister Bowen! Mister Bowen! Mister Bowen, come back!'

I did not.

Lavelle's laughter was riotous, a different kind of music amid the empty, half-built streets of Bloomsbury, echoing through the skeletons of the mass building site. He ran and I ran, following him in his dazzling display. I was always running after him; is that the nature of love? We ran until we crossed the Theobalds Road, breathlessly diving back into the old city, and all the while, I did not know what it meant that he was back.

Soon, Lavelle and I were pushing into the heart of London's iniquity. Whores stood on the street corners of St Giles, their cheeks painted like fairy-tale red apples, their eyes hard with need. A tooth puller had gathered a crowd as he pinned a guardsman down and plunged his pliers deeper and deeper into the soldier's bloodied mouth. The patient's legs squirmed and kicked as each great rooted tooth was extracted. The taverns roared with drinkers, and men sat in the gutter, cross-eyed with gin, their wigs slipping from their heads. Lavelle said that we should walk down to the river at Vauxhall and go across on a night barge to the torchlit pleasure gardens. There will be diversion there, he said, and laughed salaciously. We could catch a carriage down to Westminster Bridge. 'Let's walk through the meadows at Pimlico and even on to Chelsea, if you don't mind getting your shoes wet in the bog.'

'It's the middle of the night,' I said. 'I am not going on a country walk. We'll get robbed.'

'What do you want to do, then?' he asked.

'I want to talk.'

He arched an eyebrow. 'We are back in London, where sin is king. What is there to talk about in London? In London, people don't talk. They buy. They fuck. They drink.'

He turned away from me. I understood he was afraid of what I might say. Near us was a young man, perhaps seventeen or eighteen years old, with red hair back-combed up into a simulacrum of a woman's wig. He wore rouge on his cheeks and through his unbuttoned shirt his chest was bare and muscular. His 'wig' was decorated with a crown of pale narcissus buds, like a fairy-tale Christ come to give absolution with his arse. He was one of the molly boys who sold themselves openly in this part of town, and who patterned the streets from here all the way down to Covent Garden. Before I went on Tour, I hadn't known that such boys existed. This was not the education my mother had anticipated.

'All right, duckie?' the young man asked, eyeing Lavelle and me directly, but speaking softly, prettily. 'Looking for some diversion, is it?' He arched his eyebrow so high I thought it might peel over the top of his head. ''Cause I've got something you could both divert right up.'

Lavelle laughed, enjoying the filth. 'Did your mother teach you to speak like that?'

The molly boy gave a curt, intelligent smile. 'No, sir, it was your father. He's my best customer.'

'My father is dead,' Lavelle said, grinning.

The molly boy pursed his lips. 'What did he die of, sir? Embarrassment, was it?'

Lavelle obviously liked his cheek. The molly boy seemed to know precisely what to say, and where his power lay.

'I want to talk,' I said again. Lavelle looked at me. Something twitched on his forehead. The night was all around us, London lit by torches, but its darkness – and retribution – seething all around. I knew then that my mother was right: I was staring at the Devil, with whom I was still in love.

We pushed through the noise and debauchery to a tavern on the northern end of Endell Street. Lavelle fetched a serving girl to bring us tankards of ale while I went to sit down in a quiet corner, away from the fainting heat of a fire on which the bodies of piglets had been suspended. I found a small, latched window and opened it. The air ran in, clearing the tobacco smoke and sickly-sweet smell of crackling pork fat. I watched Lavelle talking to the girl. I saw how he kept his eyes on her attentively, said something saucy which made her laugh. I could see his charm and handsomeness at work. Another version of him could have been a great success in society – a friend to everyone. But he had wrecked his own chances, whether by accident or design I did not know.

Once he was sitting, we stared at each other for what felt like such a long time. He grinned marvellously, awfully, the whole while. The serving girl returned with two pewter tankards, foaming with pinkish ale.

'Want some piglet, loveys?' she asked. I shook my head. 'A penny a slice.'

'No, thank you,' I said and she smiled and turned on her heel, her eyes lingering on Lavelle for a second, but this time he did not reciprocate. Her smile faded.

'Listen to you,' Lavelle said, 'with your fine English manners.'

'Edgar died,' I said. 'Did you hear?'

He nodded. 'I knew.'

He was staring at me very intently. 'From whom did you find out?' I asked.

A small, knowing smile was on his lips. 'An old friend of yours.'

'Who?'

'Augusta Anson,' he said.

'How do *you* know Augusta Anson?'

'I don't, or at least I didn't. After you left, I lived for a while with a cardinal in Ravenna.' He flicked his eyebrows up and down. 'He desired me for a catamite, but the old fool could hardly get it up so it was good money for little inconvenience.' He wanted me to laugh but I could not. His eyes hovered on mine, uncertain for a moment. He took another sip of his drink. 'Are you going to drink your ale?'

'Are you going to answer my questions?' I picked up my tankard and drank. He wiped the slick of foam from my lips.

'Have you not heard of her scandal, Benjamin?' he asked. I had not. 'She had a child, unmarried. She is quite ruined.'

This amazed me, not because I could not believe it of her, but that such a thing could have been allowed to become common knowledge: a child born out of wedlock to a well-born woman. Her family would have moved heaven and earth to keep the secret. It seemed so ridiculous.

'Was it you who started this rumour, Horace?'

He laughed uproariously. 'How clever! Oh, I wish I had, but no. It's a delicious rumour, isn't it?'

He sipped his ale. Was it conceivably true about Augusta? Such a story of destruction, even for one as heartless as she, gave me no pleasure. Augusta's soul was as black as the bottom of the sea, but I did not want her destroyed. Some part of me would rather she were in a mountaintop *castello* somewhere, gloriously beautiful and severe, married to a Lombard prince. 'Edgar's death …' I began to say. 'I ought to blame you for what you did, revealing the secret I told you about us – what, just to hurt us?'

He stared at me pitilessly. 'Suicides have their self-destruction in them, like a disease. Nobody else can be blamed for someone taking their own life.'

I suspected this was true, but it irritated me that he could so easily remove himself from blame. 'But you must have known what damage it would cause, telling English people about who – what – my brother and I were.'

'What about the hurt you caused me?' he said.

'What hurt?'

'When you told me to leave.' He shrugged. 'Didn't you see how much you wounded me?'

I was amazed at his cheek. 'What about that boy at Isola Sacra? Have you forgotten him, Horace?'

His eyes flared with annoyance. 'Oh, what about him?' I grunted in disbelief. 'No, go on, what about him? Could your feelings for me be so weak as not to withstand *that*?

You want to play bourgeois fools' games with me? Let's go. I will eviscerate you, and you know it.' His fury silenced me. Seeing that, he relented. I don't think he wanted to batter me, or even to upset me. And this was Lavelle, who would garrotte his own grandmother if need be. 'Look,' he began again, 'I am sorry Edgar is dead. What I did was mean, cruel – it was …' He searched for the right words. 'I was unhappy. I felt like you had abandoned me. But what Edgar did, he did to himself.'

What he said about abandonment struck hard. I understood so much of who Lavelle was. That revelation felt as close to the truth as almost anything he had ever said to me. I began to feel the air moving in from the window growing colder, and suddenly it felt like autumn again. 'Can we shut that?' I asked, getting up to pull the window closed. Immediately, the air inside the tavern became thick with a fug of pig fat and tobacco smoke. I felt beads of sweat pricking between my shoulder blades, beads that broke and ran down the skin along my spine. Lavelle signalled to the barmaid – renewing his winking charm – to bring more drinks, though I had hardly started mine.

We took turns telling versions of the last year of our lives. Lavelle's was all strangeness, whereas mine was all convention. He told me how, after I had left Rome, he had been filled with despair. He said this in a matter-of-fact way, not expecting me to feel shame or to apologise. Some weeks later, he met a young heiress of great wealth whom he hoped to deflower and either marry or blackmail. The heiress's father sent ruffians to break his skull, and he barely escaped with his life. After that, he went north and met his impotent cardinal. There had been some argument over money – I would guess that Lavelle had stolen from him. He then drifted through Italy and back to France, pursued by creditors all the way. He told me all this as if it were a mildly funny tale in which someone else were the protagonist. But it was not funny, not at all.

'And what of you?' he asked. 'What is your story?' I spoke to him of my sense of disappointment, of defeat, of deep unhappiness, of the sense that I had imprisoned myself. When I was done, his fingers fell on my forearm and rubbed it gently. It was a brazen act, there in the middle of London. Englishmen do not touch each other. To do so is to condemn themselves in the eyes of their friends and wives. I stared at his hand touching me, its broad knuckles, the skin still freckled by the sun, the fat, blueish veins running to his wrist. I looked up at him and asked the only question I had left: 'Why are you back, Horace?'

He held my gaze. 'You know why,' he whispered.

My chest tightened. 'Do I?' Three disgusting words: would he say them? No, of course he would not. I think, in his mind, he had just said three words – 'You know why' – and he believed I would infer from them what he really meant. 'I don't know if I can forgive you,' I said.

He sat watching me, saying nothing. Then his gaze fell away to one side. 'Benjamin, you have already decided to forgive me.'

'What?'

He repeated with total command. 'Benjamin, you have already decided to forgive me.' He was staring at me like a fairground hypnotist. 'You have already decided to forgive me, and you already know it, too.'

I was staring at him, but the awful truth was that he was right. I had. There was nothing in the universe that could stop me forgiving him.

'Finish your drink,' I said.

He grinned and as he stood I saw the line of his penis hardening in his breeches. And I cannot deny its effect on me, the knowledge that just my proximity – and the proximity of sex with me – could make that happen.

We went back to his lodging-house, in the Huguenot district around Soho Square, only a few minutes' walk away. I entered his room, which was small and tattered. He lit a solitary candle. There was a bed, a wash bowl, a jug and a mirror – nothing more, save his clothes slung around the room.

Closing the door, he lifted his hand and softly touched my cheek, stroking it with his finger. His hand was still on my face, his thumb moving to touch my lips. My penis grew hard as he reached in to kiss me. A man's penis is always a traitor to his best intentions. We lowered down onto the little bed. He removed his shirt, and I reached up to try to keep my mouth connected with his. There was not a scrap of fat on him. I slipped my breeches down, not even past the knee. We were still kissing as I did it, so that we became a mistimed dance of hands and mouths. As he moved, he removed his breeches too. Then he was entirely naked, and I almost wholly dressed. His penis was huge and hard before me. I remember the feeling of it as it brushed my buttocks and found my hole. I held my breath, waited for the pain and then, when that passed, felt the thrill of our connection, the sensation of his weight as he turned me over and pressed himself deeper inside me. His hands, flat and warm, pushing my shirt up my back. After that, I remember nothing, nothing at all, nothing except a blinding sense of completeness. Of happiness.

His orgasm immediately followed mine. Then he slipped out of my body and fell against me, turning my face to his, laughing, his kisses finding my wet mouth when our faces had not an inch between them. Afterwards, we lay silent on the bed, dazed, slick with sweat and panting. Only slowly did the peremptory command of our desire reveal itself: I was still wearing my shoes and my breeches were a tourniquet around my ankles. I kicked off my shoes which clonked down onto the floorboards, and I pulled off the breeches completely, laughing at our ridiculousness. I turned against his body. His arm swept lightly over mine.

'I have thought of you so much,' I said, feeling him shift his body – still raging with heat – closer to mine until we were entirely face to face.

'Of what did you think?'

'All the nonsense you said to me.'

'Ha! I meant every word.'

'I know you did.'

'I never lie.' He was looking straight at me. We were silent a while. He moved his face downwards slightly, his lips just brushing my shoulder. 'What shall we do next?' he asked.

'Next?' I did not understand.

'How shall we continue our great adventure? Shall we stay here, or go away? We can chase girls, or we can do this, or we can go back to Venice, or off to New York, and find a new way of being.'

'Do you mean that you and I should leave London?' He said yes. He said, of course, as if it were ludicrous that we might not. 'And how should we live, Horace?'

'We are young and we are beautiful,' he said, self-satirising. 'And you, you have all your erudition – and me, I have whatever it is that I am.' I laughed as he said it, and he laughed too. But then his laughter stopped. 'Or do you want to stay here, in your brand-new house and live your parents' dreams, and spend years waiting to become the greatest passenger-liner owner in the world, and when you are eighty years old look back at your life and think only of me and your regrets?'

'No,' I said. 'I don't want that.'

'We will go away,' he said, more to himself than to me. 'The two of us ...' He smiled.

'I thought you wanted to reject my love, the fake marriage.'

'Who said anything about such things?' he said. 'We will fuck who we want to fuck. We will be free. We will live as two souls intertwined, not as man and wife chained together, as miserable as galley slaves. Who wants to be a husband? Who wants to be a wife? I never said that I did not want to be with you, Benjamin; in fact, I want quite the reverse. But if you come to me hoping for a ring and a sweet proposal, I am not that person.'

'Reject, reject, reject,' I drawled.

'Do your best to accept me as I am,' he said. 'And I will do my best to accept you too.'

There is very little acceptance in the world, least of all in love.

'On what should we live, then?' I asked.

'On our wits, of course. Our youth. Our beauty. Our *feral* intelligence.' He grinned and squeezed his arm around me more tightly. 'And your parents' money.'

I could not help but laugh. 'Oh, they will be only too thrilled to pay for us to gad off to the Colonies together. I am sure they will be very quick to open their coffers for us to fill our pockets.'

He was blinking so gently, like the softest heart-beat. 'I mean it,' he said. 'We should take their money.' His eyes were gleaming. 'We should take what we deserve.'

He slipped away from me and padded barefoot, naked except for his shirt, across the room. Moonlight fell on him from the tiny window, so that his taut limbs were painted pale and long. He walked to a little console table and opened the drawer. From inside, he pulled something wrapped in an old piece of hessian. He brought this to me and placed it before me on the bed. 'What is this?' I asked. 'A present?'

He laughed. 'With what should I buy presents? Air?' he said. 'Unwrap it.'

I put my hands to the rough cloth, its fibre so raw it pricked the skin, first one fold and then another, to reveal what was inside: a small, sharp fruit knife. I glanced up at him. 'What is this, Horace?'

'To protect ourselves,' he said. I did not understand.

'From whom do we need protection?'

'From whoever comes to harm us now,' he said. Then he smiled, reached down and picked up the knife and the hessian from the bed, wrapped it and put it back into the drawer.

'Why are you back, Horace?' I asked.

He stepped towards me and took my face in his hands, drawing his mouth close to mine, but not quite kissing. Of course he did not answer. And all the while, the knife was in the drawer.

The morning was crisp and autumnal – light and yellow. I walked from Soho to Red Lion Square, not even ten minutes, but every footstep growing heavier than the last. I was fearful, yes, but not quite frightened. I felt brave even as I felt trepidation. I had the truth on my side; or my version of the truth, at least. When I got home, the surfaces were still shivering and the servants deep in gloom. I guessed that my father had spent the morning shouting.

My parents were waiting for me, like executioners, seated around the table in the drawing room. Here, over two years before, we had conceived a plan. More than a year and a half ago, we all made oaths we did not know we would not be able to keep. My father, for the first time in years, had not gone down to Moorgate on a weekday. He had remained at the house to confront me. It would be a reckoning, I knew. My mother's face was white with rage, its pallor framed by her shroud of black satin and lace.

As soon as I closed the drawing-room door, my father told me to sit. I pulled out a chair and immediately he started to rage. He had been woken at first light by a servant holding a note from Jennings. She had never known such a thing: a host – 'a *parvenu* host' – leaving his own debut! How can such a thing be countenanced? How can such a situation be explained or saved? 'Ruination,' she had written, that most frightening thing for the English. All through my father's rage, my mother's eyes were fixed on me, her jaw set hard.

'You fled your own party?' my father was asking uncomprehendingly.

'I did not flee,' I protested thinly.

'Jennings told us everything, Benjamin,' he said. 'She told us how you were not good company to everyone! She told us how you ran away from your own party! I cannot imagine this thing! To run away from your own party? To run away from everything we have carefully planned!'

I lifted my head slightly backwards and closed my eyes, just for a moment. 'I did not run away,' I repeated, but of course, that was precisely what I had done.

My mother finally spoke. 'Why can you not be better?'

She asked it so seriously, with a scientist's curiosity, my surprise made me open my eyes. We were looking at each other nakedly. 'Better, Mother?'

'A better son,' she said firmly. 'A better man. A better thinker. A better ... a better *human being*.' Her hand curled into a tight ball and thumped the table. 'Why have you done this to us? After everything we have done for you, Benjamin, after Edgar has died—'

I had had enough. 'Oh, stop it, Mother, please – this has nothing to do with Edgar's death. You created this plan for me. For Edgar and me. But now I realise that it's not possible to just instruct someone to want a particular life. People can want whatever life they want and you can't stop them from wanting other things to you.' Of course, the truth is that it is perfectly possible to do so, but what is not possible is to guarantee the person will agree to it. My parents were staring at me, not just as though I were a madman, but also quite possibly their own assassin.

'Want?' my father cried. 'What has "want" got to do with it?'

My thoughts about my father's life flew back at me, overwhelming me with anger. 'Didn't you get the things you wanted, Father? You came to London, you had to work hard – I admire how hard you worked – but wasn't it what you wanted? And this plan, it's what *you* – what you two – want. Your whole life has been what *you* want, Father. But what about what *I* want? Don't I get to ask what *I* want?'

My father let out a hard, dismissive cluck of laughter. 'There is hardly a man in London who would refuse what your mother and I have devised for you.'

He had walked straight into a trap I had not meant to construct. 'You are right, Father, there are very few. And yet here I am and I don't want it. I want something else.'

He slammed the table with the flat of his palm. 'Do you know how much I have spent on this house? You know the plan that we have made, Benjamin, and how much we spent on your education? You know that the plan was that you should progress from what we have created, that you should become accepted, make good friends—'

'I never asked you for any of this, Father!' I yelled, so forcefully that my parents fell silent. 'This was your plan, and it was an idiotic one. You and Mother educated us, filled our heads with Voltaire and Montesquieu and Latin grammar and fucking Suetonius, and you told us all we had to do was recite poetry and speak French, and we would be accepted. But we were not accepted—'

'Lies!' my mother cried. 'In Paris, Edgar had many fine friends—'

I could stand it no further. How dare she accuse me of lies? She who had founded our whole lives on lies! 'We met your cousin, Mother, in Paris. Did Edgar write and tell you that?'

My father's back went rigid. My mother blinked in surprise. Her lips moved very slightly. 'What?' she whispered, confused.

'Yes, your cousin.'

'I don't understand, Benjamin – my cousin?'

I paused a moment. I let the moment billow out into seconds. I was looking at my mother, Mrs Rachel Bowen.

'A man named Cardoso, from Amsterdam.'

Her jawline tensed.

'Say nothing,' my father hissed at me. 'Keep your mouth fucking shut, Benjamin!'

My mother breathed out, a short, sharp, panicked breath. She raised her chin, in the imminence of the blow.

'He told us all about you, Mother. He told us that you were a Jew, and that you have been ostracised by your community. I see now that is why we shut ourselves up in this house, away from the world, so that no one could ever point at us and say: "Jew."'

I am not sure what I expected from her then: rage or relief, revelation or retribution. She gazed at me blankly, coldly, in the manner of one who is almost glad their crime has been discovered. Finally, they can stop running. 'Do you want to know what killed Edgar, Mother? Do you? All those years, you thought if you sequestered us here, the world would not find out who we truly were. You thought you could turn us into these perfect little Englishmen. You thought if you never mentioned your people, your faith, we could not be impugned by its fact. But the world doesn't do things, or forget things, or not find things out just because you and Father rule it should not. When the world did find out, Edgar and I were not ready for it. So, Mother, do you really want to know why Edgar killed himself?'

'Be quiet!' my father commanded. 'I am your father and I order you to be silent!'

'Someone found out that we were half-Jews, Mother, and they told us that we would never be accepted in society, and Edgar went and drowned himself in the harbour. If you had raised us to know that truth, we would have been all right. We would have found a way to survive, just like your relatives, your cousin in Paris, did. It might have been hard at first, but it would have been all right. We might have been proud. We might have asked you questions. We might have not been made to feel ashamed or afraid. You raised us to be a secret from ourselves. And now Edgar is dead—'

My mother was silent. My father flickered with fury.

'You miserable *cunt*,' he hissed. He screamed that he was going to tear out my fucking tongue and launched himself at me across the table, scattering the china and the candelabra to the floor. As I fell backwards out of my seat, he started to slap my face, his hand smacking hard against my skin. Then my mother was pulling him off me, screaming at him to stop. A footman, hearing hubbub and fearing a robber or villain had entered, arrived, but upon seeing the scene he crept back into the doorway. He dared not intervene. Finally, under my mother's influence, my father let me go. My mother covered her face with her hands, sobbing softly. My father hung there, silent, staring at the floor, his shoulders hunched. I knew that I had to leave. I said that I was going to my room, and neither of them resisted. But leaving the drawing room, I turned right, walked down the stairs, and went out onto Red Lion Square. Only as the front door slammed behind me did I hear my mother yelling my name.

The sun had grown strong by the time I reached Soho; it must have been near midday. At the top of Greek Street, I came out onto Soho Square where groups of French Huguenots were gathered primly in its shadowed corners. Arriving at Lavelle's lodging-house, I climbed the dark stairs to his room. Inside, in the place where our bodies had come back together, Lavelle was still sprawled naked on his bed. 'You look like you have eaten a spoonful of mustard,' he said. I thought for a moment that I should tell him what had happened, but instinctively, I knew I must stay silent. He would be satirical, ironic, brutal, and I did not want that. I just wanted to lie next to him quietly, wrapped in his arms. I didn't want anything else from him just then. I took my clothes off and moved back down onto the bed, and without saying anything, he drew my body towards his. In a few minutes, he had fallen back to sleep, and I closed my eyes, lulled by the rhythm of his breathing.

Later, we decided to go for a walk from Soho into Mayfair, with its not-quite-new houses, already out of fashion. From there, we strolled down towards Piccadilly, where they were now building houses out as far as Hyde Park Corner. Lavelle was amazed. He asked when on earth they would stop building in London. Never, I joked – but the joke has turned out to be true. As we walked, people of fashion – expensively dressed, exquisitely confident – squawked like parakeets. Lavelle made loud remarks about them: 'My God, the idiocy just drips off him!' 'Her décolletage is low enough to see what is left of her soul!' Now and then, I nudged and shushed him, but all to no avail. And what avail did I desire? I wanted him like this – awful, fearless and awe-inspiring in equal measure.

We reached the Park and dawdled around Kensington Gore's open, muddy fields. Lavelle said that he hated the countryside, leaning forwards and peering through gnarled hawthorn branches at the hidey-holes beyond. We walked back towards the more manicured paths, now given over to afternoon strollers and teashops. We sat at one which advertised the latest thing in London, Chelsea buns. Girls dressed as milkmaids poured thin tea from huge pots decorated in a faux country style. It was the very zenith of new refinement, the sort where metropolitans sit and pretend that they have always done so, since before Chelsea buns were even invented. In groups, men just like Sir Gideon Hervey or Sir Percy Paget guffawed loudly to each other about things they bellowed were *de trop*. Or they paid court to confident, pretty ladies, in full wig and lead-white *maquillage*. The ladies teased or ignored them or laughed at their jokes, in some unending, circular game. Now and then one would punctuate the game to marvel: 'Well, this is nice, isn't it?' Overhearing this, Lavelle and I only had to look at each other and we'd burst into laughter.

The lightest breeze was moving up the gradual incline of the Park to whisper to the vast city that lay to its east. 'We shall have to go away,' I said. I was not looking at him but I saw him turn to look at me. 'We shall have to live elsewhere.' I turned to him. 'Will you come with me?'

'You know I am coming with you. You *know* I am.' It felt good that he said it that way. 'But I have asked you before, Benjamin, on what shall we live?'

I thought about this. I had learned much in the shipping office – but did I want the two of us to run away, two tumbling lovers, so that I could sit the rest of my life doing the very thing from which I was fleeing? 'We could teach English.'

He laughed. 'To whom?'

I shrugged. 'To German princesses who hope to become the next Queen of Great Britain.'

He laughed again. 'Oh, the poor cows.' He paused. 'Who wants to be a teacher? It's just another living death.'

We finished our tea and I paid, then we walked across the gentle slopes of the Park. 'But we will need money,' he said. 'I have already told you what I think we should do.'

I tried to remember. 'Have you, Horace?'

'We will get money from your parents. We will take half of what they have and support ourselves on that.'

'*Half?*'

'I set my sights high,' he said self-mockingly. 'You cannot blame me for being ambitious.' I rolled my eyes, which did not please him. 'Why do they have any greater right to it than us?' he asked, in brighter outrage.

'They earned it. I think there must be some justice where those who earn get to spend.'

'*Justice?*' he cried, genuinely outraged. 'Are we not revolutionaries? Who cares who earned what? What do your parents care about fairness? When your father grinds some competitor into the dust, or charges too much for a ticket to New York, does he care about justice? They earned that money for you, in truth, because they love you, or some such nonsense, but they cannot give you conditions for their love, can they? What is the value of a love that comes with a contract?'

A very valid question for those who will never marry. 'Whatever has happened, I still love my parents, Horace. I don't want to harm them. I know you probably think I should reject some filial link, but I love them—'

'Do you?' he asked. '*Why?* Your parents are liars and manipulators and to whom did they lie and whom did they manipulate? You and your dead brother!'

Did I want from him softness, understanding? This was Lavelle: marvellous, maddening, unrepentant Lavelle. You love a man and then ask him not to be the person you fell in love with: a fool's game.

*N*ow was the point where we should – somehow – have turned and walked away. We could have gone down to the docks, with no money to buy a ticket. We could have stowed away on one of my father's ships and vanished to New York. Maybe we would have been happy and everything would have worked out for the best. We should have done that, but we did not.

Instead, we walked to where the new bridge at Westminster had been built a decade earlier by the famous architect James Gibbs. Stone columns rose like great petrified water-reeds out of the river. Cage-scaffolds made of cane had been thrown up around them, upon which the craftsmen had once performed like acrobats, unafraid of the crunching tides below. But now, only a few spare rods remained, rotting slowly, consumed by the water. Near the Parliament, green meadow had more or less been replaced by houses and shops.

We moved on from the elegant newness of Westminster back to rough old London. We followed the Thames to where the two cities touch, beneath the Savoy Hospital.

On such fine days, down there it was teeming with players and musicians, hawkers frying food or selling corn dollies or cheap fans for the heat. The river, glinting in the sun, was crammed with barges. Each one had a boy with a pole at the front, calling to his comrades as they negotiated the bridge. We pointed out things that amused us as we picked our way through the streets around old Charing Cross, past St Martin-in-the-Fields. Was this what our lives would be like when we left London, endless days like this? I suddenly became aware of people looking at us, but I did not know why.

I did not understand that people who hate sodomites are seers of a sort. They can divine a pervert's presence quite easily, and when we walk in couples, they will not stand for our provocations. In some ways, they are the best kind of moralist too. I saw the grimacing, grinning faces of those standing at their market stalls, as some silent whisper passed around about us. 'Where are *you* from, duckie?' cried one stall-holder. Another stepped out in front of our path. 'Hey, he asked you a question! Where are you from? Don't poofs like you answer questions from ordinary folk?'

I felt myself shudder with fear, but Lavelle rose to his full height. When he spoke, his voice was coldly amused and dismissive. 'I am Mister Horace Lavelle and this is Mister Benjamin Bowen, of the Bowen Maritime Company.' He paused and smiled brutally. 'And who are you?'

'Oh!' the first questioner said. 'Shipping, very nice!' He turned around to a gathering crowd. 'Does that mean you like it up the Leeward Passage, then, eh?' Everywhere, there erupted loud derisive laughter – that most violent, fear-inducing of sounds. Yet another man now began to shout from behind his stall: 'Shameless fucking mollies! Dirty fucking madge!' It was then I felt the horror, the shame. I remembered the article Herr Hof had cut out for me, of the two young men hanged at Tyburn for being lovers. A woman at the stall-holder's side, probably his wife, yelled too: 'This city is full of mollies these days – oh, they're fucking *disgusting*!'

I can feel it even now: the mounting hatred, the inevitability of violence, the fear in your gut, the knife brandished, suddenly, shockingly pointed at you. *At you*. The man who had stood in front of us lifted his fist and lunged at Lavelle, punching him in the face. All I heard was the deep thud of bone being struck. Other men joined in, throwing punches, braver now they were in company. The street's fists gathered in cowardly number, shrieking names: molly, sodomite, madge, faggot, poof. 'Kill them!' a young woman was shrieking, holding her baby close to her body. '*Kill them!*'

As in a nightmare, I heard Lavelle's screams as hands ripped at his clothes and tore at his unwigged scalp. Did I imagine seeing wafts of his hair, clawed from his scalp by good Christian fingers, glowing flaxen as they floated sunlit in the air? Feet kicked at our bodies. I felt blows against my back. Lavelle started to throw punches, but it was useless – we were engulfed by a murderous tide of fists and feet and fingers, viciously scratching, gouging, pounding and kicking. I knew they would kill us, that it was their moral duty to do so.

The men of St Giles rushed at us again, their blows rained down in a relentless rush; the women of St Giles demanded our deaths. It was their honour at stake. Our screams split the air. Somewhere a voice could be heard:

'It's gone too far!' But then another, in response: 'Punch the filthy things!' I felt those punches on me – the mob's hammer blows, the city's justice. We were finally those fennel bulbs ready to be thrown on a fire.

With the desperate energy of a drowning man breaking the surface of the water, I broke free of our attackers and became a mad whirr of fists. What did I know of fighting? Nothing. But that day – when we were close to death, closer than I had ever been – with what animal knowledge I cannot guess, I punched one man so hard I heard his cheekbone split.

The crowd drew back. Brave men in mobs falter when they see damage can be done to them. The normal man never expects the sodomite to strike him back: that is not the social contract. Normal men expect sodomites to be killed – that is their value, all they are worth. They certainly do not expect to be killed back – that is an unacceptable inversion.

I managed to drag Lavelle up from the ground, where he had fallen under stamping feet. Blood was everywhere, some of it ours, but mostly the other men's. A woman was screaming, not for what happened to us, but for the blood splattered on her unharmed face.

We began to run, bleeding but not vanquished, up Monmouth Street, pushing into the bodies of shocked onlookers. A sea parted before us: women pulled their children or their slaves out of our way, turned polite faces aside less we asked for help. The slave girls looked at these well-read, confused white ladies as if to say: from what violence do you think you are saving me?

Eventually we were north of the Theobalds Road, crossing into half-built Bloomsbury, until we came breathless to a stop. And as we did, we stared at each other, shocked and ashamed, terrorised – just as the good people of London had planned. Violence is humiliation. That is only half its power. But those who hurt the vulnerable know violence also brings shame. The people who beat us, and those polite ladies with their slaves – they all know this truth, perhaps society's only real truth. It is the centre of their power..

'We must get away from this city as soon as we can!' Lavelle was yelling, on the verge of tears.

'And go where?' I asked.

He shook his head. He did not answer my question.

'Your parents' money is yours,' he said. 'We cannot wait any longer. London is going to kill us. We could see any of these people again.' It shocked me, hearing how afraid he was. 'We are not safe here. I want to escape. I want to feel – I want *us* to feel safe.'

I saw tears in his eyes. 'We are utterly friendless. I know what you need to see,' he whispered. I had no idea what he meant. I went to touch his arm but he pulled away from me. 'Come with me,' he barked. 'I know what you need to see.'

'Where are you taking me, Horace?' I asked, but he stalked off before I had even finished the question. All I could do was follow him. I asked him again, what did he mean? But now he did not speak at all.

We staggered back west, in a haphazard direction, past the new British Museum, what used to be Montagu House. We crossed Bloomsbury Street; the road hardly laid there. We were darting around, but Lavelle seemed to know where he was headed. At some point, I realised that I had hurt my ankle. I was starting to limp a little, but I said nothing and neither did he. Finally, we arrived at a new square that had been built by the Duke of Bedford. It was very large with grand, modern houses on either side, and in the centre, a little garden was in the middle of being planted. Small trees grown in tubs had been taken out, lined in hessian, and waited for ground to be dug for them to be planted. Abruptly, Lavelle came to a stop on the square's west side, and plonked himself down on a half-finished pavement. I did not know if it was from exhaustion or confusion. 'Do you not want to sit in the garden?' I asked. There was space to do so even if it was still in progress.

'No,' he growled. 'I want to sit here.'

There was an odd determination to him.

'What is this, Horace?' I asked. He did not reply. 'Why are we stopping here?' Again, he said nothing. I sat down beside him, and watched him staring furiously out at the street and the beautiful, expensive houses beyond. 'Why are we here?' I asked again.

He did not return my gaze once. 'You'll see.' He was breathing slowly, very deeply, as if the guts of his lungs were filled with bile or blood. He was going to drown there, in the middle of Bedford Square.

'Can you give me a clue?' I half-laughed, but the laugh was a lie.

'I have lied to you,' he said. 'I want you to see the lie. You need to see the lie in order to know that I am speaking the truth about what we need to do.'

'What lie?' I asked. 'What are you talking about?' But again, he did not answer.

An hour passed in silence. I thought I might say that I would leave unless he told me the truth, but I did not.

I decided instead to let this play out, whatever this was. The time passed slowly, and I became more and more aware of the painful bruising on my body. Someone had stamped on my foot. Another had kicked my shoulder; the whole socket ached now. I thought of those people, all except the broken-cheeked man, sitting in taverns like heroes, telling tales of how they had saved London from two perverts.

Eventually, a carriage rolled up in front of the house we were facing. It was a tasteful and elegant Landau-type, with light-green painted panels and fine cherry-wood trims. The wheels were large and thin, very expensive but discreetly so. As the vehicle stopped, I could hear a woman's laughter: light, sharp and knowing. It seemed familiar, but my concentration broke as Lavelle got to his feet. He murmured, 'Come on.'

He marched towards the carriage. I followed him, just in time to see a very fashionably dressed gentleman helping a young woman out from the door. At the last moment, Lavelle stepped back a little so that I was standing in front, between him and the young couple. It was then I recognised the woman's laughter – arch and watchful – as she, beautiful and blue-eyed, smart in well-chosen, pale clothes, looked at me. It was Augusta Anson.

'Mister ... Bowen.'

She stood before me, and even in her momentary shock, how elegant, how perfect, how refined she looked. The man at her side asked, in one of those impenetrable, declamatory English voices:

'Gussie, who are these two *jagged* boys?'

Her blue eyes hovered over mine before switching to the fashionable young man at her side.

'May I present to you, Georgie, Mister Benjamin Bowen. Is it Bowen or *Bouen* now?' She smiled in her malicious way, then momentarily – a little confused – looked at my dishevelled appearance. 'Benjamin, this is the Earl of Mulford.' I bowed a little – he did not; it was not necessary for him to do so. 'Lord Mulford is my husband.'

Her husband? I flashed a look at Lavelle. 'But you said she was ruined. You said she had had a child in Italy.'

'I say—' began Lord Mulford.

'What?' Augusta cried, both amused and appalled. 'Who is this fellow, Benjamin? Why would he tell you such a thing?'

'Who *are* these scruffians, Gussie?' the Earl asked for a second time.

Augusta started inspecting my battered appearance again. 'Have you been fighting, Benjamin? In Paris, you were always very ...' she sighed, a sigh that knows well how to carve an insult '... neat.' Then she tittered. 'Did you *truly* think I had a baby?'

My emotions were running like water. 'He's dead. You know he's dead?' I said.

'Do you mean your brother?' she asked. 'Of course I know. Everyone in Italy heard the whole remarkable story.' English people use adjectives as weapons. To them, Edgar's death had been just another titbit – one of an endless line of anecdotes and gossip about fools one used *to have to* know. 'What's this about a baby?' She tittered again, her lovely, ugly laugh. 'Your friend is pulling your leg.'

I am not sure what made me continue into humiliation. 'I wondered if the baby had been Edgar's—'

'Edgar's?' she cried, again simultaneously amused and appalled. 'Oh, good grief, Benjamin, there is no baby! I never made it any further than Milan. I met Lord Mulford, Georgie here, at a ball there to receive the Archduchess of Austria and we fell in love—' She laughed again, both prettily and derisorily. A love match? It sickened me. In every romance you'll ever read, love is a reward for goodness. But here was Augusta Anson – one of the worst, least kind, least humane people I had ever met – richly rewarded with love, a magnificent house, an earl for a husband. Her poison and cruelty had brought her nothing but riches and happiness. And all the while, Edgar was still lying in an unvisited, flowerless grave in a Neapolitan churchyard. 'I never had cause to have a baby with your poor, dead brother. Good grief – me, mother of a ship captain's bastard!'

Her cruelty was so magnificent. Did its unrepentant enormity intimidate even the Devil? It must have, for Lavelle bolted again. As he ran, the heels of his shoes clattered, echoing in the four sides of the square. At once, I remembered the sound of my brother's shoes – ghost echoes – as he fled from me in the lanes that last day in Naples. A deep terror flooded in me. Those touched by suicide never forget the terror it brings.

I ran too. 'How extraordinary!' His Lordship observed witheringly. 'No, how ridiculous!' responded Her Ladyship, contemptuous.

I chased after Lavelle, calling his name. Near Tottenham Court Road, he stopped and doubled over, out of breath. Finally, he turned to face me, and put up his arms to hold me fast. 'I lied to you.'

'But why?' I asked. I realised my eyes were full of tears.

'I wanted you to think that Augusta Anson had been punished. I wanted you to think that there was some justice in the universe – but there is none. Just like I told you, justice is a myth. Look what just happened to us, our punishment for being who we are. Don't you see, Benjamin?' he said. 'You can't wait for justice to happen. It doesn't exist.'

Do the dead still love? Can the dead nurse broken hearts? Do they stare on jealously as the objects of their love live on, happily, unremorseful, hardly even remembering their existence? To what do we owe the dead, hearing their names besmirched by insults that they cannot hear themselves? Maybe nothing. Maybe what we owe, we owe to ourselves, to the living. I saw that Lavelle was right. Justice would not save us. We had to save ourselves, because no one else in the world would even think to protect us.

Everything became clear: I would go to my parents, I would ask them for money, and Lavelle and I would go away. Maybe I would say that one day we might come back, but I did not really believe that we would. Sometimes, I thought that Lavelle had come to save me. Once or twice, I thought that I had been sent to save him. But now I saw the truth: our task was to save each other.

I touched his hand. He looked at me. 'All right,' I said. He did not understand. 'What?'

'I'll do it. I'll go to my parents and ask them for money. We can go away.' A smile broke on his face. It was the most glorious, encompassing relief – from fear, from destruction, from death. 'But, Horace, I don't want to hurt them any more than I have to. I don't want to make things worse than they have to be.'

He nodded. 'All right.'

And then a dark little question appeared in my head. 'Do you have the fruit knife, Horace?'

'What?'

My voice became firmer. 'Do you have the knife?'

'Of course not,' he said. I started to pat the front of his coat to see if the knife would be revealed. My hands slammed against his chest, but all I could feel was the bone and muscle of his body. 'Stop it,' he cried. 'Benjamin, stop it! I don't have any knife!'

I felt a curious, seasick feeling. A form of dread I could hardly explain, which drove me to ask the question again:

'You don't have the fruit knife?'

'No,' he laughed.

'Are you sure?' I asked.

'Of course I don't!'

What can you do but trust the person you love?

We walked with purpose, in silence. No plans were made, no intricate murderous plots. We did not draw detailed maps or arm ourselves with pistols and gags. I said nothing more about the fruit knife, but its existence did not leave my head, not for a second. I began to wonder: is this really happening? Are we really going to do this? I turned and glanced at him. Lavelle was staring straight ahead, his eyes fixed on our future.

We crossed the Theobalds Road and soon arrived at Red Lion Square. The two of us stood looking up at the house in which I had grown up. Lavelle had never seen it before. We walked up to the front door, paused a second, and then I pulled the bell. Almost at once, the door opened and, from within, the footman bowed to me. 'Master Benjamin ...' I stepped over the threshold and then Lavelle did the same, causing the footman to step back. I asked if my father was home and the man said no, not yet. It was only a quarter to six. Suddenly dry-mouthed, I turned back to the footman. My eyes were flickering. I felt faint.

'Will you tell my mother that I am here with Mister Lavelle?'

The footman bowed and left. Lavelle turned and looked at me, his bright eyes flickering and flitting like butterflies over a summer meadow. I felt afraid, not of him precisely, but of what we might have become over the course of that day. Still, I ushered him inside my parents' home.

We walked upstairs to the drawing room. Once there, he did not look around or sit down. He walked straight to the bay window that faced out over the square. A breeze was in the trees, so that as the branches moved, diamonds of sunlight were cut on the glass in the window panes. I turned to him, the sickness in my stomach pulsing up into my chest and throat. 'I'm frightened,' I said.

'Don't be,' he replied. 'After today, we will be free.' He seemed so certain, and I felt anything but. The drawing-room door opened. My mother was, as was her way now, swathed in black – even her grey wig was covered with heavy black lace. Upon seeing Lavelle, a sudden coldness possessed her. Was she shocked by his beauty, or by his dishevelment, or maybe the surprise that he was, in fact, real, and not just a nightmare? Her eyes blazed with anger. Lavelle bowed and extended his hand to take hers to kiss; she recoiled from him. He reacted to her disgust. 'Madame,' he whispered softly, yet piquant with irony.

'You brought him here, Benjamin?' my mother said, looking to me. 'Why?' She gave a short, sarcastic laugh. 'You brought him here to hurt me, of course.'

'Mother, that's not true—' I started.

She spoke over me. 'Sit down, both of you. Whatever cruel game this is, let's get it done.' We did as instructed, and my mother began to inspect our appearance. 'Benjamin, have you … Have you been fighting?'

'No,' I murmured. Fear passes, but shame sticks to the soul.

'No, Madame,' Lavelle added, 'we were attacked in the street.'

Something in my mother stirred at hearing that her child had been attacked. 'Attacked? My God, are you all right?' We were not, of course, but shame drives you to say yes. '*Why* were you attacked?'

Lavelle's eyes switched to mine, and seemed amused. But it was not funny, none of it was funny. Only a few hours before, I had been lost in love. A day before that, I had been lost in despair. Now, we were running away. Violence had intervened and forced change.

'It doesn't matter, Mother,' I said.

'Doesn't matter?' she cried. 'I can see you have been hurt, Benjamin!'

Lavelle spread his hands like an innocent Christ. 'To perceive is to suffer,' he said. I saw my mother's cheek twitch. He had refreshed her anger.

'You quote Aristotle at me, sir? You quote Aristotle when you grind up my sons' bodies before my eyes?'

Lavelle's smile was darker than anything I had ever seen in him before. Once, in Vicenza, I had said to him that he was fascinated by my mother. I realised now that, in fact, he hated her. He was disgusted by her. But I did not understand why.

'I don't want to fight!' I yelled. 'I just want to say what we have to say and then leave.'

My mother let out a sharp gasp. 'Leave, Benjamin? What do you mean, leave?'

'I am going to go away, Mother. I cannot stay in London.'

A quick panic passed over her face. 'For how long will you go away, Benjamin? *For how long?*'

'I don't know,' I said. 'Maybe forever.'

Her eyes glazed over in a moment of confusion and emotion, but she did not cry. Instead she became cold and hard. 'And now you bring this beast here! The man who killed my Edgar! The man who drove him to his death!'

'Oh, for God's sake, Mother, no one killed Edgar. He killed himself.'

My mother started to protest, but Lavelle began to speak, with the most gorgeous, unflappable cool. 'Benjamin met me, and he changed, and I changed too. He realised that you had lied to him in the most appalling, unforgivable way – deceived him as no mother ever should – and he decided to live his own way and refuse your lies. Is it this you cannot forgive, more than the death of your son when he found out your lies?'

My mother's eyes flared. She had always believed in her own rightness, which was the same as believing in your own blamelessness.

'You killed my son, Mister Lavelle, I know it,' she hissed.

Lavelle sighed lightly, almost prettily. 'Oh, shall we play the Minute Game?' he asked. My mother's brow furrowed. I was suddenly swept back to that awful carriage ride from Aosta to Vicenza, when he had gutted Edgar, playing with him like a cat and mouse. 'Benjamin?' he said, keeping his eyes on my mother. 'Should you like to play the Minute Game?'

I took a step forward, put my hand on his arm to stop him. My mother's eyes – seeing us touch – flashed with repulsion. Perhaps I might have saved her if she had not done that. I let his arm go.

'I shall speak for one minute on the subject of the Bowen family and their rise through English society. I shall tell a story of a Welshman and a Jewess who met and fell in love, and how the lady's husband died so the two were free to marry.' He clucked with black delight. 'Oh, it *is* quite like a fairy tale! I shall tell how they sired two splendid sons, with bright brains and bookish interests, and told those boys that they were good Englishmen too, and bound to be loved by Englishmen. But you see, Madame, it was all a lie, as well you know. Englishmen are pickled in prejudice. Towards race and creed, of course – that is obvious to any sensible person – but more importantly, prejudiced to what they every day believe, so that when anything presents itself that might persuade them to change, they stand together, chorus-like, and holler: "No!"'

'Stop it,' my mother growled.

'Then how about the short version, Madame? If anyone killed your son, you did, for you failed to tell him the one thing he needed to know about himself: that he was different, that he had something in him that heartless good people would use against him. You didn't tell him that, and when he found out, he killed himself.' My mother's jaw was set, her eyes resistant.

Lavelle turned to me. 'Do you know why I have asked you so many questions about your mother? She is quite a fascinating person. Here is a woman who was clever, young and well-read. She understood that the true existence of Beauty was not in ephemeral things, but in books and philosophy and art. How blessed is the person who is both beautiful and who understands the true nature of Beauty. And yet the world had for her only a bitter truth. She was poor and so she married to acquire wealth, and when her husband died, she married again for love, and what did the world – or her world at least – do in response? It rejected her. It rejected her for who she was, and who the man she loved was. And what did your mother learn? Nothing. This intelligent woman looked at the world that had rejected her so harshly and she whispered to it, "Please, take my sons. Take my sons and love them. I will trust you, world, *despite everything*." What a cruel and stupid trick.'

Reject, reject, reject: now I saw the truth of what revolted him about Rachel Bowen, who had been Fonseca and, before that, Cardoso. But in that moment, I felt something different. Yes, I had come to resent my mother, her command, her coercion, her intolerance. I see now that I had been unfair. I had not understood who she was, and how she had become this person. She was running from her past, from the truth of those who had raised her and then rejected her. My mother's pain was revealed to me: the family that had rejected her, the hand that life had dealt her, that her declaration of independence had come at enormous cost – the loss of who she had once been, of everyone who remembered that young woman. Her people erased her from her own past, scrubbed bleach over her memory, and walked away. My mother had rejected *all* that had first rejected her. In that respect, she and Lavelle were the same, and this was precisely why Lavelle hated her. What had happened to my mother, in his view, should have made her a revolutionary. Instead, it made her a conformist, and it disgusted him.

We heard the front door slam below us. Fear rushed through me: my father was home. My mother got to her feet and I did the same. Lavelle watched us with amusement. Only a second later, the drawing-room door opened. My father breezed in, and seeing the strange scene, feeling its tension, he froze, his eyes on me, and then on Lavelle.

'What is this?' he asked coolly. A footman tumbled in behind him, bowing, starting to explain that he had not had a chance to say anything. My father waved him away. I indicated to Lavelle, who was now rising to bow to my father.

'Father, this is Horace Lavelle,' I said.

'Lavelle?' my father repeated, with dark recognition. 'Lavelle? The debaucher?'

An amused giggle escaped Lavelle's throat. I was still reeling from the words used against my mother, and my head was spinning.

'Father, you must be calm—' I said.

'Calm?' he cried.

Somewhere, a clock began to chime. It was six o'clock. Precisely on time – my father liked time to be precise – servants started to enter, carrying tureens and plates and silverware. Someone had forgotten to inform the kitchen that there was company, and to check if dinner should be served. On the sideboard, the servants began to place the cutlery and serving dishes. My father swung around. 'Get out!' he yelled. 'Get out, you fucking idiots!' The servants, panicking, went to pick up the cutlery and dishes but he would not even give them that. 'Go on, get out and don't come back until you are told!' The room shook with his voice. Lavelle paused a moment. Perhaps, he was thinking, in my father he had found a worthy adversary. The servants withdrew, leaving behind their tureens, meat forks and silver spoons.

'What is this?' my father growled. 'Why did you bring your *fiend* here?'

Lavelle couldn't help but snigger. '*Fiend.*' My father glared at him, in full knowledge of his own power. I wanted to warn Lavelle: be careful. But Lavelle pulled himself up tall and turned to my father. 'Benjamin and I have come to tell you that you will settle upon us half your wealth and we shall go away, the two of us. It is Benjamin's money. You have no right to keep it from him. If you refuse, we shall cause scandal.'

'What scandal?' my father asked, disbelieving.

My mother looked at me directly and openly, more fully than she had since I had got back from Italy. 'I want you to stop this, Benjamin. I want you to see what you are doing to us and to stop this …'

Hearing my mother's alarm, my father became more unsettled. 'What scandal?'

Lavelle let the presence of threat sink in. 'How about the poor but clever girl who rose from nothing, married well, took a lover, and founded an empire? But no, that is not what scandal is – scandal has to matter more than that. How about that you killed your first husband, Madame Bowen?'

My mother's eyes widened. '*What?*'

Lavelle gave a light, sensuous laugh. 'Benjamin told me everything!'

It took me a second to remember what he was talking about. It had been in Siena, after we left the opera, before

I told him my secret. But it had been a joke! And it was he that had said it, not me, and I had laughed – because, yes, it was a joke!

'Horace!' I cried. 'I did not say that. You said it.' I shook my head. 'Don't be ridiculous. It was a joke.'

'A *joke*?' my mother echoed. She narrowed her eyes. 'Benjamin, what have you become? How can you say such awful things are a *joke*?'

Her disgust was his nourishment. 'How *dare* you, Madame? How dare you pose as the arbiter of who should be ashamed? You, who could have been free. You, who could have run away with your lover and your books, and let loose your hair as you ran? You, who flouted all convention and made such brave decisions, and then, at the last moment, damned your sons to the chains of convention, and so killed them—'

My father growled. Lavelle did not react, just kept talking. 'You will give us half of everything – say, ten thousand guineas – and we shall go away.' Ten thousand guineas was an incredible sum of money. With the financial knowledge I had gained from working at the Company, something Lavelle had never done, I knew it would take months to realise ten thousand guineas. Ships would have to be sold. The house in Bloomsbury as well. It seemed so innocent of Lavelle – so stupidly innocent of him – to ask for it.

'You ridiculous, prancing fool,' my father spat. 'Look at you, here, pretending you are the big man.' He took a step forward. I caught it then, just momentarily: Lavelle's instinctive recoil. 'I have snapped necks of men far nastier than you, you filthy nancy.' The word tore through the room, simultaneously scalding and ridiculous. It was aimed at him, and then at me. 'Do you think I would not do it to you? Ten thousand guineas, you fool! I could destroy you with the snap of my fingers—' My father's hand flew out at Lavelle's face, his fingers snapped as loud as a hammer on an anvil.

My mother yelled at him to stop and he, her adorer, obeyed. 'William, what kind of man are you? How can you have allowed this to go on so long? Do you not protect your wife and family any more?'

My father loved my mother so very much. He walked to the sideboard, where the serving dishes and cutlery sat abandoned. Lavelle started to say something scornful, not feeling any fear. My father picked up the meat fork and slammed his body into Lavelle's, sending him hurtling to the floor. Lavelle landed hard on the floor, so hard that I thought he might have knocked himself out. I threw myself at my father, who, still on his feet, stuck out a hand and stopped me dead. He drew the fork back, poised to strike at my face. It was then that fear truly hit me. My father might kill me. And if he would even contemplate killing me, what else would he do?

My mother stepped forwards and grabbed my arm, pushing me back. My father fell to his knees on top of Lavelle, who groaned heavily with the impact. He half-laughed, as though my parents were making such delicious fools of themselves. My father pressed the sharpened fork close to Lavelle's throat, but still he did not seem frightened.

'You are not about to leave!' my mother yelled at me, the bark of the person never to be contradicted in the moment of realising she might have lost. But the person who comes to control can never admit defeat – they can only redouble their efforts to control. 'Benjamin!' my mother sneered. 'You think you can survive in this world without me, without my help? You won't last five minutes out in the real world, Benjamin. I know what it is to suffer. I know what it is to worry about starvation. You – you know nothing of these things.'

My mother's eyes were on me, focused and imperious. How many times had she employed her stares and harsh, sudden words to control Edgar and me? But I knew now that only you can concede to dominance, and only you can turn away from it.

'I will survive, Mother,' I said.

She shook her head as she spoke. 'I am not going to give you a penny. Not a single farthing. Go, if you must, but it is without a penny from me.' My mother's eyes were hard, sharp, burning bright – like light through a lens. 'Go into the world, the two of you. Go, see how you prosper.'

I looked at Lavelle, weighted down by my father. He was watching my mother – his adversary – speak. 'How do you think about that, Mister Lavelle?' she said. 'Do you still want to love my son? If there is nothing, not a penny, do you love him still?' My father was staring down at Lavelle, still pressing the fork to his throat. 'Mister Lavelle,' my mother continued, 'what if we give you five hundred pounds now? How long could you live on that for – five years? Six, seven? Five hundred pounds to leave now, and never see my son again. You can accept it tonight and go. We will not harm you. In fact, make it six hundred and never come back. How does that sound?'

The words left my mother's mouth and the air in the room seemed to split apart. I was watching my lover. He was not looking at me. He was going to accept it. That was my fear: that he would betray me and say yes. My mother could smell victory.

'What about seven?' Lavelle asked. Horror overwhelmed me. But of course Lavelle was going to betray me. They would let him go. He would collect his money, grin at me, shrug and vanish. 'What about eight?' he then asked. It might take a little while to collect the money, but then they would hand it to him and that would be it. And we would all return to their plan, as if nothing had changed. They would have won, and I, their son, would have lost – just as my mother always needed. Then Lavelle looked very directly at me.

He kept speaking, and grew more satirical with each word. 'What about nine hundred, one thousand, two, twenty thousand, forty, eighty?' My mother was silent now. She realised the power of his sarcasm and his refusal. 'Madame, there is no sum of money in all the world that will make me give up your son. I love him.' The three words, after a fashion. 'And he loves me. And all your money can't change that. We have love, and so we have power over you.'

My father looked up at me and I saw the most terrible vulnerability in him. I understood at once what it was: the death of a man's dreams. He looked beyond me at my mother. She had started weeping. I had hardly ever seen my mother cry.

Then he pushed the meat fork into Lavelle's neck.

His flesh burst open. Blood poured out of him. His body went rigid, then began wildly kicking. I started screaming and ran to Lavelle.

All these years later, I try to piece it back together. How quickly he died. I don't remember a scream. Did he die instantly? Can someone as bright, as brilliant, as all-encompassingly alive as Lavelle, just be snuffed out like that? I remember not the silence of his blood as it bloomed out over his body and the floor, but the smell – that rich, toxic smell of death. I remember picking up his body. I remember my screaming, my father's shriek of horror, Lavelle's blood all over him and me, his eyes already milky white, the strange, fading gurgle in his throat.

I remember my mother put her hand on my head and held it there, until I had stopped screaming. *Shh*, she was saying, *shh*, as mothers whisper to sons when they are small and in need of soothing – or of silencing. Gradually, Lavelle's blood passed to my body, and through me, passed to her. 'Your father has protected you, Benjamin.' She was crying, her body heaving with violent sobs. 'We have protected you.' Then she said something like: 'We love you, Benjamin. We still love you.' But all I could feel was the weight of her hands pushing down on my skull. 'We have protected you. From this demon. You were intoxicated. You were in-toxicated. You thought you were in love, but you were wrong, Benjamin. You were …' she sighed painfully, and in that sigh, I heard all her terrors, and disappointments, and lies ' ... *intoxicated.*'

I passed into a still kind of shock. Two footmen came, alerted by the screams. Were they shocked when they entered, seeing the scene? Or did they jump for joy, thinking, we're rich men now for knowing this strange family's dark secrets? My father told them to be calm, I think. I remember hearing him telling the footmen that the three of them would wrap the body and take it down to the river. They were to find some hessian and some rope and anything heavy with which to sink a weight. He promised them five guineas now and an extra guinea a year if they were to go along with it. They were to say nothing. Be silent, say nothing, and the truth will never find us. *Say nothing.*

The house grew quiet, I remember that. In the wake of a death, silence eventually descends like snowfall. I heard voices kept low, the same wintry hush, my father and his henchmen, after the fact. A door slammed and the carriage was pulled around. My father knew how to drive a carriage still; he was not born a gentleman. He and the footmen were going to the river, to get rid of a body.

When it was late, my mother came to my room. She appeared in the gloom of the unlit doorway, holding a candle in one hand so that only she was illuminated. I was lying on my bed, dazed. I turned to see her there.

There was such a ring of horror around her then, at the events that had just happened, and events that were yet to come.

She walked into my room and closed the door behind her, so that any remaining, unimplicated servants could not hear. At the edge of my bed, candlelit, she hovered above me like a medieval apparition. She let out a long, tearful breath, her forehead crumpling. The light made her tears shine golden.

'Mother, did you know that Father would do that?'

'No,' she said in a neutral tone.

I didn't believe her. My mother was breathing heavily, her chest hollow with tears. She went to say something, but paused to clear her throat. She started to speak again, but again had to clear her throat. I heard the tears catch in her chest. 'I want you to know,' she said carefully, 'that your father is a good person.'

I shook my head, closed my eyes. 'No, Mother, he is not. And neither are you.'

She took a breath. 'We have protected you,' she said. The loor of her drawing room was covered in a stranger's blood. Her husband had gone to get rid of that stranger's body. The stranger was her son's lover. And her other son was dead. When she spoke of protection, she meant she had protected what she – they – had wanted. Nothing else, ultimately, had mattered much at all.

I wondered at my mother. She had always sought to dominate us whilst claiming she was merely protecting us. I thought of the clever girl whose life had turned out to be a trick. Was her grasping at control her attempt to avoid more pain? By governing what happened, could she stop anyone judging her, hurting her, hurting us? If that was the case, she had failed spectacularly, because oppression can never bring happiness. And so she had destroyed us as much as protected us. She had sent us to our deaths when she sent us to our glorious futures. 'Did you kill Solomon Fonseca, Mother?'

It seemed the only question I had remaining. 'No,' she said.

'Did Father?'

She did not miss a beat. 'No.'

'I don't believe you, Mother. I don't believe a word you say any more.' I heard the crack in her throat. She said nothing. Here I was, one of the devotees she had created, telling her that I had lost my faith. She sighed, turned and left the room. She did not lock the door. She did not say goodbye.

My mother and I never spoke again. In the dead of night, before my father returned, I slipped away from my parents' house without a penny to my name. Dazed by Lavelle's death, I staggered back westwards through St Giles and Soho. I drifted through London's night, vanishing into the city's throng.

Many years have passed since these events. I did not see my parents again. I found out in passing that seven years later my mother died. I had moved to Paris by then and was reading a London newspaper, several weeks old, describing a grand wedding at a big house in Bloomsbury. William Bowen of the Bowen Maritime Company, labelled a widower without children, had married a second time to a much younger woman of some learning, whose family were 'mercantile'. I knew nothing of the circumstances of my mother's death, and nothing of what my father might have told his new wife. Assuming my father would have further children, I wondered what he might tell them about his past. After all, he and my mother had told us so little of theirs. Did he tell them of the sons he had before, sons he had loved, sons he no longer thought of?

Now and then I think I might write and ask for the letters that Edgar sent to our mother, but of course I do not. I have no right to do so, and perhaps they no longer exist anyway, burned on a fire long ago. No one remembers the names of Rachel Fonseca or Rahel Cardoso or Edgar Bowen any more. I too no longer exist in the stories that someone somewhere must tell about my family. All that history is dead. Should I regret its passing? Why should I? History is filled with lies.

People want love. People demand love. They prescribe love. They proscribe it, too. People make mistakes, and people grow afraid, and they fail and hurt each other. Some people talk about love like drunkards, and their words end up meaning nothing. But some people cannot talk about love; it kills them to do so. And with time, passing straight through the hurt itself, we come to see the nature of their love. We come to see how transformative it was, and what an honour it was to have it in our lives.

I think of him all the time. Sometimes I feel I am thinking of him every second of my waking life. And then at night, I dream of me and him again, our naked bodies, young and beautiful, alone in the clear water of the Lido, looking for fishes in the water, his joy at seeing their darting silver forms. There, in that dream, he and I have found a sort of happiness. We have negotiated a love that fulfils us both completely. And then I wake. It's a fantasy, of course. No such love exists. All a couple can do is walk together, holding hands in the street, hopeful, trusting in their future. Except some couples don't have that trust. They would be attacked if they even tried.

Half a lifetime has passed. I have lived in Paris a long time now, making my living as a writer, a teacher of English – Lavelle's living death! – and, occasionally, when things have been hard, in other ways. I have loved again many times, happily, briefly, heartbrokenly, enduringly. And each time that I love, and each time love ends, I think of Lavelle. His love defines me still. My love bears his ghostly imprints, his brilliant traces. Sometimes I wish his ghost away. And other times I am glad to have known a love like this. But I have to tell you, my mother's plans were smashed to pieces. You see, I never ended up a good person. Not even remotely.

Now and then I see new generations of Tourists arrive. The fashion of wig, the position of beauty spot, the shade of silk might change, but the people do not. Sometimes I stare at them ironically and sometimes I want to leap up and tear the wig off their heads. They are the good people. I am not. Who won? *Who?*

Everything about me was changed by Lavelle, but the world did not change. The world never changes. It lumbers on, crushing good people and making kings of the most appalling. No, the world never changes. It just keeps on spinning, turning and turning on its fixed axis. In Paris, in the last few weeks, there have been protests, riots in streets that were once rigidly controlled. Ordinary people finally – after centuries of oppression – are demanding their voices be heard. They have stopped feeling fear; or rather, have learned that their fear will never stop unless they stop it themselves. For the first time, unimaginably, the lowest class of Parisian yells his ideas for the future at aristocrats, at the stupid king and his idiotic queen, who crawl around, already relics of a suddenly dead past. I don't know what will follow. All I know is that the world must change, or else it may as well stop spinning altogether.

'We are all of us fallible,' Voltaire wrote. 'So let's forgive each other's follies.' It was my mother's favourite quote. Let's forgive each other's follies. How nice for the normal man, all this forgiveness on which he insists. Forgive, in the name of Jesus Christ, who does his merry dance up on his cross to save our souls, though we never asked him to. Lavelle did not forgive. He came to crush. And that's precisely what normal men deserve. So, like Lavelle said many years ago, fuck Voltaire. And fuck forgiveness. The world needs change, not forgiveness.

Paris, July 1789

ACKNOWLEDGEMENTS

Thank you to my agent, Veronique Baxter; to my editor, Jocasta Hamilton, and everyone who worked on the book at Penguin Random House; to the members of the North London Writers' Group; to Adi Bloom, Alix Christie, Emma Flint and Zoe Gilbert, for their words of encouragement at moments when (they didn't necessarily realise) I needed it; and most of all, to Zahid.

I would also like to mention my beautiful friend, Martin Pepperell, who the last time I saw him before he died, asked me when I was going to take my writing seriously. It was a good question.

READ ON FOR AN EXTRACT FROM
NEIL BLACKMORE'S NEW NOVEL

COMING OUT ON 15 JULY 2021

ON THE SUBJECT OF HYPOCRISY, SODOMY & ALL-ROUND TOMFOOLERY

Everyone says I am the cleverest man in England. *Everyone*. But in this country, it's a worthless thing to be clever. Which books you've read, which poets you can quote, matter nothing. In fact, such fripperies disgust my fellow Englishmen. (Or, at best, they do not see the point.) Knowledge revolts people, its application enrages them. Because in England, in our times at least, only two things matter: the nobility of one's lineage and the exquisiteness of a boy's face. *That's not fair*, you bluestockings protest. But this is England, where life is not fair, where life does not give a shit what you think, unless you are an earl – or a pretty boy with a tight hole, lolling in the bed of our good King James. This, I'm afraid you will have to accept, is the truth.

And what of me, you ask? Francis Bacon? Polymath, politician, philosopher, all-round know-it-all. (I am being ironic.) I am long past forty years of age, and in those years I have published books on what people call a 'bewildering' range of subjects (then how easily are people bewildered!). Frankly, hardly anyone has read them. I have no title, no great position. I have been a Member of Parliament, a legal advisor to the Crown, even risen to the post of Solicitor-General, but still I spend more money than I earn (I even went once – briefly – to debtor's prison). I am not Baron This or the Earl of That. I have no children, and no likelihood of ever acquiring any. My family, despite its intellectual and reformist connections, was not aristocratic. I was raised by a father who loyally served old Queen Elizabeth as the Lord Keeper of the Great Seal and died with nothing, and a mother who was in contact with some of the greatest minds of the age, but could not feed her servants. After years of hard work at court, *years* of doing first the old Queen's and now the current King's bidding, why do I still have so little to show? I deserve success, but deserving things and getting them are distinct propositions.

When I was still a very young man, I published my first great work, *The Essays*. It was then that men first called me a genius who had invented the essay, but of course, those men have not read Montaigne or Castiglione. If you have not either, just nod and look *as if* you have. (That's England, right there, in that knowing nod.) Then, in my *Advancement of Learning*, I suggested that philosophy might be separated from theology, that human beings might have things in their lives that are not explained by God. (They could have burned me at the stake for that suggestion.) Continental scholars said that I was going to transform the approach to knowledge, create a new empiricism, a rational approach to life in which scientific evidence might actually matter. A new and modern world. I was going to be the great philosopher of our age, those scholars said. All of which stands to prove one thing: *people talk the most awful shit.*

After all this time, I have no money, and not enough power. I remain an outsider. But suddenly, something has changed. King James called me to Theobalds, his favourite palace. And so that was how, one pale, misty morning, I rode the two hours north from London. What had changed was that the King was going to make me Attorney-General of England, the kingdom's most senior lawyer, one of his closest advisors, and – I was sure – I was in with a chance of finally being rich. *Oh*, you say. *Philosophers must not care about such things.* Well, philosophers love the same things as most fellows: money, position, parties, cock. It's just that they make their name pretending that they do not.

On the open fields before the palace were arranged the most august bodies in the land: the King himself, his court and advisors, and the noblemen of England, feathered hats on heads, muskets in hands. It was a shooting day; the air shivered with the sound of guns just discharged. Smoke sifted, birds had fallen from the air and dogs were running off into woodland scrub, snuffling for avian corpses. Away from the shoot, the ladies with their starched ruff collars and high bejewelled wigs had gathered to watch the game. Some wore gloves and carried small, pearl-handled pistols. Others glugged down wine though it was not yet eleven o'clock; this is the way of the court. Around this coterie, the court dwarves sat patiently and buffoons performed, all of them waiting for the inevitable pinches – and punches – that would come as their mistresses became soused.

An ice-pick voice rose on my approach, clear and aristocratic. The Earl of Southampton: the most avowed of all my enemies. He is a glamorous fellow, clever in some ways, one of the first to invest in America, a distinguished and tasteful patron. But he sees no advantage in the intelligence of others, or the possibility that a man could – or should – rise in life. So he hates me. (There are other reasons he hates me, but more of that later.) Know this, though: My Lord of Southampton, he would kill me if he could.

'Look, fellow noblemen, here comes *Mister* Bacon!' he spat, the insult being that I was knighted by the old Queen, but such an honour means nothing to someone of his background. He turned to the Earl of Suffolk, member of the Howard dynasty, which regards itself as a true whiff of England, several notches above our *Scottish* royal family. These two men – very seriously – are my enemies. When their eyes met, Southampton's handsome face glimmered with malice, and then he looked back at me. I bowed to him, most decorous, but then I immediately turned from them. The whole while, he and Suffolk glared at me.

As I turned, I saw the King: James I of England, VI of Scotland, uniter of our island. With his accession back in 1603, for the first time in history, England, Scotland, Wales and Ireland had a single ruler. So now it was ten years since he arrived from Edinburgh following the death of the old Queen, who was his cousin. She had kept him hanging on so long, that when she finally died, standing on her feet to almost the last moment – which should tell you everything that was marvellous and infuriating about her – he almost did not believe that his ship had finally come in. He had waited since he had ascended the Scottish throne at ten months old, the king of nowhere, to become the king of *somewhere*: England. He left for London and never went back.

He was not alone in his flight south. About half the kingdom of Scotland followed him to this land of (relative) milk and honey, bollock-eyed and open-mouthed at all they were about to gorge themselves upon. But the true prize was not the green pastures of England but the scabby, heartless riches of London. At the time, Londoners had complained about all these Scots coming down here and taking over, but I knew which side the future was on. So I wrote my *Discourse on the Union*, which put forward the idea of a single 'British' state. The King had loved it, and I thought his favour was secured. But quickly, I was reminded of the truths of this country. Under the King, as it had been under the old Queen, the pretty face rises quickly, and the aristocratic title never falls. Everyone else just bobs around, sometimes inching upwards, sometimes plummeting down. But now I was finally getting my reward.

The King was sprawled on a makeshift gold-painted wooden throne, watching other, fitter men shoot birds, a huge tankard of wine slopping in one hand. Physically, he was unremarkable in every possible way – not tall but not short, his body wrought by high living and laziness, in the way that any man who lives on meat and wine would be. His red hair was frizzy and unattractive and gone brown-grey with age; his tongue was too large for his mouth so that he spat at you as he spoke in his intense yet uninteresting way; his lips were stained purple with so much claret.

Every day he drinks from waking until he collapses into bed at night, and he eats only meat and candied sweets. No wonder his health is bad. He is not alone: people at court refuse to eat fruits and vegetables, believing they are bad for the constitution. It's chicken and venison, pastry and pies, all washed down with bottle after bottle of wine. How he lives has now, in middle age, begun to take its toll on his body. His gout is so bad now, and his feet and legs so covered with ulcers, he can no longer stand long enough to shoot birds. (No doubt, there will eventually be a science of food and health that will explain very many errors of belief and behaviour.)

On that makeshift throne, and on the royal lap, something – *someone* – was writhing and giggling. It was his lover, Robert Carr: vicious, beautiful Robert Carr – as pretty as a bauble, with a heart as black as jet. The King was slobbering red-wine kisses all over the boy's neck, while the boy – who was really a man – writhed and laughed and sometimes accepted them. The whole court stood around, pretending not to notice.

In case you are one of those types that hears 'sodomite' and thinks 'pederast', let me make clear that Carr was not so much of a boy any more. He was nearing thirty, but it was important that the world continued to see him as a boy. That way, it could pretend that this was some elegant Platonic ideal of the older man leading the youth to adulthood. Carr had been the King's favourite for six or seven years by then, a long time in the firmament of these things. At the King's request, revoltingly, he calls him 'Daddy', for then we can all pretend that they are the paradigm of that thing called father and son. But we all of us know that this is not what is going on; we all of us know into which slot the royal favour truly goes. What the King does to Robert Carr, I am pretty sure fathers should not do to their sons.

All of Europe knew about the King's desires, yet there are some who point to various dreadful (I mean, insightful!) works the King has written to attest he cannot be a sodomite. Oh, yes, the King is a scholar too: a fucking dreadful one. In his *Daemonologie*, for example, he railed nonsensically about how to catch witches. (When he asks if I believe in them, I say, 'I have never seen one, sire, flying across the moon, have you?' and he laughs.) Meanwhile, in his terrible book on kingship, *Basilikon Doron*, he denounced swearing, drinking and sodomy. But here he was, on a spring afternoon, pretty much doing all three. People believe whatever they need to. They shut their eyes to the obvious truth, and find it very easy to lie to themselves. This is how scholars make terrible fools of themselves.

'*Beicon*, there ye fucking are!' the King yelled, turning his mouth from Robert Carr's. He has never truly mastered the English language, speaking instead some hybrid half-Scots. I bowed deeply. He rose forward on his throne, Carr half-tipping, half-slipping from his lap as he did so.

'Sire,' I said, 'you summoned me.'

'Ach, aye!' he hooted. 'That I fucking *did*!'

There is one other thing you should know about Robert Carr. For the last few months, he has been blackmailing me, saying he wants a thousand pounds from me to convince the King that it was a good idea to appoint me as Attorney-General of England. If I didn't pay, he would speak against me, so that the King would not consider me for further promotion. A thousand pounds! He might as well have asked me for my soul. But I paid it (mortgaging my country house, inherited from my father, at Gorhambury, out near St Albans, again, borrowing even more again) and here we all were.

Boom, boom, boom! A musket fired into the air. A dove thumped to the ground, smashed to bloodied bits but still – just about – alive. Its mess of guts and dislocated wings heaved around, its beak arched open, its head thrashing against the ground. I looked away, thinking I could puke, and at once saw Carr staring at me, the hint of a smirk on his face. But that face was beautiful like no other at the English court, and therein lies his dominance. That court is a world of diamond-hard lineages into which ordinary people could not break. But fate had handed young men like Carr a specific opportunity: intense physical attractiveness at the specific time that a monarch reigned who openly craved such things. Beauty was their skill, as much as working stone was a sculptor's. And power, in its many forms, was their prize. They want access to power in its simplest, most aggressive sense: riches, titles, control over men and the affairs of the world. Sometimes, they just want the power that comes with the authority of another's age, or access to a cultured man's knowledge and understanding of the world. They want the power that comes with being young and beautiful and desired and they want it from those that are none of those things. This, then, is a story about power. *Nothing else.*

The King has had several favourites here in England, and more famously in Scotland, where among the thin-mouthed northern Puritans, his preferences got him into trouble. But no one has ruled him so absolutely as Carr does. He came here with that half-kingdom of hungry Scots who drifted south after the old Queen died. At some point between

Edinburgh and London, he was befriended by one Sir Thomas Overbury, who is every bit as awful as Carr. Overbury has the meanest mouth at court, and they say that he saw in the then-innocent Carr his opportunity to make a fortune for them both. It is said that it was he who trained Carr to be a favourite, crimped his hair, cleared up his spots and shaved his arse, and taught him how to ensnare the King, that it was he who set up their first meeting, which ended in Carr breaking his leg at a tournament, and the King rushing to scoop up the broken, beautiful boy whom had entranced him that day ... and every day since. No two Scots were hungrier than Carr and Overbury, and no two have done better among all those who came south.

Now Carr rules the King not with kindness, not even with sex (despite what my spy in the Royal Bedchamber reports about their twice-a-day activities). It's the blowing through of terrible moods that gives Carr such mastery over the King: lightning sulks, ferocious tantrums, sparkling gales of laughter, seemingly earnest declarations – and then sudden withdrawals – of love. The King grew up entirely without love – abandoned by his mother, that flame-haired fool Mary Stuart, queen of idiots, gobbled up by the sharp beaks of his vulture-aristocrats. In Carr, love came not as salvation but as tropical hurricane, as icy North Sea storm. (Note to self: I shall write something on some future science of the mind, in which its practitioners will be able to understand what makes men behave the way they do. If I ever live to see this mind-science, I shall recommend they study first the love of our own King James for Robert Carr.)

His eyes still on me a moment longer, Carr sauntered away towards his best friend, Overbury. The King watched his lover's smooth, egg-domed buttocks sashaying away in perfectly pert silk britches, his furry red tongue moving over his cracked purple lips, growling to himself, transfixed. All these years and nothing has abated his desire for Carr; nothing has even come close to threatening it. Only when his lover was gone did the King's eyes flick to me. He grinned and said, utterly without warning: 'I know that ye tried to fuck my Rabbie once, you know, *Beicon*.'

So here is another thing you should know about Robert Carr. I had indeed tried to fuck him once – years before – and he'd turned me down. He told me I was too poor, too low-born, for him to consider. I did not realise then that he had his eyes on a much, much bigger prize than me. Still now, a rigid fright went through me, hearing the King say those words. 'Majesty,' I said with alarm. 'I . . . I do not know what you mean –'

Understand this, before we proceed: power is a game. A deadly game. A game of enormous losses and enormous rewards. And in the game of power, you must always be alert to the threat in its moment. When a king says something like this, what does he want? To warn you? To humiliate you? To give notice that trouble is coming? Or just to gloat?

'Sire . . .' I began to gabble, pressure at my temples, a pulsing against my throat. 'What you refer to was many years ago, before you and Rabbie . . . I mean, Robert . . . And nothing happened!'

The King began to laugh. '*Beicon!* I am just teasing ye, man. Do not worry, I am not sending ye to the fucking Tower yet, y'know!' His laughter rained around me, hard and heartless. 'These pretty boys, they're all the same. They think with their pussies as much as their noggins, *eh*?!' He rapped the side of his head with his knuckles,

314

to imply an empty skull, when his was the emptiest of all. I bowed and smiled, and felt my fear recede – for now. But fear is in the nature of proximity to kings.

Sighing happily, the King took a greedy gulp of wine from his tankard. Then he declared, 'Us two, *Beicon*, we are the *real* fucking intellectuals. I want to talk to ye about *intellectual* things!' Then he belched so loudly that a bird in a tree above us took fright and flew off, and some random earl fired a musket at it, missing.

Oh, God, I thought. *Why? Why do people see me and want to talk about 'intellectual' things?* The King is the worst type of idiot: one who thinks himself intelligent. But I bowed; what else could I do? He is the King, the sun around which the rest of us orbit (according to Mister Galilei, at least). He did not blink but gazed at me, through his alcoholic haze.

'Tell me, *Beicon*, what are ye scribbling these days? Some fucking *conundrum*, I should not wonder!'

How I did not want to talk about this. 'I am working on a critique of Aristotle, sire.'

'*Aristotle?*' he cried. Wine spittle splattered on my face. I smiled. I did not dare wipe it away. 'A fucking critique of Aristotle? What is there bad to say about Aristotle? Every cunt loves Aristotle!'

Well, indeed. *Every cunt loves Aristotle.* That's the problem, a problem that has ruined European civilisation. All of Christian thinking in Europe is founded on the work of Aristotle. He created a methodology for knowledge – specifically, scientific discovery – which has been the cornerstone of all correct thinking for hundreds of years. The foundation of his method is the pronouncement of existing, accepted ideas which the scientist or philosopher

315

is then instructed to prove, from which they can *deduce* the facts.

Except *I* have realised it is wrong. And so, I, Francis Bacon, disagree with Aristotle. I believe that rather than starting with the premise and using the data at all costs to prove it, the scientist should start with the data and work up from that, to outcomes that are unknown, ever-openingly unknown. My idea is that the scientist should not assume he knows answers before he searches for evidence. If they looked for evidence and then *induced* answers, that, I believe, could transform knowledge, create the foundations of a modern, *scientific* world.

Science could become a kind of revolution, a tool for the betterment of all people's lives that could revolutionise medicine, technology, industry, everything. This change, I believe, could be the foundation of a new, modern world of ever-expanding knowledge.

I explained all this news to the King and he just hooted: 'What nonsense you will pick at, *Beicon!* Thank goodness you're clever for you're nae kind of looker, are ye! Maybe that's why Rabbie never gave ye a second look!'

I smiled at the insult, for what else can one do? (I did not reply that Carr's objection to me was his precise attraction to the King: I had no money, and precious little power, whereas the King had plenty of both. I am too nice to point out such things, you know!) He rolled his eyes around in his head like marbles knocking together. He tried and failed to let out a small burp. The King's attention had moved on; the child was growing bored. 'So, let me tell ye my good news.'

I held my breath. 'News, sire?'

'I have decided to offer ye the post of Attorney General, *Beicon*. What do ye say to *that*?'

What did I say to that? What did I say? I felt every knotted year of tension in my shoulders release, I felt every waking night worrying that I might have to go back to the debtors' prison vanish. I looked over at Southampton and Suffolk who were watching me with the King, like two bulldogs that had just been lapping bowls of sour verjuice. I felt my enemies' hands around my throat . . . letting go.

'Thank you, sire,' I said, bowing deeply. 'Thank you, I am honoured.'

'Ha!' went the King. 'Of course ye fucking are!' Then he lifted his glass up high and called for more wine. 'Wine for me! Aye, and wine for the . . .' He waggled his bushy eyebrows. '*Attur*-ney-General!'

With me marvelling at my new fortune (minus the thousand pounds I had given Carr), we turned to watch the shooting. The numbers on the field increased. Queen Anne had arrived with her ladies, but to little fanfare. A Danish princess by birth, she was very tall, towering over most of the bow-legged men of her husband's court, with a great fizz of blonde hair on her head and pale blue eyes that could intensely peer at one and yet reveal nothing, something that people mistook for emptiness. She was speaking to her ladies – and then to her dogs – in her loud, deep Scandinavian voice. Most people say that the Queen is an idiot. Or perhaps not an idiot: a nincompoop, a cipher, a tomfool, a goose-egg, a void. Most people say those things about the Queen – but they are wrong. I always liked the Queen and she me.

She was accompanied by her only surviving son, the young Prince Charles. Of the Queen's seven children, only he and his sister, the Electress Elizabeth, survived, but the sixteen-year-old girl had recently left to Germany to live with her new husband, the Elector Palatine of the Rhine. We would likely never see her again. The Queen's eldest son, Prince Henry, had died a year before. Intelligent and energetic, the Prince had been the hope of these nations, but then one day, a strapping lad of eighteen, he had gone swimming with friends, caught a fever and just died. He had slipped away so fast, everyone was stunned: the court, the country, *everyone*. Each day for four weeks after his death, Londoners queued, a thousand deep, to see his body at Westminster Abbey. Even the old Queen hadn't got such a send-off. The King and Queen had, like most parents, lost other children, infants and babies, but the Prince's death, on the cusp of manhood, was shattering. It was especially hard for the Queen, however. Only now had she reached even the most fragile level of stability. But do not misunderstand: she was tough. Her life – so very privileged and so very neglected – had made her tough.

Just as the shooters, the Queen included, took up their positions, a tiny spaniel ran up to me, yapping at my heels. Carr had given the dog to the King as a gift, and so it was much prized – thoroughly spoiled, in fact. 'Ritchie, *stop!*' the King cried. 'Fucking dog! Ach, I do love him ... Ritchie, stop!' The dog did not stop; its teeth were so close to my ankles that I could feel the air whip against my stockings. 'Ritchie, fucking stop it!' the King kept on yelling. Still the dog did not stop. *Do not bite me, you little mutt*, I thought. '*Ritchie, fucking stop it!*'

A musket went off. The dog scampered away in the direction of Carr. There was a moment of silence then loud laughter. I looked up and there were Carr and Overbury, bent over guffawing, each of them a few feet either side of the Queen, who was holding her still-smoking musket. Only then did I notice on the floor the still, dead body of a bird. It was a crow. The Queen must have shot it by mistake. I did not understand, for she was an excellent markswoman. Had something been said to make her miss?

Then came Overbury's unpleasant squawk: 'Oh, madam, all you brought down was a crow, a bird hardly fit for eating. Madam, have you not read Leviticus? The raven is not an eating bird! It is an *unclean* bird! Do they not teach that in Denmark? Or is it the Swedes who scoff down crows?'

Laughter everywhere! Even the Earl of Suffolk was laughing. I did not understand. Suffolk, proud English Howard, despised Carr, common Scottish whore. Something was afoot, I could sense, but did not know what. But more than that, I thought of the Queen, now just emerging from the horror of her grief. She deserved better than their cruelty.

'Sire,' I began to say to the King, 'I think perhaps the Queen is unhappy.'

The King slurped some wine then licked his lips. 'Ach, no,' he said, 'she's as happy as a fucking *clam, Beicon!*'

I saw her raise her musket and point it directly at the dog, Ritchie, sitting at Carr's feet. *Oh, shit,* I thought. *She is going to shoot the ugly little mutt.* 'Majesty!' I cried, meaning to call to the Queen, not the King. *Boom!* A puff of dirt. The dog yelped. I caught my breath. Then the King, realising what had happened, started to scream. '*Ritchie!* No! Ritchie, Ritchie!' The whole court – all those cruel laughers – fell silent. Carr started howling; Overbury's face was white with shock; the Queen had struck back. The puff of dirt cleared; there was the dog, whimpering, cowering on the ground, not dead. Carr was shrieking like a fox caught in a trap. The King staggered to his gouty feet, yelling at everyone to *calm the fuck down.* His yelling calmed no one. Then, miraculously, as cool as an icicle, the Queen looked directly at me and smiled.

'Oh, Bacon!' she called to me, without a care in the world. 'What a pleasure to see you!' I walked towards her, bowing a little. Meanwhile Carr was running towards the King, still screaming his head off. 'How did you like the shooting?' the Queen asked as I came up to her.

'I thought it extraordinary, madam.'

'The crow or the dog?' she asked with a small smirk.

'Neither, madam. I was thinking more of Robert Carr.'

Behind us, there was bedlam. 'Bacon, you are as sly as a snake,' the Queen said, majestically ignoring the din.

I bowed. 'You insult me, madam?'

'No, I compliment you. I like snakes. Snakes catch rats.'

Finally, without a single flicker of worry, she looked back at the commotion. Carr was crying hot, enraged tears; the King was pleading with him to calm down; the dog was whining; and Overbury looked like he had crapped in his own britches. Momentarily there was a cool smile on her lips, then it passed and she looked back at me and said, 'Did you pay Carr his bribe, Bacon?'

'Yes.'

'*Ha!*' the Queen cried, turning to leave. 'Good day, Bacon. Let me know if you ever want to catch a rat for me.' She gazed at me very directly, and then looked away, returning to her ladies, who gathered around her to whisper and giggle at what their mistress had just achieved.